Fish Bone Alley 2

David F Burrows

978-1-9164050-2-8
Illustrations by Steve Royce Griffin
www.steveroycegriffin.co.uk

David F Burrows
www.dfburrows.co.uk

Published by Platen Publishing an imprint of David F Burrows

David F Burrows was born and raised in Suffolk. He lives there to this day with his wife Jenny. They have two grown up daughters and three grandchildren.

Having had a few short comedies published over the years David still looked on his writing as a relaxing fun hobby. Now that he is semi-retired, he has had a lot more time to devote to his writing, resulting in the unique Fish Bone Alley Series of short stories. This is the second book in the Fish Bone Alley collection. The first was published in January 2019.

To find out more about David and his work please visit his website at: www.dfburrows.co.uk

For Jen, Mel, and Nat. Wish for it enough and it will eventually arrive.

Contents

Jack the Flasher

Betty and I are in bed enjoying our morning cuppa with biscuits. It is bloody freezing and we are wrapped up in our dressing gowns over our nightgowns and both wearing woolly hats, mine is blue and Betty's is pink. The window is iced up inside and the air is clouded with our breath. I dunk my digestive only to see the wet bit break off and plonk down into my tea just before it reaches my mouth.

"You really are messy sometimes, Detective Inspector," grates Betty. "You've splashed tea on the quilt."

"Sorry my little vixen. My hand shivered with the cold and wobbled the soggy bit off."

"We'll have to stop having tea in bed, Detective Inspector if you keep making a mess."

"Understood," says I, placing my cup and saucer down on the bedside cabinet. "How about I try dunking something else instead?"

Betty giggles, but gives me the 'you'll be lucky look'. "You stick that in your tea and it'll get scalded."

"I didn't mean stick it my tea."

"I know that," she grins. "Anyway, you've no time for naughties. You'll be late for work. It's nearly eight, Detective Sergeant Head will be here in half an hour."

"He will indeed," sighs I. "I best get a move on." Swinging my legs out of the bed I head for the bathroom. After the usual ablutions I dress and go downstairs to find Betty, still in her nightwear, cooking eggs on the stove. On a plate on the kitchen table sits a two-inch-thick lump of ham beside a plate of doorstop crusty rounds of bread splodged with lumps of near frozen butter.

"The ham's a bit thick, Detective Inspector," says Betty shooting me a glance over her shoulder. "I couldn't cut it any thinner it kept slipping all over the place."

I tip it on its side, stab a fork into it and go at it with the carving knife. Expertly I slice off a third of it for Betty only for the knife to slip and shoot her piece off the table and on to the floor. Quickly I pick it up, peruse it for any dirty bits, decide it's fine and drop it on her plate.

"Nearly ready," she says.

"Lovely," says I. Feeling guilty I transfer Betty's ham to my plate and give her mine, but my bit's too big a swap, slipping the bit that fell onto the floor into my jacket pocket I have another go at what's left and manage to cut it, more or less, in half. I plonk a piece on each plate just as Betty swings away from the stove and comes over with the frying pan. She dumps two sunny side up eggs on my plate and one onto hers, puts the frying pan down and comes and sits opposite me.

"That ham doesn't appear so big now you've cut it up, Detective Inspector. Have you eaten some of it already?"

"No."

She narrows her eyes. "Well tuck in or it'll get cold."

We tuck in and just finish when Head raps on the door. I don my coat and bowler, slip my revolver in its holster and am ready to go.

Betty fusses over my tie and gives me a peck on the lips. "Be careful you don't slip on the icy pavements," says she, buttoning up my coat. "And keep warm! If it starts to snow heavily like it did last night find some shelter."

"I will my little hot water bottle." I hug her to me and then make for the door. Betty sees me out. She and Head exchange pleasantries before Head and I head off towards the end of the road where we intend to catch a tram, if they're running, followed by more trams and finally the Underground to Hyde Park.

Head's breath pants out of him like a steam train. "Bloody cold isn't it, sir?" says he, rubbing his hands together. "I should have worn gloves like Chloe told me to, but I didn't listen."

"We rarely do," says I, feeling my feet slip on the cracking ice. "And I should have put on a stout pair of walking boots instead of shoes, just like Betty advised."

Head's entire body goes through a rhythmic spasm of shivering. "It's-it's, brass bloody monkeys!" he grates as his teeth chatter.

It certainly is cold. There is a good covering of snow on the rooves where icicles hang down from the eves like shimmering spears in a bright sun that still manages to pierce through the smog that hangs over the houses. Trees and bushes are coated with blue ice and fluffed layers of snow, they appear statuesque and add to the general aura of the season. It is only six days until Christmas Day but shoppers are nowhere to be seen and what little traffic is out on the treacherous icy roads is taking things very cautiously.

"It's fireside weather, sir," whines Head.

"I agree with you there, Sergeant. A good book, a glass of Scotch and your nuts roasting on the grate. Wonderful."

"Wonderful," sulks Head. "I really didn't want to leave my bed this morning especially as I'll bet we're on nothing more than a wild duck chase." We come to a halt and face each other. "I mean, sir, what flasher in his right mind is going to get it out in this cold and wag it about. I said to Chloe earlier, I said, Chloe can you imagine some pervert jumping out in front of you and going, 'Hey, lady what do you think of this?' Why, it will have shrunk to the size of a peanut it's that bloody cold and you'd need binoculars to even see it!"

"Exactly." We walk on and I wait for Head to go on again about the case we are on. He hasn't stopped moaning about it since Clump instructed us to take it over from the plods who had gotten nowhere with it. Sure enough he starts.

"It's a bloody disgrace, sir," he growls, kicking a cat that sidled up to him for a bit of leg brushing. "Two of the Yard's finest chasing a bloody flashing pervert with a wonky willy when we should be chasing mass murderers and such like."

"As I have said, Sergeant. We are being made an example of. It is a punishment meted out by the new Commissioner to send a message to every copper in the Met' that even the finest must tow the line and not think they are above the law."

"Well it's bad enough not getting promoted as we should have been, but to be ridiculed like this is tantamount to being mentally castrated."

"I wouldn't go that far," says I as we reach the main road and come to a halt at a tram stop. "Look, Sergeant. We have escaped prosecution for helping ourselves to, shall we say, rewards we weren't entitled to. We haven't been demoted or drummed out of the force, but we have to accept promotion is not on the boiler for now and we will have to swallow such crappy cases as this one until the Commissioner feels we have learnt our lesson. That is how it is and the sooner we accept the fact the better we shall be. However, there is a bonus; at least we are not likely to come to too much harm chasing a flasher."

"Probably not, sir. Even so, the sooner we're back on cases more suited to our talents the better."

At last the horse drawn tram skids up and we climb on board and take a seat downstairs, it is virtually empty. Twenty minutes later we get off and take another tram and then the underground. Thirty minutes later we are standing forlorn and miserable in Hyde Park wondering what the hell is the point of us being here.

"There's barely a soul out, sir," moans Head. "Even the bloody urchins aren't about. This is a waste of bloody time."

"Even so, we should at least do something. Come on." I lead the way around a snow-covered path and then slip into a bunch of evergreen bushes to hide while keeping an eye out.

Head takes out a hip flash, he takes a long swallow and then kindly passes it to me, I take a short swallow as it is nearly empty.

"That's better," says Head retrieving the flask and putting it back in his pocket. "I feel a bit more cheerful now."

"Good. Look, here comes a pair of nannies…"

"What, goats?"

"No, Sergeant. Child nannies pushing perambulators."

"Oh, yes, I see them. Do you think the flasher will go for them?"

"He might. He's conducted more flashing in Hyde Park than anywhere else."

We watch and wait. Will the flasher jump out from his hiding place, open his coat and shout boo? I doubt it. The women pass by unhindered, thick fog descends and in minutes visibility is down to barely fifteen feet.

"This is bollocks," moans Head. "We may as well bugger off home."

"Just what I was thinking," shivers I while slapping my arms around my chest and stamping my feet. "I'll tell you what, Sergeant. It is too early to sneak off home. What we'll do is go and re-interview some of the women who have been confronted by the flasher. That way we'll get to warm up and may even get offered a hot drink or two."

"Good idea, sir. I'll need a pee first. This cold doesn't half set you off."

"It does," says I, deciding I best try for one myself in case I don't make it to the public toilets. Just as I extract my manhood a voice booms through the fog, "Right! Out you come you dirty git."

Through a gap in the hedge I spy a pair of plods, truncheons drawn, staring straight at me. "I am having a urination!" snaps I. "You will have to wait."

"We are officers of the law, come out *now* or we'll come in and get you."

"Piss off we're busy," growls Head.

"There's two of 'em Bert!"

"Doin' it, is they Bill? Right you pair of perverts, out now or we'll brain ya."

"We are also police officers," grates I, shaking the drips off and trying to put my manhood back where it belongs but finding my hands are so cold I can't seem to keep hold of the stupid thing as it's shrunk back like a snail's head into its shell.

"They all say that," growls Bert. "Now *out* or we come in."

We go out to face a pair of old fashioned plods, helmet badges gleaming, thick bushy moustaches speckled with frost and truncheons raised ready to strike.

The one called Bill points at me. "I know you. You're that famous detective called Jerry Pot."

"Detective Inspector Gerald Potter, to be precise and this is my colleague, Detective Sergeant Head."

"Sorry to have to accost you, gentlemen. But you were in a bush together with your whatnots out."

Head goes for it, "That's because we're out on surveillance looking for the flasher and needed to pee because we're so bloody cold we can't hold it in!"

"How was we ta know that?" says Bill. "Anyway, just because you're detectives it don't mean you can't be a pair of funnies."

"Well we aren't," snaps Head.

"All right, don't get nasty about it, it was an easy mistake to make. Anyway, shouldn't you two be chasing mass murderers instead of hiding out in bushes."

"It is a long story," says I. "Now, which way is Upper Brook Street?"

He points across the park, "Walk straight through the fog and you'll come to an exit, cross over Park Lane and you're there."

I thank him, we wish them a merry Christmas and head off. Taking out my notebook I note the house number and check what the plod who originally interviewed a Miss Delphinium Spencer and a Miss Rosebud Spencer had told me earlier when we took over the case. One thing's for certain, these 'ladies' are apparently as nutty as coconuts. But, they recently sent a message to the Yard saying they have some new information about 'Jack the Flasher' so we best see them first, plus the plod stated that warming refreshments were gladly given. Presently we arrive at a semi-detached four storey white stone, modern house, with a small frontage surrounded by iron railings and a fancy scrolled gate leading up a short flight of stone steps to a posh black painted door. We climb the slippery steps and I pull the bell chain. The door swings open and we are confronted by a middle-aged, massive bulldog of a woman disguised as a maid.

"Yes! Can I help you?" sneers she, as the warming aroma of fresh baking manages to squeeze past her bulk to tickle our taste buds.

We flash our warrant cards, I introduce us and demand, "We have come to speak with your mistresses."

"For what reason?"

"For whatever reason it is."

"What is it then?"

"I do not wish to discuss delicate matters concerning your mistresses on the doorstep, madam. So, perhaps you should just allow us to enter."

"I can't stand here letting all the heat out. State your business or go away."

"Madam, I doubt very much that any heat at all would even dare to try and escape when you are on guard duty even if there was enough room for it to get past."

She shakes her head. "No one enters this austere establishment while I'm on duty unless they fully state their business."

"And what if that business is far too personal for a mere servant to hear?"

"I am privy to my mistresses' deepest secrets. They tell me everything. Now, for the last time; for what reason do you wish to speak to my mistresses?"

"Look, misses," puts in Head. "The Inspector keeps trying to tell you that it is too personal for a mere servant to hear. Now either you move your fat arse out of the way and let us in or…"

She slams the door in our faces.

"That didn't quite work, Sergeant," says I ringing the bell again. The maid's face appears at the window, she sticks her tongue out and gives us a two-fingered salute.

"Cheeky cow," grates Head.

"Let us in," I mouth to bulldog features.

"Clear off," she mouths back.

I hold up a hand. "Very well," I mouth. "You win."

She grins and draws her face back.

"I wouldn't tell that lump anything," grates Head. "Nosy cow."

"Fear not, Sergeant. I do not intend telling her the real reason why we are here."

The door opens. "Let's start again," smirks bulldog. "Can I help you gentlemen?"

I reintroduce us and then say, "We wish to converse with the Spencer sisters on a matter of the utmost importance."

"What importance?"

"We have reason to believe the sisters have secretly been laundering money for Chinese Triad drug smuggling gangs."

"What!" She lowers her voice, "I don't believe you, the sisters have never done a bit of laundry work in their entire lives. God forbid they should even wash out their own skiddy drawers let alone wash money."

"Nevertheless madam, it is imperative we speak to them if only to prove their innocence regarding this matter."

Narrowing her eyes, she appears thoughtful as she rubs her bristly chin. "Very well. You may enter. But wipe your cruddy feet."

We enter and she shuts the door. "Wait here," says she and wobbles off to disappear down a long picture galleried hallway.

We wipe our feet on a coconut mat and then look around. A seriously crafted mahogany staircase curls up towards the bedrooms. Aspidistra plants in colourful pots on white china stands that sit on expensive blue and white shiny tiles all herald the wealth and status that whoever lives in a house like this are bloody lucky sods. The house also has central heating.

"Not short of a few bob," says Head.

"Indeed not, Sergeant."

Bulldog returns. "My mistresses will see you right away. Give me your hats and coats."

We hand her our bowlers and coats which she throws on the floor. "Now follow me."

We follow her bouncing, wobbly bum down to a door that opens into a very plush parlour where two old birds sit side by side on high backed mahogany chairs with their backs to a roaring fire and their fronts at a huge oval table covered with a heavily embroidered cloth. On that cloth sits a silver cake stand with fancy cakes on it, besides the stand there is a blue patterned porcelain tea service that looks like it's worth more than my house. The old birds gaze at us studiously through sharp blue bloodshot eyes, they look like twins with their starchy grey hair poking out beneath matching bonnets, one lilac, the other bright yellow, they wear dresses that complement their bonnets. They have thin pinched noses and are heavily wrinkled, in truth they both appear as mad as March hares

Bulldog introduces us and pink bonnet says, "Sit down gentlemen."

We take seats opposite them and my backside sinks into the luxury of a well-padded seat.

Pink bonnet addresses Bulldog, "Malcom, make a fresh pot of Charley for the policemen and be quick about it."

"Yes madam," she snaps and turning away she stomps out like a bad-tempered baby elephant. Obviously she wanted to stay and earwig.

"Nosy fat slug," sneers lilac bonnet.

"I am Delphinium Spencer," says pink bonnet. "And this is my twin sister, Rosebud. How may we assist you lovely men?"

"We appreciate, ladies, that you have already been interviewed regarding your, um… unfortunate encounter with the flasher, but if you do not mind we would like to go through it again, and I believe you have some new information for us."

"We do have new information, Inspector. And we do not mind in the least going over what we have already said," says Delphinium. "There is nothing we'd like more. Is there dear?"

"No, indeed not," smiles Rosebud. "Spare not our blushes, Inspector, for we are women of the world. Are we not, dear?"

"We are indeed, Inspector. Rosebud and I have travelled the world. Father was a foreign diplomat you see. We have lived in Africa, India and even South America. We have seen it all, from bare bottomed barbarians to totally nudie natives. We have even seen the Dinka men swinging their big sticks at each other. Fascinating, Inspector. Have you been to Africa to visit the Dinka?"

"I cannot say that I have."

"And you, Sergeant?"

He shakes his head, "I went to France once."

"Oh, you won't find any Dinka there, I'm afraid."

"Walloping great handsome brutes," says Rosebud. "Strapping men, all muscles and no clothes. They like to fight each other, don't you know, Inspector."

"They do indeed," smiles Delphinium. "Goodness, they whack the shit out of each other, don't they dear?"

"They certainly do. Why they swing their whacking great big sticks all over the place. Whacking each other on the head, the back and even the buttocks. Anywhere's fair game, but they do try and avoid the manhood areas. But it can still be pretty bloody."

"It sounds gruesome," says I, trying to imagine two men going at it totally naked while whacking each other with big sticks. "I should think you ladies were glad to get away from these, um… Dinka men."

"Good God no, Inspector," laughs Delphinium. "We love them so much we go back every year for a month or so. Don't we dear?"

"Wouldn't miss it for the world. And they adore us too. Don't they dear?"

"Yes, they do. And it isn't just because we treat them to things they need to survive."

"What, like pots and tools?" asks I.

"Good grief, no. Rifles, Inspector. Rifles. They need them to shoot their neighbours before they shoot them."

"We always buy them a few rifles," smiles Rosebud. "They are so appreciative they hold a stick fight in our honour."

Luckily, Malcom comes back in with cups, saucers and a pot of tea on a silver tray which she sets down on the table between Head and I.

"Help yourselves, gentlemen," says Delphinium. "Malcom, pass the policemen the sugar bowl."

Malcom goes around to the sisters' side of the table, picks up the sugar bowl and then brings it around to us. Why Delphinium couldn't have just pushed it over herself I have no idea.

"Malcom, tell cook to plate up a few sausage rolls and beef patties for the policemen and look quick about it, they are in need of something to heat them up. Now, where has that lazy parlour maid got to?"

"She's in a cupboard with the gardener, madam."

"Gardener! Gardener! What's he doing indoors? He should be outside cutting the grass and pruning the roses."

"Everywhere's covered in snow and ice, madam. Gardening's a no go."

"Well go and tell the lazy bastard to go and clear it off so we can see the grass."

"Yes, madam. Anything else?"

"No, thank you, Malcom."

Malcom leaves and I ask, "Your maid has a very unusual name, Miss Spencer. Is it her surname?"

"Oh, it's not her surname or her Christian name, her real name's… What is her real name, dear?"

"Fuck knows."

"Is it really? That's it Inspector. Her real name was so rude we renamed her Malcom. It's easier to remember as we have a brother called Malcom."

Head shoots me a 'they're as mad as hell' look. I smile, that much is obvious. "Now, can you good ladies recall exactly what happened when you were accosted by the flasher?" I take out my notebook and flick through to the relevant page. "Leave nothing out even if it is embarrassing for you."

"You wish to know *every* little detail from that fateful day?" says Delphinium.

"We do, madam and we shall be taking notes."

"Very well. I arose at nine o'clock and went for a poo."

I hold up my hand. "Sorry, can you stop there. Omit everything until you were in the park and were accosted."

"Very well, Inspector. Rosebud and I were catching the air while enjoying a stroll around the lake. It was a sunny day and quite mild for the time of the year. But that was before the wind changed and blew all that white crap our way. We were in good spirits but as we veered off and went through a wooded area on a narrow footpath this man, dressed all in black, suddenly jumped out in front of us, threw open his ankle length coat and shouted out, 'Feast your eyes on this beauty, girls.'

"You must have been dreadfully shocked," says I.

She smiles and shakes her head. "What, by that piddling piddler? No, Inspector, not only were we unfazed by the sight of it, Rosebud and I burst into laughter. Especially as it was bent, well, sort of curved."

"In what way?"

"Imagine a banana, Inspector. It was just like that."

"Was it yellow?"

"No, more of an off white."

"I hate to ask, madam, was it in a state of arousal?"

"It was in a state, Inspector. Ugliest one I've ever seen. Far too much skin hanging off the end, wasn't there dear?"

"Oh, yes, far too much," joins in Rosebud. "Why it reminded me of the thin end of a sausage roll when you get that tapered pastry with no meat in it."

I am losing the plot here. "What happened next?"

Delphinium takes up the baton again, "He wagged it about for a while, which made us laugh even more, which seemed to make him really angry as he snarled out, 'Ain't you old bags horrified by the sight of my beauty?' We said, 'No, not really' Then Rosebud asked if she could sketch him. She always carries drawing equipment around with her in her handbag. Don't you dear?"

"I do indeed. I adore impromptu sketching, Inspector. If something unusual catches my eye I just have to get it down."

"How did the flasher respond to your request?"

"Oh, he was very keen to be immortalised in one of my sketches."

"So, we went into the woods for more privacy," says Delphinium. "Rosebud and I sat down on a fallen tree trunk and Rosebud got out her sketchpad and charcoal and set to it while the flasher posed."

I am amazed by this revelation. "You actually have a sketch of the flasher?"

"We do. Which is, of course, the new information we have. Do you wish to see it?"

I nod as words fail me.

Rosebud gets up and goes over to an ornate sideboard, opens a drawer and brings back a small sketchpad which she opens and passes over to me before retaking her seat and studying me expectantly through excited eyes. I study the sketch and pass it to Head. Rosebud has drawn the flasher in his entirety including his exposed banana. Beside and beyond the figure she has scribbled in a few trees for effect. It is very accomplished.

"Turn the page, Sergeant," urges Rosebud.

Head does so, frowns pointedly and hands the pad back to me. I gaze upon an enlarged detailed sketch of the offending object. It is graphic to the point of covering every wrinkle. I close the pad but hang on to it. "I found no reference to these sketches in the notes taken by the constable who originally interviewed you Miss Rosebud. Why was that?"

"Oh, he was very shy, Inspector. Why his face was as red as a baboon's bum and he sweated profusely throughout the interview and obviously couldn't wait to finish up and bugger off. So, we didn't actually get around to showing him the sketches, and we wondered whether we should even mention the sketches in case it should offend you good people."

"We are not offended, madam. May I borrow your sketches so our photographer can take copies?"

"Certainly, providing you realise that copyright remains with me."

"Of course. And I will return the pad as soon as I possibly can."

"Goody," she smiles just as there is a knock on the door.

"Come," bellows out Delphinium.

The door opens and in comes Malcom accompanied by a younger and much slimmer maid. Malcom is also carrying a plate with a steaming hot collection of pastries on it which she sets down on the table, again between Head and I.

"Thank you, Malcom," says Delphinium. "You may leave, but you, Rolland, remain."

Malcom flounces out and slams the door behind her while 'Rolland' stands to attention.

"Now, Rolland. Tell me what you were up to in the cupboard with the gardener when you know full well the manure smelling creature isn't allowed indoors without express permission from myself or Mistress Rosebud?"

"There's mice in that there cupboard Miss. I asked him in to clear them out because I is terrified of the little monsters."

"They are *bastard* creatures. Weeing all over the place and running up your drawers. That being the case you are let off. Off you go, Rolland. We shall say no more about it."

She leaves and Delphinium smiles at us. "Help yourselves to pastries, gentlemen." Reaching over she takes a sausage roll, splits the pastry and taking out the meat goes over to the door and squashes it in the key hole and then retakes her seat. "That'll block the nosy slugs' view," she grins. "I cannot abide snouty servants. What say you Inspector?"

"Agreed," says I, as Head and I try a similar patty-shaped pastry. It contains beef chunks with horseradish and is deliciously hot. "Your cook is very accomplished, madam. These pastries are delicious."

"Good. I'm glad you like them, Inspector."

She and Rosebud reach across and grab a fist full of pastries each and then tuck into them as if they're in a race to see who can scoff them the quickest. Not bothering with plates, crumbs fall all over the table and they even wipe their mouths with the back of their hands.

I grab a sausage roll before they all disappear and take a gulp of tea. Head grabs another beef patty and rams it in his gob.

At last the pastries have all gone and the sisters return to normal, well their impression of normal.

Delphinium asks, "Will that be all, gentlemen? Rosebud has a couple of models turning up very shortly. She's recreating that scene in her studio when Adam gives it to Eve in the Garden of Eden."

I take it she means when Adam gives Eve the apple, at least I hope that's what she means. "Just one or two more questions if you don't mind. Did the flasher say anything else while he was being sketched?"

"Yes, he did. He said, 'Ladies this is very kind of you. Can I have the sketches to keep?'"

Rosebud cuts in, "I said he could once I'd taken them back to my studio to polish them up and would he like our address so he could pick them up the next day. However, he declined my offer and once the rudimentary outlines had been done, he took a quick peek and then went away whistling."

"Interesting," says I. "Is there anything else you can think of that may help us in our investigations?"

"Yes, there is," smiles Delphinium. "He didn't have any ginger nuts on him."

"Why would he have biscuits on him?"

"No, not biscuits. Ginger nuts! Look, Inspector, the sketch is in charcoal pencil, his hair appears black around his privates as indeed it was, as does his beard and moustache. But in truth his facial hair was ginger. So, either he dyes his facial hair ginger or he dyes his private hairs black."

"Or more likely he was wearing a false beard," says Head.

The ladies clap their hands together. "Of course," says Rosebud. "I said as much to Delphinium. Didn't I dear?"

"You did dear. But I poo-pooed it."

"Thank you, ladies," says I, picking up the sketch pad and getting to my feet. "You have been very helpful."

Delphinium rings her bell and Rolland comes in and curtsies.

"Show the gentlemen out, please Rolland. Oh, one more thing Inspector. The flasher spoke like a commoner when he first addressed us, but during the sketching he dropped his *accent* and attempted to speak in a more cultured tone. Also, he was quite boyish, a bit squeaky, almost girlish really."

Rolland leads the way back to the hallway where she fetches our hats and coats then shows us to the door.

"May I ask, what are your and Malcom's real names?" says I slipping into my coat, donning my hat and shoving the sketchpad into the wide 'poacher's' pocket inside my coat.

"We have the same forenames, we is both Margarets and that's why the mistresses call us men's names so they don't get confused."

"Do they get confused a lot?"

She shrugs as she opens the door, "All I'll say, sir, is take everything they say wiv a bucket of salt."

"Thank you, Margaret," says I as Head and I step back out into the cold, but at least the smog seems to have lifted and the sun is out.

A smell of manure assaults my nostrils as a tall skinny man who's scraping the ice off the steps and tossing on grit straightens up and touches his cap. "Mornin, gov'. Bloody cold innit?"

"Brass bloody monkeys," shivers Head.

"I 'ave information on Jack the Flasher, for a couple of bob," says the smelly man who is obviously the gardener.

"What is it?" says I.

He raises bushy grey eyebrows. "Promise you'll pay up?"

"If your information is sound. I promise."

"Rumour has it that the flasher's a gent'. A real posh bugger. My mate Harry Long works at Parkins, the gent's tailors down Oxford Street an' 'e recently measured up this clean-shaven bloke for a black suit, long black coat an' top hat."

"Why would he assume that the man he measured up might be the flasher? Surely he is forever measuring up all manner of men for the same outfits?"

"True, but get this. Harry's ol' woman, Mable, works next door in the costume shop an' the same gent went in there and bought a couple of false ginger beards right after 'is fittin'. Two weeks later the flashing starts an' Mable gets flashed an' recognises the dirty bastard's ginger beard plus knowing his coat an' stuff came from Parkins."

I ponder over this Mable's surname, but cannot recall it in the notes I have. "Did this Mable Long report the incident to the authorities?"

He shakes his head, "Nah. She weren't that fussed by it. Besides, she weren't goin' to report no gent to the coppers in case it come back on her. You know 'ow it is? There's them an' us."

"Perhaps we should go and talk to the Longs, sir," says Head.

"They won't speak to ya," frowns smelly scratching his wiry hair beneath his cap. "They'll deny ever sayin' anythin' to me."

I realise of course I could be being taken for a ride just so the gardener can con me out of a few bob, and what he knows about the ginger beard was told to him by Rolland who'd obviously been earwigging her mistresses' conversations. Even so, we have little to go on as it is. "Do you know the name of this man?"

Leaning closer and nearly bowling me over with his unctuous odour he says smugly, "You want 'is name an' it'll cost ya another three bob. That's um... 'Ow much is two an' three?"

"Four," says I, holding out a hand.

"Four bob it is then, gov'." We shake hands on it. "Oswald Standridge Carter is 'is name."

"Any relation to Sir Stanley Standridge Carter, the famous explorer?"

"'Is son."

"I know where Sir Stanley lives when he's in London. I also know he and Lady Standridge Carter are in India killing tigers and won't be back for months. Now, have you any idea where I might find this, Oswald?"

"No. No one does. 'E was stayin' at their big 'ouse in Belgravia. But apparently the ol' man kicked 'im out just before 'e an' 'is misses went off on their travels. 'E caught 'im rogering the 'ousekeeper. The 'ol man was furious 'cause 'e thought 'e was the only one rogering the 'ousekeeper, but it turns out everyone was, includin' the butler."

"This housekeeper sounds a woman of very low morals," says I sternly.

"Not really. She just likes a bit of 'ow's ya father."

"How do you know all this?"

"Mable's sister, Beryl, works at the 'ouse as a chambermaid."

I thank him and hand him his four shillings and tell him to contact me at Scotland Yard should he hear anything else. Head and I continue on our way.

"I wonder how much of what we've learnt today is just a load of old rubbish, sir," says Head.

"I am thinking the same, Sergeant. But for lack of anything more we shall have to follow up on this information. I suggest we head off to Sir Stanley's house in Belgravia and question this Beryl, the housekeeper and, Oswald, if he has deemed to return home now his father's out of the way. If nothing comes of it we'll journey to Oxford Street tomorrow and question the Longs."

"If they'll even talk to us."

"If indeed," sighs I. "The sooner we solve this ridiculous case and get back to normal the better."

It doesn't make sense, I ponder to myself as we stroll along. Sir Stanley I know for a fact is devoted to his wife and wouldn't risk ruining his marriage or the ensuing scandal by giving one to his housekeeper. Servant gossip that has become twisted beyond reality and got out of hand is what this is all about. Oswald and the housekeeper were at it and as a consequence Sir Stanley threw them both out. Oswald is probably no more the flasher than I am. The other thing is, Rosebud's sketch of the flasher doesn't really match the description given by the majority of his other victims, especially the colour of his beard - they nearly all said it was black. Although one said it was greyish like a dirty old man's and another said it was orange, while several more said they didn't know because they weren't looking at his beard anyway and also failed to notice what colour his pubic hair was.

We head back in silence into Hyde Park and skirting Park Lane make our way towards Belgrave Square where Sir Stanley's house is close by in Chester Street. Suddenly I feel something poking around my left flank.

"You have a new friend, sir," grins Head.

I look down to see a black labrador sniffing at my left hip. "Clear off," orders I trying to shoo the thing away. I am met by a growl and a wagging tail.

"Do you want me to shoot it?" offers Head kindly. "It might have rabies."

"No thank you, Sergeant. It's healthier than you and I. I just want it to stop slavering at my side and clear off."

"There must be something on your coat that it likes the smell of. Perhaps it can smell the pastries on you."

"Of course." I eyeball the dog and say, "Sorry, old chap, but we have nothing for you, we have scoffed the lot."

"He doesn't look like he believes you, sir, he keeps licking his lips."

"Look, doggy, I've told you they are all gone. Now clear off before I lose my temper."

I spy a pair of urchins up ahead building snowmen. "Let us go and talk to those boys, Sergeant. Perhaps the dog belongs to then."

We go up to the urchins, who are wrapped up well in thick, cut-down adults' coats. They have woollen hats and gloves on that look suspiciously like the ones Betty knits and gives to poor kids such as they.

"Does this dog belong to you?" I ask the tall lanky one who gazes at me through squinting eyes as a big dew drop falls from his nose. Both boys are obviously freezing cold despite their warm clothes and shivering like jellies.

"Nuffin' to do wiv us, mister. It's been runnin' 'round 'ere the past hour or more. Do you want to buy a snowman?"

"How much is it?" asks Head.

"Sixpence," grins the shorter one, his red nose running green candles down to his chapped lips where it quickly gets licked away.

"What would we do with it if we did buy it?" asks I.

"How should we know?" snaps Lanky. "Do ya want it or not?"

I shake my head, "No thank you."

"I know," says Shorty. "You could take it 'ome an' put it in ya garden."

"And how shall I get it home? It isn't easy carrying a snowman you know."

"We can deliver," says Lanky. "For another sixpence."

Suddenly the dog sinks its teeth into my coat, making me jump. I give it a ringer around its floppy lug and it backs off growling. Then a bell rings in my head. Unbuttoning my coat, I slip in a hand and take out the chunk of ham that I slipped into my jacket pocket at breakfast and hold it up high, which causes the dog to set up an excited barking while trying to leap up high enough to grab the ham. I pass the ham to Head. "Hold this for a bit, Sergeant. But do not eat it."

"Can't say I really fancy it, sir," says he holding it right up in the air.

While the dogs jumping up at Head, I speak to the boys. "Can either of you read?"

"I can," says Lanky giving me a puzzled frown.

"Good." I take out my note pad and a pencil and quickly scribble down my address and a short note to Betty. Tearing out the page I hand it to Lanky and fish around in my trouser pockets for a few coins, coming up with a half a crown. "Here's the deal. Takes yourselves down to Holborn way and go to that address. The lady who lives there is my wife and also the lady who knitted those woollies you are wearing. Her name is Mrs Betty Potter."

"We knows 'er an' this street," amazes Lanky wide eyed. "We call her Betty the Diamond. Everyone luvs 'er, 'cause she's so kind and has a great body."

I ignore the body comment, even though it's true. "Give Mrs Potter the note. She will let you in and will want you to build snowmen with her. That's outside the house, not inside. No doubt she'll even give you something hot to eat and drink. Now, while you're there you will conduct yourselves appropriately. If you nick anything, piss on the floor or upset Betty in anyway, you will have me to deal with. Understand?"

They both nod frantically. I hand Lanky the half crown and he whistles in appreciation, but then says, "What's the catch, mister?"

"You take that mutt with you for a short way, give it the piece of ham and then lose the bloody thing. Agreed?"

"Agreed," he takes off a glove, spits in his hand and offers it to me.

We touch hands and then I wipe mine on the dog's silky coat before taking the ham from Head and passing it to Lanky.

"Cor," says he. "That's a big chunk of 'am. Can't me and Mikey 'ave a bit of it as well as the bloomin' dog?"

"Why not," says I. "Now get going before you catch your deaths."

The boys go off with the dog trotting alongside. Head and I continue on our way.

"What was that all about, sir?" says Head, shooting me an old-fashioned look. "I know you wanted to get rid of the dog, but handing over a half crown to those little devils doesn't make sense. They'll probably eat all the ham and just bugger off home with the money. If they've got a home that is."

"They've got a home, Sergeant. And decent parents too. Poor, but honest and hardworking."

"How do you know all this?"

"I recognised the tall one's coat. It's been cut down, but once it was on my back. I had a clear out of clothes a few months back and gave my cast-offs to one Joe Clements. He's a jobbing builder who has done the odd job for me and the father of those boys. Clements lives a couple of streets from me and if those boys don't do as I told them I will call on Joe and he'll sort them out."

"What if Betty doesn't want those boys around?"

"She will. Betty's been a bit down. Another Christmas approaching without the patter of tiny feet around the place. She will love having those boys around. She'll be out back making snowmen and throwing snowballs. Then she'll feed them up, give them each a handknitted new jumper before marching them back home."

"You never fail to amaze me, sir. Your kindness and generosity are often at odds with the hardnosed, brutal copper that most criminals know and hate."

"Thank you, Sergeant for that stirring accolade. I love you too."

He shoots me an odd look and then quickens his pace. We carry on in silence until we reach Sir Stanley Standridge Carter's home. It is a huge detached late Georgian white fronted house with a sweeping driveway big enough to take half a dozen carriages. The property is ringed by an eight-foot-high red brick wall and the scrolled black iron gates make the usual statement: Keep out and piss off if you are a hawker, a low life, a beggar, etc. Ignoring the written version on the wall we try the gates; they are unlocked so we swing one open enough to pass through and then shut it behind us. Head suddenly claps his hands together and then sticks two fingers in his mouth and whistles loud enough to wake the dead.

"We're safe to continue," says he. "If there were any vicious guard dogs loose they'd have been flying at us from out of nowhere by now."

We cross the driveway, climb the steps up to a pair of imposing doors painted bright red and Head pulls the bell cord in the wall. Two minutes later the door opens and we are confronted by a tall, erect footman with plastered down dark hair and a neatly trimmed thin moustache. He appears rather splendid in his red livery complete with shiny brass buttons.

"Good morning, gentlemen," says he amiably. "May I help you?"

We flash our warrant cards and I introduce us. "We wish to talk with Master Oswald Standridge Carter, the chambermaid called Beryl and the housekeeper, regarding a rather delicate matter."

"Please come in," says he, stepping aside.

We enter and turn to face him as he closes the door.

"Master Oswald has moved on to pastures new," says he.

"Has he moved into a field?" asks Head.

Sometimes I have no idea whether Head is joking or just plain stupid.

The footman grins, "I have no idea, Sergeant. Neither less do I care. Beryl is out on an errand, but should be back within the hour. The housekeeper, Miss Janice Palmer, has also moved on and is no longer employed at this establishment."

"Ah…" says I, wondering what to say next.

"May I enquire what this is about, Inspector."

"You may."

"Thank you. What is this about?"

"My Sergeant and I are investigating the recent incidents regarding a certain individual who exposes himself to innocent ladies in order that he may obtain some kind of sexual pressure from the distress he catapults them into."

"Do you not mean sexual *pleasure*?"

"That as well."

"I suppose you will also want to speak to Miss Amelia and Miss Rebecca Richardson."

The names ring a bell. I fish out my notebook and flick through the pages. The women are twin sisters and were interviewed two weeks ago having been accosted by the flasher in Saint James' Park.

"According to my notes the sisters were originally interviewed over this matter in a house in Berkeley Street. May I ask why they are here?"

"You may."

"Why are they here?"

"They are house sitting for Sir Stanley. He does not like leaving the house without a housekeeper and butler to maintain order. The sisters, being his nieces, were happy to temporarily move in here and take control until the master returns from his travels."

"What happened to the butler?" asks Head.

"He ran off with the housekeeper the lucky bastard."

"That lovely, is she?" sympathises Head.

The footman drops his head and stares reflectively at his shiny black shoes. When he raises his eyes, they have gone a bit watery. "I shall inform the ladies of your arrival," chokes he.

"Cor, he's *well* smitten," says Head once the footman's out of earshot. "This housekeeper must be one hell of a girl. I wish I could meet her."

I change the subject as I peruse the hall. "I thought the Spencer's house was posh, Sergeant, but this place takes opulence to the extreme."

"It certainly does, sir," says he gazing all around a hall that would do Buckingham Palace proud. "I don't suppose Chloe and me will ever live in a place like this."

"Nor me and Betty. Unless I mysteriously inherit a fortune from a long lost relative, which is extremely unlikely."

"You'd have to rob a bank to get enough to buy a place like this."

I throw him my serious look. "We could do that, Sergeant. If you fancy it."

"Do what?"

"Rob a bank."

"What and get caught then spend the next twenty years in clink?"

"Or not get caught and spend the rest of our lives in luxury."

Thoughtfully he rubs at his chin. "I don't know, sir. I mean, this place is out of our world, but is it worth risking your freedom for?"

"My thoughts exactly, Richard. I would rather be tucked up safe and sound in bed with my lovely Betty than shivering all alone in a cold grey cell on a lumpy straw mattress."

"And having to poo into a rusty old bucket and slop out in the morning when it's had all night to gas you to death."

"Eating watery porridge and mouldy cheese."

"Communal showering in cold water and never daring to bend over to pick up your dropped soap, in case you get rogered by some hairy-arsed psychopath who's fallen hopelessly in love with you."

"Shaving with a blunt razor."

"Having your hair shaved off. No *thank you*… On reflection, sir, I'm happy as I am."

"Good. So am I. Besides, who knows what might be around the next corner."

The footman returns, "The ladies will see you now, gentlemen. Allow me to take your hats and coats and then please follow me."

I take the sketchpad from my pocket and we do as we were bid. This time our coats are hung up in a cloakroom and our hats set down on a black velvet covered shelf before we follow the footman down a seemingly never-ending corridor festooned with lots of wild animal heads stuck all over its orange painted walls. There's so many, from every continent, that there is very little space for anymore heads unless they are from mice.

"What a rotten colour that orange is," whispers Head.

"Does it matter? There's barely ten percent of visible wall."

"Too many bloody heads. It's a wonder there's any wildlife left in some of these countries the way this lot blasts away at them."

"It is overkill on an industrial scale, Sergeant."

At last we come to a halt at the entrance to the drawing room. I know it is the drawing room because it says so on a silver plaque on the door. Footman opens the door and steps inside with us edging in behind him. The room is seriously decadent with its exquisite French furnishings and gold velvet curtains that are tied back at two huge windows that gaze out over a massive landscaped garden that is magically enhanced by its covering of blue tinged snow. On a settee large enough to accommodate half of London sit two elegant young women perched on the very edge of the heavily embroidered seat as their bustles demand. Both have dark silky hair piled up just so, they are fine featured and dressed in white gowns embroidered with tiny flowers, the one on my left has roses, the one on my right chrysanthemums. Delicate hands rest on their laps, they are demure, reserved and gaze up at us with apprehension through soft hazel eyes, their china white skin flushing prettily in their cheeks. I fall in love.

"Please sit, gentlemen," says Footman waving a hand towards a pair of armchairs opposite the settee.

We sit down, the chairs are so big you could house a slum family of four in them. Between us and the young ladies is a bow-legged gold leafed coffee table bigger than my kitchen table. The floor is decked in a fabulous Persian carpet that would be well worth pinching but would need four men to carry it off, it's *that* huge.

"Would you gentlemen care for refreshments?" asks Footman.

"A coffee would be nice, thank you," says I.

"And for me, please," says Head.

Footman goes off and I introduce myself and Head.

"I am Amelia Richardson," says the one on my left in a trembling tone. "This is my younger sister by ten minutes, Rebecca. How may we assist you, Inspector?"

They smile timidly, displaying perfect white teeth surrounded by slightly sulky very kissable pink lips. I estimate their ages at between eighteen and twenty.

"We have an image of the man who may have accosted you in Saint James' park. We would like you both to look at it and confirm if you recognise it as being the same man."

Amelia's eyes open extraordinarily wide in apparent shock. "Oh! I don't know. I had hoped never to see that awful man's face ever again."

"Nor I," croaks Rebecca.

I recall the notes up in my head that were taken at the time by a plod. "In your original statement, Miss Rebecca, you said you did not see the assailant's face. Are you now saying you did?"

She blushes deep red and sets to wringing with her hands. "I didn't see his face. All I saw was that *disgusting* thing hanging out of his trousers. Amelia described the brute to me later on and now I have to suffer awful visions of the monster coming for me while I lay helpless in my bed."

She starts to sob, burying her face in her hands as her entire body shakes with emotion. I breathe in deep, this isn't going to be easy and I wish I had not come.

"Try not to upset yourself so, Miss Rebecca. We have the culprit in our sights and hope to arrest him much later than sooner. Anyway, you are safe here and provided you only go out escorted by, say a bodyguard, you will have no further trouble."

"That is exactly what father said," says Amelia. "And that is alright to say, but we haven't dared to venture out in fear of our very lives."

"Why your lives?"

"We came near to heart attacks, Inspector. We came close to dying! Oh, God! It was the most terrible of situations. Just the two of us, all alone in the park and to be practically jumped on by that revolting creature." She sweeps a dramatic hand across her brow before flopping back on the settee in an apparent faint.

A maid enters carrying a silver tray with coffee pot and all that goes with it, including a small tray of mint chocolate squares. On seeing her mistresses' distress she raises admonishing eyebrows, dumps the tray on the table, shakes her head in frustration and walks back out.

Head throws me a questioning look that says it all. The sisters are grossly exaggerating their symptoms, overacting and taking us for fools and I am thinking the sooner we get out of here the better, plus I have fallen out of love with the pair of them.

Amelia comes around and sitting up straight gazes right into my eyes. "I apologize, Inspector. To you and the Sergeant." She smiles sweetly at Head and I can feel his melting beneath her sparkling hazel eyes. "It really has been such a trauma."

"Perhaps we should leave it for now, Miss. We shall come back when you are more composed."

"Needs must, Inspector. Let us get it over with rather than drag it on. We will be brave, I promise you. Won't we Rebecca?"

Rebecca recovers her composure and I note there is not a single tear in her eye, but when she speaks her bottom lip quivers oh… so… prettily. "I will be a brave little soldier. Show us your picture, Inspector. But do not be surprised if we swoon away."

"Part of the picture contains a graphic image," warns I. "Do you wish me to cover the thing up?"

"Oh! The thing! The thing!" cries Rebecca. "That disgusting object. Never have I seen such a *revolting* sight in all my life. But still I must go on, I must face my demons if ever I am to return to normality again."

Bloody roll on, I grate to myself. She would have seen hundreds of horses' knobs in her life unless she goes around with her eyes permanently closed. There isn't much difference between man and beast anyway other than size.

"I'll pour the coffee," says Head. "Would you ladies care for a cup?"

They shake their heads and Amelia says, "I shall require something more fortifying than mere coffee if I am to survive this ordeal."

Getting to her feet she goes over to a bell cord beside the window and gives it several angry tugs. Almost immediately the maid comes in, no doubt she had been earwigging on the other side of the door.

"Bring the brandy and four glasses," demands Amelia. "Or I shall die of exasperation."

Or overacting, muses I.

The maid goes over to the drinks cabinet and returns with a crystal decanter half full with brandy and four small glasses on another silver tray which she sets down on the table before curtsying and then leaving.

They have a good deal of silver in the place and I'm wondering if I might take a few bits home with me for Christmas. "Shall I pour, Miss?"

"Thank you, but *we* must do it," croaks Amelia sitting back down. "But if we cannot manage it I am sure the Sergeant will assist us."

With trembling hands Rebecca takes hold of a glass, Amelia takes the stopper from the decanter and then holding the decanter with both hands tips its towards the glass.

"Pour it now," sobs Rebecca.

"I'm trying," cries Amelia, tipping the decanter enough for a few drops to plink into the glass. "You are *not* keeping the glass still!"

"I am! It's you who keeps moving the decanter about. Just tip it *up* a little more."

Amelia does and at last the glass has a good tot in it. Setting the decanter down she flops back on the settee again, "Oh, *God*, I am *exhausted* from the effort."

"Exhausted! Exhausted!" cries Rebecca as she clasps her hands in prayer and stares up at the crystal chandelier for divine intervention.

I give it to her, "Sergeant, take over and pour the brandies before we *all* faint away." Truly I have had enough of their shenanigans.

Head leans over the table and grabs the decanter and all three glasses. He pours a tot in one and pushes it back over before filling the other two close to the brim and passing me one.

"Cheers," says I lifting the glass to my mouth and swallowing half the contents down. It is as smooth as silk, even better than Clump's finest whisky. Head takes a good swallow while the sisters take a demure sip before chucking the rest down in a *very* unladylike fashion. They pass their glasses back to Head. He half fills each one and pushes them back.

I open the sketchpad to the full-length sketch of the flasher and pass it over to Amelia. "Is this the same man who accosted you in the park?"

She nods and shows it to Rebecca.

Rebecca nods and says, "I recognise his *thing*."

I reach out and take back the pad, close it and set it down on the table.

"What colour was his beard?" I ask directing my question to Amelia.

"It was black."

"Are you sure it wasn't red?"

She nods. "Definitely black just like in the sketch."

"And you are both sure this was the man who accosted you on that fateful day?"

They both nod before raising their glasses and again chucking the brandy down in one go. Rebecca chokes a little and Amelia shudders, but it is obvious both of them are well used to drinking alcohol and I am wondering just exactly what kind of 'ladies' I am dealing with here. They certainly are *not* shrinking violets.

"Did the flasher speak to you?"

Amelia drops her eyes and stares at the carpet, "Only to say, 'Look at this, girls.'"

"Was his accent lower class or upper class?"

She meets my eyes and shrugs, "I'm not sure, Inspector. Perhaps somewhere in between."

I down the rest of my brandy, take hold of the sketch pad and get to my feet. Head, empties his glass and also stands up. It is time we left.

"We shall leave you in peace, ladies," says I. "Just one more thing. Do you know where Oswald has gone?"

They shake their heads and stare up at me with expressions of pure innocence. "No idea, Inspector," says Amelia. "He could be abroad for all anyone knows."

"Do you know why he disappeared?"

Amelia nods solemnly, "He had been having a, shall we say, inappropriate relationship with one of the servants."

I smile, "Thank you for your time and we are truly sorry for upsetting you both. Please forgive us."

"We do. We do," urges Amelia. "Don't we Rebecca?"

"Yes… Yes of course."

"Well good afternoon to you both," says I. "And thank you again for all your help. We'll see ourselves out."

Head and I head for the door, once back in the hallway I gently close the door, put a finger to my lips and then bob down to spy through the key hole. Head presses an ear to the door and we wait. It doesn't take a minute before the sisters are up on their feet and embracing each other before splitting away and laughing loud enough for us to clearly hear.

"What a hoot!" guffaws Amelia.

"Priceless darling. Utterly priceless," snorts Rebecca.

"I do believe we should be on the stage, darling. Why we'd give that *bloody* Langtry woman a run for her money."

"What did you think of our intrepid policemen?"

"Nice enough, I suppose. For *commoners*."

"That Sergeant was quite sweet."

"I quite liked the Inspector. He was a bit more cultured. A bit of upper class breeding somewhere down the line, no doubt."

"Out of wedlock of course."

"The maid and the master."

They collapse back on the settee in fits of laughter and I have heard enough. "Let's go, Sergeant," says I, standing up.

"What a pair of spoilt tarts," grates Head as we head back to the hallway. "They both need a bloody sharp lesson in life on how to be a lady."

"Such as?"

"A kick up the proverbial for a starter."

"Fear not, Sergeant. I have a feeling we shall be meeting those 'ladies' again, but next time it will be on our terms."

We reach the hall where Footman is sat on a chair talking to another pretty, rather busty young maid who is standing almost to attention.

"This is Beryl Jones sir," says he, rising to his feet.

Beryl appears somewhat apprehensive. I quickly put her at her ease and ask her to confirm all that the gardener had told us. She does exactly that, except for adding that it is only a suspicion that Oswald could be the flasher because he once exposed himself to a scullery maid when she went into his bedroom to clean out his grate, and that she mentioned that to her sister in the strictest confidence. She has nothing else to add except that she believes the Richardson sisters *do* know exactly where Oswald is, and that they are so close to him they would know whether or not he *is* the flasher. But, would lie through their teeth to protect him because he's one of their own.

"Them sisters are terrible snobs," she adds, her mouth twisting up with frustration. "If you're not from their class then you don't count. Ain't that right, Jim?"

"They're like a pair of beautiful birds, Inspector. You gaze up at them in awe while they gaze down at you with contempt before dropping a sloppy plop on you."

"Spoilt rotten," grates Head. "The sort who'll fall into a sewer and come up wearing a new dress."

"Perhaps," says I. "But everyone has to pay the piper one day, Sergeant. Even the privileged." I thank Beryl and Jim for their time. Head and I don our coats and hats and once again we venture out into the cold.

"Where to now, sir?" asks Head as we cross the road once a coal waggon has gone by and an urchin riding on the back hurls a couple of lumps of coal at us but misses spectacularly because we are seasoned duckers.

I check my fob watch. "It's three o'clock, Sergeant. I suggest we bugger off home before it gets dark because in truth, I have had enough of the cold for one day. Plus, look at that sky coming over."

Head gazes up and whistles. "It's full of it, sir. There must be half the North Pole up there waiting to fall down on us."

We head for the nearest Underground station, discussing all we have learnt this day.

"I don't know who was the worst," says Head. "Those batty old birds or the batty young birds. I mean, who do you believe? The old girls insisted the flasher had a red beard, but the other two insisted he had a black beard."

"They might all be telling the truth, Sergeant. If the flasher does indeed wear false beards then he can change colours whenever he wants too. But, as nearly everyone who has been interviewed so far, except for the Spencers, has insisted that he sported a black beard, then I am inclined to think the Spencers lied to us, or we have a copycat flasher to also contend with."

"The old girls are mad, sir, and probably made it all up just for attention. Best to forget them. But those other two, well I'd like to go back there and give those brats a real good grilling, because I think they were lying *and* acting a part just for a laugh. Stick the fear of a truncheon up the pair of them that's what I'd threaten them with and make them tell us the truth because I think they know a lot more than they are saying."

"The trouble is, they may well be telling the truth. If we go at them like a couple of bullies we shall be the ones hauled over hot coals, Sergeant. We are not dealing with ordinary people, we are dealing with two extremely privileged young ladies who can call upon a wealth of powerful men to ensure the likes of you and I are not only slapped down but booted in the bollocks as well, metaphorically speaking that is."

"Um…" sighs Head. "Don't it just piss you off sometimes, sir, being hamstrung just because you weren't born with a silver spoon in your gob?"

"I try not to allow it to bother me. Anyway, on a different note, I intended to ask for a photograph of this Oswald fellow so we might compare his features to our sketch. That way we can either condemn him or exonerate him while exposing both sets of sisters as liars or indeed innocents."

"We could go back."

I shake my head, "A roaring fire, a wonderful wife and a delicious beef stew await, Sergeant. The twins, the Longs and the bloody flasher can all wait until tomorrow. What say you?"

"A roaring fire also waits for me, sir, along with the comforting arms of my lovely Chloe. But as for a delicious stew; God knows what I'll get, Chloe can't fry an egg without cremating it."

"She'll learn, Sergeant. The main thing is you love her and she is an accomplished housewife in every other way."

"I'm dreading Christmas Day," he frowns, "Undercooked turkey. Hard roasties. Sloppy veg and a gravy thinner than a gnat's urine."

We come to a halt and face each other just before we descend towards the Underground. "Then come to ours on Christmas Day.

Come early and then Betty can teach Chloe the essence of planning, preparing and cooking a *superb* Christmas dinner. Crack that and Chloe will be half way there."

"That sounds lovely, sir. But shouldn't you ask Betty first. I mean she may have asked loads around for dinner already and can't handle any more. Besides that, she might not want us around on the big day anyway."

"She will. She loves company, especially you and Chloe's. Besides, as her sister and her five, unbelievably noisy, unruly brats have moved up north because of her husband's promotion on the railways only Betty's parents have been invited, making it a very quiet Christmas indeed. So, we'll have plenty of room, lots of food, drink, crackers, nuts and festive everything.

Head looks doubtful. "Perhaps you should confirm with Betty that it will be alright before I tell Chloe."

"Look, Richard. I am fully in charge when Betty's out. It will be fine, trust me."

"Then, Gerald," smiles he holding out his hand. "Chloe and I look forward to sitting at your table on Christmas Day."

"Good man," says I shaking his hand. "Now, let's get home before the sky opens up."

I finally arrive home looking like the Abominable Snowman, I'm that covered in snow. The front door is only half visible because of drifting snow, the wind cuts you in half and I fear my balls have dropped off from frost bite. I decide to go around back because if I open this door the snow will fly into the hallway and then I probably won't be able to shut the door until I've shovelled the snow away, doing that will let all the heat out and Betty will have a moan. Trudging around back I can just make out three sizable, well-crafted snowmen through the blizzarding snow. Slapping off as much of the icy snow from my coat as I can I turn the backdoor knob, step inside and quickly shut the door.

"Goodness, me," cries Betty as she turns away from the range to face me. "You must be frozen, Detective Inspector. Did I not tell you to seek shelter if it snowed heavily?"

"You, d…d…did indeed," says I, my teeth chattering as Betty comes over to me.

"Let's get you out of this coat," says she going for my buttons. "And don't you dare move off that door mat before I tell you."

I wouldn't dare, thinks I. Coat off, Betty hangs it on the hook on the door to drip dry, removes my bowler and hangs that up before giving me a peck on my frozen cheek.

"Stamp your feet and then go and stand by the range and get warmed up, Detective Inspector."

"I'd rather, g…g… go sit by the fire."

"You're too wet to go into the parlour just yet. I'll go and get you some warm socks and your slippers, and a nice tumbler of scotch."

Doing as I've been told I practically hug the range while drinking in the wonderful aroma of the stew gently bubbling away on the plate. Betty returns in a minute, hands me the scotch, drags over a chair and tells me to sit. Once sat she bobs down, takes off my shoes and socks, puts on a welcoming pair of warmed, thick handknitted socks, slips my slippers on and then stands up while gazing down at me like a loving mother. My hands are shaking so much I have to hold my glass up to my mouth with both hands.

"B…body warmth is the b…best way to get warm," says I gazing up into her beautiful face. She truly is an angel. Not many women would do what she'd just done without having a go about my uncut nails and cheesy feet.

"Body warmth later. After you've washed your smelly feet and cut your toenails, Detective Inspector."

Avoiding the subject, I ask, "How did you get on with those boys? I… I saw the s… snowmen in the garden."

She smiles her 'I love you' smile. "It was pure magic. Mikey and Jack were lovely. Polite, friendly and bundles of fun. We built three snowmen, had a snowball fight and then I fed and watered them with stew and a hot drink. I then walked them home before the snow fell down. That was a lovely thing you did Detective Inspector and I really did appreciate it. How was your day?"

I tell her all. She laughs about the Spencer sisters, frowns about the Richardsons and is intrigued to see the sketches of the flasher, which luckily, I find have remained dry once I had fetched them from my coat pocket. We chat for a while until I am ready for the fireside and another scotch. Betty takes my glass and puts it down on the kitchen table. Taking my hand, she leads me into the hallway and I am thinking we are about to go upstairs. We are not. Instead Betty stops at the parlour door and orders me to close my eyes and not to open them until she says so under pain of no 'body warmth' for a week. I do as I am told. I am led into the parlour where I hear the crackle and spit from the fire and feel its heat enveloping the room. I can also smell pine, that earthy smell you get from a Christmas tree.

"Open your eyes, Detective Inspector."

I do so, in front of the drawn curtains stands a majestic highly decorated Christmas tree sat in a large flower pot with red coloured crepe paper draped around it. The tree stands seven feet high and is adorned on its top with a golden winged angel that gazes down at you with sobriety and love. Shiny multi-coloured balls, tinsel, little soldiers in red and black uniforms. Tiny candles with fake glass flames are illuminated by the flickering yellow and blue flames from the oil lamps situated around the room. Beneath the tree are several more presents, wrapped in coloured paper, than I would normally expect to see. In fact, a *hell* of a lot more presents than I would normally expect to see. I really am in for a treat this Christmas.

"Well?" says Betty. "What do you think?"

"It is truly magnificent," says I. Turning to face her I pull her into me and wrap my arms around her waist.

"The greengrocer brought it round *just* after you had left and I managed to *just* finish decorating it *just* as the boys knocked on the door."

"That's a lot of justs," grins I. "Just as there seems to be an awful lot of presents under that tree."

She breaks away from me and goes over to the sideboard. "I fancy a nice drop of port," she says cagily. "Do you want one?"

"I'll have another scotch," says I, knowing I am about to hear something I may not like.

"Shall we sit down, Detective Inspector?"

"We shall," says I taking the glass held out to me. I take my armchair to the right of the fire and Betty takes the one to the left of the fire. We do this because the left side doesn't suffer as much draught from the door. "So, my little slippery minx. What do you have to tell me?"

She takes a sip of her port and looks at me with trepidation in her eyes. "Joe Clements, that's Mikey and Jack's father."

"I know who he is," cuts in I.

"Well, Joe broke his leg falling off a ladder a few weeks back and hasn't been able to work since. He *is* on the mend, but because of his incapacity the family have had to survive on his wife taking in laundry and the boys earning whatever they can. Hence the reason they were out in all that biting cold hoping to raise a little extra money for Christmas."

"Hence the reason there are so many more presents under the tree," frowns I. "You have not only bought them presents from my hard-earnt money, but I will bet you have also invited them for Christmas dinner which will cost me *even more*."

Betty turns on her 'I know I've been naughty cute kitten' look which would melt an ice cap. I can also understand so very well why she would love to have those young lads around for Christmas Day. Especially as we haven't got hardly any guests anyway. She loves a full house.

"What is done is done," grates I. "But really Betty, sometimes you go too far with this charitable heart of yours. I am a police officer not a bloody banker."

"Sorry, Detective Inspector," says she sulkily in that way she does when there is more to come. "I couldn't just ask the boys without asking the rest of the family, now could I?"

"You certainly couldn't!" I lift my eyes to the ceiling and suck in air before I face her and say, "Remind me, do Joe Clements and his wife Judith, have three girls as well as two boys?" Betty nods guiltily. "And doesn't Joe's widowed mother live with them as well?"

"She does," says Betty in a barely audible croak.

I raise challenging eyebrows. "I have also invited Richard and Chloe."

"Oh, lovely. Mother and father are coming of course. And…um…so…"

This one gets me out of my chair and onto my feet. "Don't tell me your sister and her tribe are going to be down for Christmas and are all descending on us as well?"

"They are."

"Couldn't they come on Boxing Day?"

"No. They are going to his parents on Boxing Day and so are my parents."

"How *wonderful* for them all. My first sanctioned Christmas Day *and* Boxing Day off in three years that will not only cost me a fortune, it will mean living in a sardine tin on one day and being too exhausted the next to enjoy so much as a mince pie."

"Oh, that's reminded me, Detective Inspector. I must put mincemeat on my shopping list."

I sit down again and stare into the fire. "Why not pick up a hamper or two and have them delivered to the work house while you are at it?"

"That is a right Scrooge thing to say, Detective Inspector and is unworthy of you."

I meet her admonishing eyes. "Sorry. But it doesn't detract from the fact that there will be, what, ten kids and eleven adults altogether? May I remind you our dining table seats eight, ten at a squash. Do you suggest we seat ten in the dining room, four at the kitchen table and the rest in the parlour? Or perhaps everyone might like to *stand* at the dining room table to eat their dinners while shouldering a kid and feeding it at the same time!"

"Now you are being silly."

"*I'm* being silly?"

"It's all in hand. While the men get drunk as usual in the parlour, us ladies will serve the children first in the dining room. Then, while they go into the parlour to play quietly with their Christmas presents us adults shall enjoy *our* dinner around the dining room table."

"It seems you have it all mapped out. However, I seem to recall you ordered a turkey big enough to serve six not six hundred."

"I changed the order this afternoon once I had taken the boys home."

"To what?"

"A fifteen pounder, a leg of pork, four pound of sausage meat, for stuffing and rolls, and a slipper of ham for tea."

I am incredulous, "We are to give them tea as well?"

"In for a penny."

"Debtors prison as well I have no doubt."

Betty reaches into her dress pocket and to my amazement pulls out a small wad of pound notes. "I have been putting this aside throughout the year. It is the money I earn for knitting those posh cardigans for the Wool Shop on the High Street. I haven't told you but they doubled their order in the summer because they are so popular. So, do not fear, Detective Inspector, I have saved enough to not only pay for Christmas dinner, but enough to have bought and payed for all those presents under the tree. So there."

I shrink down in my chair, swallow the rest of my scotch and wait for the rest.

"Talking about presents, Detective Inspector, I was unable to find where you have hidden *my* present."

"That's because you aren't supposed to find it as you'll only guess what it is, as usual, or *accidently* rip a little piece of the wrapping paper so you can take a sneaky peek."

"You have *got* my present?"

"Of course, I have," lies I. "It's just hidden in a safe place away from your nosy nose."

"Where is it then?"

"I am not telling you."

"What is it then?"

"I am not telling you that either."

"Well you should!"

"Why should I?"

"In case I don't like what you have bought me."

This I can understand as I am pretty useless when it comes to buying Betty presents. In my mind's eye I conjure up the image of Betty excitedly opening her first present beside our first Christmas tree as a married couple. The collectable wooden dolly didn't go down too well. Subsequent birthdays, anniversaries and Christmases faired just as badly. The too tight, risqué corsets went back along with the too big, old granny types that replaced them. The sickly-sweet cheap perfumes gave her headaches and most of the jewellery did not please. Especially the mourning brooch I got cheap from the market and the 'expensive' ring from a load of stolen jewellery I managed to recover and return, apart from that is a few pieces that went missing again into my pocket. The ring's huge diamond turned out to be glass. The 'diamond' fell out anyway and the twenty-two-carat gold ring turned Betty's finger green.

"Well my present better be under that tree by tomorrow night or you're in trouble."

"Fear not my little bossy boots, trust me it will be there."

"Um…" ums she in obvious disbelief.

What can one do when they have no idea what to buy a woman who is so special she deserves the best? I will have to have a serious ponder over the matter. But for now, it is toe warming time, more scotch and read the paper. I settle down while Betty goes off in a huff to prepare dinner. I grab the paper and am incredulous when the headlines scream out at me; 'Who is Jack the Stripper?' Jack the Flasher has been upgraded by the gutter press in an obvious pathetic attempt to compare him to Jack the Ripper, anything to sell more papers. Reading on I learn nothing that is of any help in my investigations and putting the paper down I start racking my brain over what I should get for Betty's present. It is hard work, so I fall asleep instead until my socks begin to scorch and the smell of burning toenails wake me up. Betty comes back into the room.

"Dinner is ready," says she, wrinkling up her nose. "What's that smell? Is something burning?"

Now I have to explain why I allowed my brand-new socks to become ruined. Needless to say, dinner was a solemn event, though delicious, bedtime was a non-event, love wise, and breakfast the next morning was a get it yourself and hurry up out of my sight. All this is about her Christmas present and I do not blame her. As I get ready for work I try a different tack. I'll try asking her.

"What would you *really* like for Christmas?"

Betty smiles, we both know what she would truly like, but that is in God's hands.

"I would like a basket of bathroom luxuries."

At this I start to panic, the last bathroom luxuries I bought her from a posh shop were actually for pets not people. I know I should have realised because the soap bars had pictures of little puppies on them but I *didn't* realise because I was knackered and had left it to the last minute.

Betty reads my mind, "If you go into Smithers Emporium on the High Street you will see what I want in the 'gifts for her' department. That's not the same as the gifts for him, or… the gifts for pet's department. The basket I desire says; Exquisite luxury items for the better class of lady. Or as near as. Have you got that?"

I nod just as there sounds a violent thump on the front door, obviously Head is also in a bad mood. Coat on, hat on, and this time wrapping a thick navy-blue scarf around my neck and wearing sensible walking boots I go out back and around the front to find Head with a face even more miserable looking than mine. He has also put on something else to keep warmer, but I am unsure if a Davy Crocket hat is really suitable for a man in his position.

"Good morning, Sergeant," says I lightly.

"Is it?"

"Is what, what?"

He shrews up his mouth. "A good morning."

"Do you want to talk about it?"

"I do," he says with a lopsided half smile.

We head towards the High Street, talking as we go. It turns out that Head also has no idea what to buy Chloe for a present.

"May I suggest, Sergeant, you ask her."

"Ask her? But then it won't be a surprise."

"It won't be such a bloody disappointment either! Trust me, just ask her."

We stop and face each other, "Sometimes, sir, I really do believe you are the font of all knowledge. How simple, just ask her."

He smiles broadly and we carry on, but to where first? I have no real idea other than playing it by ear. I require a picture of Oswald from Sir Stanley's house. We must interview the Longs and anyone else we can find time to re-interview, and I shall have to find time to get to the Yard and have Rosebud's sketches photographed before I return them to her. But most importantly I must pick up Betty's present.

Although it is still cold the wind has dropped, the going is easier than yesterday as fresh snow covers the ice and reduces the slip factor. The sun is out and the smoke from the chimneys is going up instead of down, therefore not covering everything with black sooty spots.

As if reading my mind, Head asks, "Where do you think all that smoke goes to, sir?"

"Heaven I expect."

"I shouldn't think they'd really want it up there, especially as everyone's dressed in white."

"I suppose not. But then it is only an assumption that everyone in heaven wears white. White being considered purity. They may actually wear purple."

"Or green. Actually, they might not wear anything at all, like Adam and Eve."

We come upon a shivering urchin trying to scrape a frozen dog's turd off the ground to put in his bucket. I feel so sorry for the skinny little runt I pause, take off my scarf and wrap it around his neck. It was itching my neck anyway.

"I feel for the 'pure' collectors in this weather, sir," says Head stepping right over the skinny kid. "Poor bastards, it's hard enough trying to make a living from picking up crap when its fresh let alone struggling with it in the freezing cold. Plus, there's not so much about this weather."

"But at least it may weigh more when it is frozen, thus increasing their revenue."

We trudge on in relative silence until we come to a tram stop and I spy a hansom cab coming our way.

"Sergeant, we shall hire a cab for the day. That way we can cover an awful lot more ground, keep a little warmer and a lot drier should it snow again." I stick a hand out and the driver slows the horse to a halt without it skidding. The road is far less dangerous as grit has been shovelled over it.

"Chester Street, cabby," says I as we board. "And spare the horses, we are in no rush."

As we trot along I note that there are far more people going about their business then there were yesterday. Shops appear busy and those with money are having their carriages loaded up by liverymen and shopkeepers with the endless goodies they've bought. Turning off the High Street we find the much narrower street virtually blocked by a pair of posh carriages that have decided to rudely park opposite each other. The driver slows the horse down and just manages to start squeezing through with barely an inch to spare either side, which presents Head and I with a golden opportunity. I reach out and grab a parcel from the back seat of the open carriage on my side and Head does the same on his side. The unsuspecting liverymen on both sides are unaware of our actions being too busy ensuring the urchins don't pinch anything. Clearing the jam, the horse returns to a steady trot.

"Works every year," grins Head as he starts ripping the brown paper off his shoe box size 'present'.

"Never fails," says I. My 'present' is in oblong box three feet long, six inches wide and about ten inches deep and wrapped also in brown paper. I rip the paper off and open the box.

"Marvellous," says Head holding up his present. "A pair of brown leather women's shoes that with luck will just fit, Chloe. What's in yours, sir?"

I hardly dare say and hold it up for him to see.

Head stares at the object in amazement. "Is that what I think it is?"

"It is. Just my bloody luck." Bitterly disappointed I toss the wooden leg out the cab where it smacks a scrawny urchin across the skull who unperturbed grabs hold of it then makes a break for it.

"If the shoes don't fit Chloe, Sergeant. I will buy them from you for Betty. They will definitely fit her."

"Right. Thank you, sir."

We carry on in silence while the rhythmic clip clopping of the horse's hooves starts sending me to sleep until at last the cab stops outside Sir Stanley's house. Head and I alight and the driver agrees to wait for us.

Stopping at the gates I find them locked and give them a frustrated shake just as a barking, tail wagging black dog comes hurtling out of nowhere towards us.

"Isn't that the labrador we saw in the park, yesterday?" says Head.

"I believe it is," says I reaching through the bars to fuss around its silky neck as it jumps up to greet me. "So, who owns you?"

"No one," counters Head. "I am very much my own man."

"I am talking to the dog, Sergeant."

"Of course, you are, sir. But I don't think you'll receive an answer."

"Perhaps not an answer in the conventional way, but an answer we shall have."

The front door to the house opens and Jim descends the steps and comes over to us.

"We have to keep the gates locked," says he as he puts a key in. "People *will* leave the gates open and of course Bobby gets out and runs off."

"He's a lovely dog," says I. "Is he yours?"

"Good grief no, Inspector. Heaven forbid a house servant would be allowed a pet dog."

He swings one gate open enough for us to step through while holding the dog back by its collar. Closes the gate and relocks it.

Bobby jumps up me and I ruffle his head. "Who did you say owns Bobby?"

"He actually belongs to Oswald. He left him behind went he got thrown out by Sir Stanley. Anyway. Good morning gentlemen. What can I do for you?"

"We require a photograph of Oswald if you don't mind asking the Richardsons to find one. And I would like to speak with Beryl again."

Jim appears unfazed by my request. "The sisters have gone back to their own home for the day, Inspector. I will look for a photograph while you speak to Beryl."

He leads the way towards the house while Bobby runs off barking towards the rear of the house before coming back, barking a bit more and running off again.

"I think he wants us to follow him, sir," says Head.

"He just wants you to play find my balls," puts in Jim. "He hides them around back near his kennel and you have to find them."

Thank God for that, muses I to myself as we follow Jim inside. He takes our coats and hats, puts them away and then requests we follow him down the long hallway of heads towards the servants' hall at the very rear of the house. A wafting aroma of roast lamb hits my nostrils as we near the hall and stepping inside reveals a short plump cook stirring a saucepan on the range, while four maids, another footman and a liveryman are sat around a large table that is set up for a meal. Everyone except the cook gawps uneasily at us and I note that Beryl in particular appears *very* worried by our sudden appearance.

Jim introduces us to those we haven't already met, he bades us to sit and orders a maid called Mary to make us tea. "I will try and find that photograph you requested, Inspector," says he. "Though I am afraid Sir Stanley has ensured that not a single image of Oswald remains anywhere in the house."

"He burnt them on a big bonfire," blurts out a thin faced maid, staring wide eyed at me from across the table.

"That will be enough from you, Jenny Partridge," snaps the cook as she whirls round to glare at the girl. "Speak only when you are spoken to in future."

Jenny drops her eyes and I see her body tremble. The servants are obviously *all* in a state of fear, all that is except Jim and the cook, or are they just better at hiding it? Something is very wrong here and I will not be leaving this house until I find out. And I wonder why I didn't pick up on it before. But then we *were* preoccupied by the Richardson sisters.

Jim goes off. Mary sets down two enamel mugs of steaming tea in front of me and Head and it seems everyone begins to relax a little. Perhaps I am reading more into this than needs be read? Perhaps the servants are merely perplexed at the presence of two policemen invading their sanctuary. And I wonder if Head and I appear somewhat fearsome to them. But then perhaps I am simply wondering too much?

I address Beryl, "I wish to speak to you in private, Beryl. Is there somewhere we may go."

She dolefully nods and gets to her feet, "We can go to the common room. If you'll follow me."

Leaving Head to his own devices, I follow Beryl out the hall and into a small room that the servants use to relax in whenever they have time. The room has half a dozen small armchairs and a coffee table with a few cheap prints of the countryside on the leaf designed wallpapered walls. A log fire crackles in the corner and there is a small decorated Christmas tree by the window.

We sit opposite each other and I take out my notebook and pencil.

"Did you want me to fetch your tea, sir?" she asks tentatively.

I shake my head. "It will keep, Beryl. Now, I want you to tell me what is bothering you."

Avoiding my eyes, she says, "I may 'ave given you the wrong idea last time. Master Oswald ain't no flasher an' I shouldn't 'ave said anythin' to Mable."

Realising Beryl has obviously been warned off I decide to up the aggression. "Holding back information that may lead to a criminal escaping justice is called perverting the cause of justice and can lead to imprisonment. Do you understand me?"

"No. I ain't no pervert. I'm just a girl who 'as to keep her job 'cause I got a sick muvva to feed."

With that she covers her face with her hands and starts to cry. Obviously, she has been threatened with dismissal for spreading rumours and ordered to keep her mouth shut in the future, no doubt by Jim or the cook. I decide to give the cook a grilling and after allowing Beryl a few minutes to regain her composure we head back to the servant's hall.

As we step into the hall the cook glares at Beryl in an obvious warning of 'You better not have said anything'. Beryl avoids her eyes and goes to sit beside Head as if for protection.

"I wish to speak to you, Mrs…?" says I directing my vision to the cook.

"About what?" snaps she clamping her hands on her ample hips.

"About whatever it is I wish to talk to you about."

"Can't you be more specific?"

"As you please. Do you wish to open your fat gob in private or in front of everyone?"

"You can't talk to *me* like that."

"Why not?"

"Because I am a respected person. A senior servant within this austere establishment. Not even Sir Stanley himself would dare to speak to me the way you just did."

"Mrs Plum!" snaps Head, joining in the affray. "I would advise you to go and talk to the Inspector right now before he loses his temper and orders me to cuff you and drag you down to the station, where we shall fling you in a cell to cool down to reflect on the error of your ways before we even attempt to question you."

"Which would probably be sometime tomorrow because we're very busy right now and will want to go home for the night," smiles I.

"Very well then," she growls stomping over towards me.

Moving out of her way I allow the sulky lump to storm out of the hall before I say to Head, "How is it going, Sergeant?"

He winks. "Keep her as long as you can, sir."

With a nod I turn and head for the common room where I find the cook already sat back in the armchair closest to the fire having hauled up her skirts to her thighs while displaying her grey stockings and warming her crotch up. I shut the door before anyone sees her.

"Madam," says I. "Your deportment isn't becoming for a woman in your position. Kindly shut your legs and sit up like a lady."

"Oh, draw your neck in copper. When Petunia Plum relaxes she couldn't give a toss about bloody deportment. Now," she points, "you go to that sideboard there, open it and pour us both a drink."

I do as I am told, although God only knows why. Opening a small door, I find a bottle of expensive brandy and a couple of tumblers. Half filling the tumblers I hand her one and then turn the armchair beside hers to face the fire instead of leaving it where it was and having to look up her skirts into Cheddar Gorge.

"Cheers," says she.

"Cheers," says I. Taking a sip the nectar from heaven invades my senses, it is silky smooth with just enough punch to lightly burn your tongue while slipping down your throat like beef dripping.

"Bleedin' good isn't it?" she grins, her dark eyes sparkling. "A couple of these and you'd feel young enough to jump in the bath with an entire team of rugby players."

This makes me smile. "I can't say it holds any attraction for me, madam."

"Of course not. You're a red-blooded male, Inspector, that much is obvious. Now, I suppose you want to question me about Oswald."

"I do, madam. What can you tell me?"

"For a start you need to forget anything those silly girls tell you. That Jenny and Beryl have always got their heads together and coming up with all sorts of rubbish. Imagination, lies and conjecture, Inspector. They can't tell their bums from their elbows at times." She fixes me with a stern stare. "That Jenny will be talking nine to the dozen to your Sergeant now I'm out of earshot as no doubt that Beryl rabbited away to you. You tell me what Beryl's told you thus far and I will then give you the real facts."

I tell her what little Beryl told me while embellishing it and making it sound more dramatic. She listens, tuts a bit, screws up her rosy face, scowls and scoffs.

"There is *some* truth in what she has told you, Inspector." She holds her tumbler out to me. "You refill these and I will then tell you the *real* truth."

I do exactly that. She pulls down her skirts, turns her chair to face me and starts talking.

"Oswald has always been a lady's man. He wears his brain between his legs and is fortunate enough to have a big brain. He and Sir Stanley had often been at odds over Oswald's philandering. Sir Stanley's a committed Christian. Very proper and righteous. He is also a staunch advocate of maintaining the status quo. Everyone has their place and everyone must stay in their place and never the twain shall fornicate. Now, he had a fondness for Janice Palmer, he respected her ability as a housekeeper despite her relative youthfulness. When by pure chance he found out Janice and Oswald were having an affair he went berserk. Even more berserk when Janice announced she was pregnant by Oswald. So, what does a man in Sir Stanley's position do about it? Well, he had to avoid a scandal, that above all else. There was also an unborn child to consider. But how to keep everyone quiet about it all because he quickly realised that practically everyone in the household had known for ages what was going on. Sir Stanley came up with a plan. It was well known that Albert Timms, the butler, was besotted with Janice, unrequited though his adoration was. Sir Stanley persuaded Janice that her best option was to spread it around that Albert was the father, marry the man and then leave the household. That way the child wouldn't be born a bastard, Janice would at least appear to be a respectable married woman and Albert, bless him, would be blissfully happy. Well it isn't everyday a sixty-five-year-old, overweight virgin gets to marry a rampant seductress less than half his age is it?"

"Indeed not. In fact, it would be enough to kill a man not fit enough for the task in hand."

"Exactly!" Petunia takes a long swallow of her brandy, smacks her lips and burps. "Sir Stanley writes Janice and Albert glowing references so they might easily find employment elsewhere despite being a couple expecting a child. He also paid them off, how much

I don't know, but what I do know is they left here arm in arm and both were smiling. Sir Stanley and Lady Sarah gathered all the staff together and informed them that Janice and Albert had sinned against God, but as they had repented and were doing the right thing all was forgiven. He also informed them that Janice and Oswald had also sinned against God and that Oswald refused to repent. However, he warned them that the matter was now closed and never to be spoken about again. Anyone who did not adhere to his demands would find themselves not only losing their position with no references but may also find themselves taken to task for spreading malicious gossip. That left Oswald to deal with. Oswald isn't like his two elder brothers. They are their father's sons. Both are serving in the Coldstream Guards out in India right now. They are God-fearing, stalwart and righteous. Oswald on the other hand is a gambling whore monger who has always abused his position and his parents. Sir Stanley viewed Oswald's affair with Janice as the ultimate betrayal and ordered Oswald to take out an immediate commission with the Army and get out of his sight and not dare to return until he had become a man of honour. Oswald told him, in not so many words, to get fucked. He demanded money, a lot of money, or he would get the money from the tabloid press for his 'story'. This tipped Sir Stanley over the edge. To everyone's amazement Sir Stanley physically threw Oswald out in just what he stood up in and warned him never to return. Oswald was banished for life. Cut out of his inheritance. Cut off from his allowance and denied taking his dog and his horse with him. Sir Stanley even burnt every photograph he could find that had Oswald in it. Since then it is as if Oswald never existed. And that, dear Inspector is that. Any questions?"

"How did Sir Stanley find out about the affair?"

"He couldn't sleep one night and went to go down stairs for a drop of port and a cigar. On passing Oswald's room he heard gasping, so he barged in to find Janice bouncing up and down on top of Oswald."

"How do you know all this?"

"Janice told me. And only me. She and Oswald managed a short goodbye in secret just before Janice left for good. You are the only one I have told this to and I trust you to not reveal your information source or I shall lose my position."

"You have my word, madam. I do not recall any of this in the press. Do I take it that Oswald *didn't* seek remuneration for his 'story'?"

She shakes her head. "Oswald tried again to threaten Sir Stanley, via a letter, that he would go to the press. Sir Stanley, we believe, payed him off because since then we haven't heard a word from Oswald."

"How do you know about the letter?"

"Jim overheard Sir Stanley discussing it with Lady Sarah in the drawing room when he went to announce the arrival of a visitor, the door was slightly ajar and forgetting himself Sir Stanley's voice was raised."

"Jim didn't mention this to me when I spoke to him."

"He wouldn't. Same as me he doesn't want to lose his position."

"Do you know where Oswald is now?"

She shrugs. "Who knows? He may have gone up north to fall on Sir Stanley's brother Edward for sanctuary. Edward has a large estate up there and has always got on well with Oswald. Peas in a pod, Inspector."

"And the rumour that Oswald could be the flasher?"

"Exactly that, merely a rumour. There is not an ounce of truth in it nor any evidence for it. Even the so-called exposure of Oswald's knob to the new scullery maid was a load of old cock and balls. The silly girl burst into Oswald's room without knocking just as Oswald got out of bed in the nude."

"One more question before I leave you in peace. How do you view the Richardson sisters?"

"As a pair of over privileged, immature, stupid tittle twats with nothing to do except make up stories and cause mischief."

"There's no love lost between you then?"

"None at all. Anyway, Inspector, I must check my lamb and get the potatoes on. Will you stay for a bite of lunch?"

"Thank you, Mrs Plum, but no, we also *must* get on. Oh, one other thing. Do you know where Janice and Albert are now?"

"No idea," smiles she, getting to her feet.

We head back to the hall to find it resounding with laughter, no doubt Head is regaling everyone with some of his risqué stories. Silence is quickly restored with a single glare from the cook. Head and I say our goodbyes and Jim escorts us to the door. He has a small photograph in his hand which he gives to me to peruse while he gets our hats and coats.

"How old would you say the boy in this photograph is, Sergeant?"

Head takes it and peruses it. "About six I'd say."

Jim steps up with our coats, my bowler and Head's stupid furry thing.

"Have you not got a more recent photograph of Oswald?" asks I.

"Sorry, Inspector, it's the only one I could find. Sir Stanley burnt the rest."

"Well it will not suffice, Jim. And I find it difficult to believe Sir Stanley burnt *every* photograph in the house."

"Well he did. Honestly he did."

"Never the less, Jim. I want to search the house, starting with Lady Sarah's bedroom."

"What if I say no?"

"I shall ignore you and carry on regardless."

"I'll have to inform, Mrs Plum."

"Inform the pope if you want but it will make no difference."

"Very well," sulks he. "Follow me."

We take charge of our hats and coats and follow Jim up the stairs, along a long corridor and into a large expensively furnished bedroom.

"This is her ladyship's bedroom," announces Jim. "Sir Stanley's is through that adjoining door."

We hand back our hats and coats to Jim and I set to searching through Lady Sarah's dressing table draws while Head goes through a mahogany chest of drawers.

"Got it, sir," announces Head holding up a small photograph album.

"Excellent, Sergeant. Let's take peep inside."

Head sets it down on top of the chest of drawers and flicks open the first page, luckily Jim stays by the door because he may be well shocked to see what's in the album.

"They're bloody filthy," whispers Head. "Would you bloody believe it?"

I am perusing two dark skinned naked men holding big sticks in their hands and smiling at the camera. Turning the pages reveals these same men, and others, obviously in battle against each other.

"I believe, Sergeant, we are looking at a stick fight between Dinka warriors."

"Of course, we are, sir. Those Spencer sisters spoke about these Dinka warriors, didn't they?"

"They did. Now look at this."

There is an inscription on the inside cover: To our darling cousin Sarah. Enjoy, but do not allow Stanley to see your enjoyment. You know what we mean? Love and hugs, Delphinium and of course, Rosebud.

"Well, well," drawls Head. "We've been conned, sir. And by a couple of old nutters to boot."

"Keep it quiet, Sergeant. Put this back and let's carry on the search."

"Any luck?" calls out Jim, obviously keen to know what we had been looking at.

"Just some photos of babies."

"Really. That'll be her 'boys' most probably."

Some boys, thinks I. Beneath a pile of letters I find a large envelope. Taking it out I open it and pull out several six by six-inch photographs and turn to face Jim. "No mother who loves a child will allow anyone to try and wipe that child from the face of the earth, even if that child is in disgrace. I would have bet money Oswald's mother would have hidden away a few photographs of her son to help remember him by."

Jim appears less than happy. "Very clever, Inspector. What now?"

"We shall select one photograph and put the rest back in the drawer and be on our way."

"Very well, Inspector. But don't you want me to confirm that they are indeed pictures of Oswald?"

"They are, trust me." I select a photograph that shows a tall slim man with a neatly trimmed beard, moustache and long sideburns. He is wearing a top hat and long coat. I slip the photograph into my coat pocket. It's time to go.

Jim sees us out and over to the gate where Bobby comes up to greet us again. A quick pat on his head and we are having the gate locked behind us.

"Do you know when Sir Stanley is due back?" I ask Jim through the bars.

"Not until the second week in January."

I thank him for his trouble and Head and I go over to our cab where we find the driver inside snoring away like a wart hog. Why he hasn't frozen to death I don't know because the sun has gone, the clouds have thickened and appear full of snow, while it has become infinitely colder than it was an hour or so ago. I give him a shake, he groans a bit, swears a bit, farts a lot and rubbing his baggy eyes gives out a hippopotamus yawn while displaying a set of teeth that should be condemned.

"What time is it, gov'?"

"Time to get on."

Groaning and swearing about his aching bones he stumbles out and still farting climbs up back to take the reins.

"Where to gov'?"

"Perkins on Oxford Street."

Settling down I ask Head to relate all he has learnt. Which turns out to be no more than we already knew.

"They don't half live the good life once the old man's away, sir. Bloody roast lamb and all the trimmings for lunch accompanied with a couple of bottles of claret no less. One thing I'm sure of is they're all hiding something."

"What struck you the most about Beryl."

"Truthfully?"

"Of course."

"Her beautiful bouncing bosom."

"What else?" frowns I.

"She seemed more evasive than the others. When I think about it, I believe Beryl is holding back more than anyone else. And she's nervous."

"Perhaps she is nervous by nature. Anyway, let me tell you how I got on with the cook."

Head's eyebrows shoot up while a grin forms on his mouth. "Now there's a wench if ever I saw one, sir. Tell me more."

Simply to tease him I say, "We'd hardly got into the common room before the dirty trollop sat down, hoisted up her skirts and spread them."

"I don't believe it! Really? Truthfully?"

"On my honour."

"Cross your heart and hope to fly?"

"I do," says I crossing my heart.

"Well… Well… You smell like you've had a tot or two into the bargain."

"A drop of the finest brandy I have ever tasted."

"Bloody hell. All I got was a waft of Beryl's apron, a mince pie and a couple of cups of tea."

"Never mind, Sergeant. Such is life."

"Um… Trouble is, sir, you have a conscience. Do you recall how terrible you felt after giving Lady Hervington one? You felt so bad you were on the point of confessing to Betty in the vain hope she'd forgive you. Not only that, you considered going to church to beg the Lord as well for forgiveness. How are you going to reconcile yourself with this one? Especially having poked a woman old enough to be your mother."

"My conscience is clear, Sergeant. Let me explain what really happened."

I tell him all. Secretly I think he is relieved that I didn't 'poke' the cook. On the rest he is thinking on the same lines as I am. We have been led up the garden path, lied to, conned and bullshitted beyond belief.

"It's a bloody conspiracy," grates Head. "All designed to throw us off track and confuse us while covering up the real truth."

"Which is?"

"Oswald's the flasher and Sir Stanley has orchestrated an elaborate scheme to cover it all up. He'd rather have the scandal of Oswald and the housekeeper exposed than see his son hauled up in court for flashing his banana."

"Exactly. The trouble is, where the *hell* is Oswald? Without him, or someone telling us the real truth, we have not one jot of evidence, just speculation, guesswork and a copper's intuition. Let's see what the Longs have to say for themselves. And whatever happens do not allow me to forget Betty's present."

We travel on in silence until we reach Parkins Gentlemen's Tailors. I inform the driver we won't be long with the Longs. Head takes the tailors and I go into the Costume Shop next door where I ask to speak to a Mrs Mable Long. Looking very similar to Beryl Jones, a short young woman wearing glasses and dressed in a dark blue dress is presented to me.

"I am Detective Inspector Gerald Potter," says I. "You are Mrs Mabel Long?"

"I knew that already," says she indifferently. "How can I help you?"

Taking out Rosebud's sketchbook and the photograph of Oswald, I ask, "I want you to look at the men in these pictures and tell me if you recognise either of them."

She takes a good look at each one in turn. "I recognise the pair of 'em."

This surprises me. "Can you tell me why you recognise them?"

"Yes."

I wait a moment for the woman to speak before I demand, "Well go on then."

"Go on what!"

"Tell me why you recognise them."

"All right, don't get grumpy! The tall one's Oswald Standridge Carter. I know of him because my husband has measured him up before now for suits and he's often in the society magazines. I don't know the other one's name, but I recognise him as being the dirty dog who flashed his thing at me."

"What colour beard did the man who flashed you have?"

"Red."

"What colour beard does he normally sport?"

Her eyebrows go up. "What kind of sport can you play using a beard?"

"Madam. I believe you are trying to bamboozle me into thinking you are an ignoramus. Please drop this silly pretence and answer my questions properly or I shall take you down the station where you can answer them from the comfort of a cell for wasting my time."

"Very well," sighs she screwing up her face. "That man," she points at the sketch, "came into the shop and bought two red beards. At the time he was clean shaven. Now, I know it was him who flashed me because I recognised his face despite the false beard and I knew the beard was one of ours. He was also wearing clothes from Parkins no doubt cut by my old man."

"Can you be certain of that, madam?"

"I'm certain because Harry's work has a distinctive style about it."

"What colour hair did he have?"

"Harry has brown hair."

"*Not* bloody Harry. The flasher."

"I don't *know* he kept his top hat on. But my Harry told me he was bald as a parrot."

"Parrots have feathers, madam. Therefore, they are not bald."

"Who cares? Look Inspector. Is that all, the owner's giving me her angry face. There's people to serve."

"That is all. Except to warn you that giving false information to a policeman doing his duty will be classed as perverting the course of justice and may lead to a criminal charge. Do you understand?"

"I do."

"Then good day to you, madam."

I leave and climb back into the cab where I find the Sergeant busy picking his grumbles.

"Any luck, Sergeant?"

Wiping his grumble on the side of the cab he says, "Lying through his teeth, sir. Sweated like a pig he did. How about you?"

"The same. They are all part and parsnip to the same conspiracy."

"Parsnip?"

"Ah… Thank you for reminding me, Sergeant. I must pick up some swede and parsnips on the way home."

"Along with Betty's present."

"Of course."

"Where to, guv?" calls the driver.

I consult my notebook and inform him of the next address.

As we trot along, Head and I compare notes and then decide how we shall continue with our investigations once we've interviewed a few more of the Flasher's victims. Head is all for the heavy-handed approach on those we believe have lied to us so far. Which is everyone.

"Have the buggers dragged down to the cells and then threaten to beat the truth out of them, sir," snarls he, punching a fist into the palm of his other hand. "Make them stand outside in the snow for a few hours in just their undergarments, that'll loosen up their tongues."

"We could chuck ice cold water over them as well, Sergeant and then wire them up to one of those new-fangled electric circuits and shove thousands of volts through their bodies. Or shove a gas pipe up their bottoms and give them a whiff or two of gas along with a lighted cigar."

"That might be going a bit too far, sir," reflects he.

"Exactly, Sergeant. As is what you suggested. No, what we need is to find Oswald. Once we have finished our interviews we shall go back to the Yard and consult with Clump and see if he'll agree to the papers putting in a 'Have You Seen This Man?' article."

Three hours later we are heading for the Yard having spoken to four more of the Flasher's victims who *all* picked Oswald out as the flasher. We had no doubts that they were all telling us the truth. We took time out to have a leisurely lunch in a pleasant pub recommended by the cab driver along with a few beers and all is now well with the world; except I still have to pick up Betty's present and the vegetables.

At the Yard we alight from the cab and Head grabs his shoes. I pay the driver off and ask him to sign a receipt so I can claim the money back on expenses. Unfortunately, he can read.

"I ain't signing that, mate," scoffs he. "It's for a pound more than you payed me."

"I'll give you two bob."

He snatches the money from my hand, signs the receipt, hops back on his cab and drives off while farting away.

Head and I make our way into the station and head off to Clump's office where we have to wait because he has someone with him. I suggest to Head that he might want to leave his Davy Crocket hat and the shoe box in our office rather than allow Clump to see them.

"I'd rather not, sir," says he. "Someone might pinch them."

"May I remind you, Sergeant that we *are* in a Police Station full of policemen."

"Exactly."

"Point taken. But at least take the shoes out of the box, remove the hat from your head and shove them both out of sight in your coat pockets."

He does exactly that and dumps the box on the floor just as Clump bawls out, "Come in men."

Taking off my bowler, we go in to find Clump behind his desk and a uniformed inspector sat opposite him who cranes his neck around to eyeball us. He is a thin faced dark-haired man who obviously didn't stand close enough to his razor when he shaved as he has a markedly stubbly chin.

"Lads, may I introduce Inspector Bristle, soon to be promoted to Chief Inspector Bristle. Inspector Bristle." He points at me and then at Head. "Detective Inspector Potter and Detective Sergeant Head."

Bristle gets to his feet, turns and holds out a hand to me. "I have heard stirring renditions of you and your Sergeant's considerable success rate in solving crime and bringing the guilty to justice, Detective Inspector Potter. It is a pleasure to meet you."

We shake hands and he turns his attention to Head. "A pleasure to meet you also, Detective Sergeant Head," says he shaking Heads hand.

"Take a seat, lads," says Clump. "Inspector Bristle is just leaving."

Clump comes around and shakes Bristle's hand and sees him to the door.

"Anything you want John, just ask."

"Thank you, Arthur. There is just one thing. My name is Bristol, not Bristle."

"Of course, it is. Merely a slip of the tongue I assure you and not a veiled attempt to highlight your um..."

"Stubble? As I have said, Arthur, I have had a severe rash and cannot shave too close to my skin for at least another week for fear of exasperating my condition."

"I see. Well God speed, John. Onwards and upwards."

Bristol leaves and Clump retakes his seat.

"I made a cock up there," says he grimacing. "I could have sworn he said his name was Bristle. Anyway, not to worry. Inspector Bristol has just transferred from North London to take over uniform while I am to have the new title of: Detective Chief Inspector, so I can concentrate all my efforts on keeping you buggers under control." Reaching into his drawer he brings out the scotch and three glasses. "First things first. Why have you got a shoe sticking out of one pocket and a cat's tail hanging out of your other coat pocket, Sergeant?"

"The shoes are a present for Chloe, sir. And it's not a cat's tail, sir, it's a racoon's tail."

"Of course, it is. How silly of me not to know that. Why have you got a racoon's tail sticking out of your coat pocket, Sergeant?"

"Because if I was wearing it on my head you might not like it being there."

"I take it that it is a dead racoon. So, why would you want to wear a dead racoon on your head?"

"It keeps my head warm."

"I see. Well put it on and let's see it."

I shrink down in my chair. Clump will explode when he realises Head has been tramping all around London while wearing his daft hat and making the force a laughing stock.

Head pulls out the hat and puts it on, straightens it out and then tips it to one side.

"Lovely," smiles Clump. "Can you get me one of those, Sergeant, so I too can look like Davy *'bloody'* Crocket!"

"What size head are you, sir?"

"Sometimes Sergeant you really do push your luck. Now, put the stupid thing away and do not ever let me catch you wearing the thing in public. Is that clear?"

"As mud, sir."

"Good." He fills the glasses up and pushes ours over. "Jack the Stripper. Where are you with the case?"

We tell him all we have discovered thus far. He tuts a bit, frowns a bit and drinks a lot. He is on his third glass before we've even finished our first. I don't think he likes where this is going at all. I show him the photograph and Rosebud's sketch.

At last he speaks, "Damned business, Inspector. I'm sure you are right about this Oswald character being the Stripper. The trouble is his father is far too an important man to have his laundry dragged out in the open unless we have cast iron proof of Oswald's guilt. Right now, I would say you do not have that proof. I would also say we cannot afford to put Oswald's mug all over the papers just yet either. Find Oswald. Bring him in and punch a confession out of him."

"The trouble is, sir, we have no idea where to start looking."

Clump scratches thoughtfully at his scruffy beard. And I'm thinking it's scruffier than Head's racoon hat. I do wish he'd take a shave.

"I always say, Inspector, search the obvious places first according to the characteristic of the person you are searching for. In Oswald's case that would be upmarket whorehouses, racetracks, gambling dens and such like. Talk to the money lenders and find out if he owes money. Use your heads. But first try and find this Janice Palmer and the butler. Take my advice and ask around at the work agencies who are always searching for upmarket service staff. If that fails then make a start at Oswald's own home in case he is hiding there and brow beat the servants and those snotty twins to open up and start spilling the milk."

"That sounds like a plan," agrees I.

"Good. Still get copies of the photograph and the sketch. I'll give them to Inspector Bristle to hand out to uniform and they can keep their eyes open when out on their beats." Suddenly a cloud clouds his eyes. "Has it crossed your mind that Oswald may actually be dead?"

"No, sir, it hasn't," says I as a bell rings in my head.

"Well he wouldn't be the first child of a wealthy famous person with strong links to the aristocracy to have been murdered to prevent a scandal, now would he?"

"He certainly wouldn't," agrees I.

"I agree," agrees Head. "But I would say searching for a live body will be easier to find because unlike a dead one they tend to move around a lot more and therefore get seen more often."

Clump's hairy brows meet in the middle, "Sergeant, that was a brilliant evaluation of the pluses and minuses of searching for someone who is alive, in preference to searching for someone who is dead. Once you have retired from the force may I suggest you write a thesis on the subject and present it to Oxford University so they may piss themselves laughing as I intend to do the second you bugger off home and leave me in peace?"

It is time to leave. We say goodbye to Clump and make our way to forensics where photographs are taken of the sketch and Oswald's photograph. They will print out loads and hand them over to uniform. Head and I exit the Yard and go back into the cold. Head puts his racoon hat back on.

"It's too bloody cold not to have a hat on, sir," says he with a grin. "I was thinking in there that time is getting on and you've still got to get Betty's present. Smithers' place closes at six."

Whipping out my watch I check the time. "Bloody hell it's five thirty! We best get a move on. If I don't come home with Betty's present tonight she will skin me alive."

"And don't forget the vegetables or you'll have none with your dinner."

Sometimes it is patently obvious that Head is an awful lot cleverer than he is given credit for I realise as we flag down a cab. Head engineered that silly rendition about bodies back in Clump's office because he knew Clump would lose the plot and tell us to piss off. That way we could make the shop in time.

Once outside Smithers Emporium, Head takes his leave and I pay off the cab and go into the shop. It is a massive place, selling everything imaginable over four floors and is fully decorated up for Christmas. Following the signs towards 'Christmas Gifts for that Special Lady in your life' I end up on floor three, staring blankly at another sign that says: Special Offer; Willow shopping baskets filled with only the most luxurious bathroom items any discerning lady could possibly want. A very smart middle-aged lady assistant slides up to me.

"May I help you, sir?"

I fucking hope so, I groan inwardly. "I wish to purchase one of your luxury bathroom baskets, but there does not appear to be any out on display."

She rubs well-manicured hands together and meets my eyes with a look that says she's reading the panic in them. "Sold the last one barely five minutes ago I am afraid, sir. They have…"

"Never mind that," cuts in I. "Who bought it and which way did they go?"

"I am afraid…"

"Well don't be," snaps I fishing out my warrant card. "Who and way?"

She scowls at me but I am not to be intimidated.

"Tell me or it's down the nick for you."

"Sod this, I didn't sign up to be a shop assistant to be bullied by a prat like you. Clear off or I shall call security."

I contemplate shooting the woman but realise it would be a bit over the top. What I must do is remain calm and think. Spinning away from the assistant I flee downstairs and out onto the pavement. I look up the road, across the road and down the road hoping to see someone carrying a wicker basket that matches the advertising picture in the shop window. I spy at least ten baskets but not one matches. The shop closes in five minutes! What if whoever just bought the last basket is still inside? Then they will be out any minute now and I'll be able to persuade them to hand over their basket of luxury bathroom goodies for a profit or a truncheon around their lugs, either or being their choice.

Exactly five minutes later the concierge is holding open the door for the last few straggling customers to leave. Not one is holding what I want. I collar the concierge before he shuts and locks the door.

"Do you know where I might purchase…?"

"No," snaps he and slamming the door he quickly locks it.

I am done for. Unless? As I head off home I go over and over the ingenious plan that has formed within my brilliant brain. But will Betty fall for it? Of course she will. She will be struck dumb with awe when I tell her that I have ordered something else for Christmas other than what she wanted. Something so wonderful, so expensive and so exclusive even the Queen couldn't get one.

Betty will then demand, 'What is it?'

I will smile and say, 'You must wait until Christmas morning to find that out.'

She will then say, 'I don't believe you, Detective Inspector. Why don't you just admit you forgot again?'

Dejected beyond belief I forget the stupid plan and resolve myself to having to face the music. A serious ear bashing would be nearer the truth.

Half way along the High Street and by now more miserable than I have ever been in my entire life the last thing I need is an urchin jumping out in front of me while pushing a rickety wheelbarrow with a dirty table cloth covering whatever is in it.

"Oy. Mister. Want ta buy ya ol' woman a special gift?"

"What is it?" sighs I. Well you never know.

"Ow 'bout this," says he excitedly. Pulling back the cover reveals a wooden leg and one that looks suspiciously like the one I 'found' earlier.

"Do I look like I need a bloody wooden leg?"

"No! It ain't for you. It's for ya ol' woman. It's a woman's wooden leg."

"Well she doesn't want a wooden leg either because she has a pair of perfectly good legs thank you."

He holds up a finger and touches his nose knowingly. "Ah… But one day she might need a wooden leg. Buy it now when it's cheap, mister an' save ya self some dosh."

I walk on hoping he'll just bugger off, but as I made the mistake of giving him a minute he will now follow me to kingdom come until I give in and buy something from him.

I stop and face him. "What else have you got?"

"What do ya want?"

"I want a willow shopping basket full of lady's luxury bathroom items."

He squints up at me through piggy little eyes. "'Ow many do ya want?"

"One will suffice," says I warily.

"Lucky ol' you. I 'ave one left."

He fishes around under the cover and then, to my utter amazement, pulls out exactly what I want complete with an embossed Smithers Emporium Luxury Gifts red ribbon tied neatly across the items. Everything appears to be there. Fancy soaps, bottles of shampoo, bath salts, creams and whatever else it is a woman needs when she gets into a bath. Personally, I am content with a bar of carbolic and a scrubbing brush.

"How much?" says I, trying not to appear too eager.

"They're two quid in the store. A pound to you."

"Ten shillings."

"Bugger off," grates he. "A quid or ya don't get it."

"Ten shillings or I arrest you for stealing."

"Mister. When I got 'it by a wooden leg earlier that flew out of a bloody cab I never dreamed the bugger who nicked it an' threw it would not only turn out ta be a bloody copper he'd later on try an' steal off *me* as well. So, arrest me an' take me down the nick if ya want ta risk it."

"A pound it is then."

I fish out a pound note and hand it over to him. He hands me the basket, grins from ear to ear and says, "Anything else ya want? 'Ow 'bout a nice pair of flower-patterned woollen drawers for the ol' woman as well. They're brand new wiv no 'oles or skids in 'em."

"She only wears fancy French bloomers."
"Lovely. Take a gander at these buggers."

I am now pushing the wheelbarrow home having had to buy that as well as I couldn't carry everything I bought. In fact, the only things I didn't buy from 'Honest Mick' was the wooden leg and the woollen drawers. Betty will be ecstatic come Christmas morning when she undoes all her presents. Which reminds me I must get some wrapping paper. But then perhaps not, Betty's bound to have lots of the stuff and I'll only buy the wrong type anyway. For once I am absolutely certain I have got it right. I hope so because I cannot return anything she doesn't like or what doesn't fit for the obvious reason.

It is hard work pushing the wheelbarrow. Made of solid wood it is very heavy and the wheel itself is wonky and keeps getting stuck in rucks of ice. At last I reach home and go around the back and park up by the backdoor.

Sticking my head in the kitchen, I call out, "*It's me.*"

Betty comes in and gives me the suspicious look. "Well come in then, Detective Inspector you're letting all the heat out."

"Not until you go away. I don't want you seeing the presents I have bought for you."

"Presents as in plural presents?" asks she excitedly.

"Lots of them," grins I. "So, take yourself off into the parlour and do some knitting or something."

"Did you get the vegetables?"

Bugger! I knew I'd forgotten something. "Um… I was so embroiled in getting your presents my little strawberry I completely forgot. Sorry."

She smiles, "You do realise dinner's going to be very late. Never mind. I shall tramp up to the grocers while you bring the presents in Detective Inspector. Can I get you anything while I'm out?"

"Do you have wrapping paper?"

"Upstairs beside the wardrobe. Help yourself. Oh, and just take the meat out and let it rest off the heat. It should be nicely done by now."

Betty goes off and a minute later I hear the front door pulled shut.

I quickly unload the wheelbarrow and then shove it over by the outhouse just as the wheel falls off. Back inside I take the roast pork out and set it down beside the hotplate. It smells wonderful. Picking off a chunk of crackling I give it a blow and eat it. It is perfectly done and tastes delicious. After a quick hand wash I go upstairs and grab Betty's bag of Christmas wrapping paper, scissors, tie ribbons, message cards and a pot of paper glue.

Back downstairs I gaze lovingly over everything I have bought for Betty now set out on the kitchen table. I reason I have twenty minutes to wrap up ten presents before she returns. That's a two-minute average for every present. I get to work, but tying up presents isn't as easy as Betty makes it look. In fact, it is a pig of a job and fifteen minutes later I have to concede defeat. A chimpanzee could have done a better job. Everything looks a right bastard.

The glue stuck at first but gradually the paper curled away from it as if it were allergic to it. The tie ribbons are all twisted and knotted when they should be flat and neat. Instead of meeting in the centre of the present they are all way off line and cross together up one end or another and over to one side. Here and there the paper doesn't quite fully cover the present, there are gaps, holes, tears, curl ups, rucks and wrinkles. One thing's for certain, I can't put this lot under the Christmas tree looking as it does. I need a plan.

To hell with it! I go and pour myself a scotch to help me think. The clock on the mantel informs me that it is now seven thirty, at most I have five minutes left before Betty returns.

The clock ticks on and sounds so loud I fear it will deafen me, how strange I never noticed before now. Two minutes left, more if she'd stopped to yak to someone.

As I pour another scotch inspiration comes to me. I rush upstairs, fish out a pillow case and fly back downstairs. Luckily all the presents fit into the pillow case with the willow basket just plugging in the top and hiding everything. Wrapping the basket was, without a doubt, my best effort and, providing you don't look underneath it, it is passable. I carry the case into the parlour and stand it up beneath the tree and then stack a few presents around it for effect. It looks wonderful. Feeling very pleased with myself I down my scotch and reward myself with another just as I hear the key in the door.

As we head towards the High Street the following morning beneath a cloudless sky I am relieved to see Head is wearing his bowler hat again, having sold the Davy Crocket hat on his way home last night to a wooden leg carrying urchin. I relate to Head all that went amiss when Betty came back with the vegetables. He is highly amused by it all and can't stop sniggering as he goes over it all *again*.

"So, once you'd cleared up the mess on the kitchen table and scraped all the glue off while Betty cooked the vegetables you then cut your finger carving the meat until finally you both sat down and ate dinner at eight thirty? By which time you were well inebriated and Betty was half cut?"

"Correct," frowns I, surveying the wad of bandage on my left index finger.

"You then left the washing up and went into the parlour intent on relaxing, where to your horror you find the pillow case had fallen over and spilled the presents out. One of the stoppers from a bottle of jasmine bath oil had come loose and spilt its contents over several of the presents. Betty then spent the next hour or more, on and off, rewrapping her *own* presents plus a few of the other presents while you tried to clean up the spilt jasmine oil. The next thing you knew you'd slipped on the oily floor and grabbed the tree to stop yourself from falling. On hearing your unholy outburst Betty rushed into the parlour to find you laid on your back with the Christmas tree on top of you and the mother in law's present of handmade luxury chocolates squashed beneath your buttocks. It then took you another hour to put the tree back to more or less how it was, by which time Betty had gone to bed and left you to it. Bloody marvellous, sir. Will she ever forgive you, do you think?"

"She already has. Although I did only get porridge for breakfast so I suspect I haven't as yet been fully forgiven."

"What happened to the chocolates?"

"We ate them despite them being all squashed up and unrecognisable. Waste not want not. However, do not let me forget to pick up another box on the way home."

"I'll try not to," grins he.

At last the subject is dropped. Having decided not to bother trying to track down the housekeeper and the butler we take a cab to Sir Stanley's house where we find the gate is unlocked and an excited Bobby is waiting to greet us. I recall the bell in my head from yesterday and this time we follow Bobby around to the back of the house. I have no intention of looking for his balls as I have a hunch that he wishes us to find something else. Four stables beside a tack room on one side and a small barn housing the family coaches on the other side come into view. Four horseheads stick out over the stable doors, one of which sets up a whinny while nodding its head up and down. Bobby trots around to the rear of the stables and we follow him where beside a pile of manure he sets to barking furiously while scrabbling at a sunken area of ground. Snow is quickly 'raked' away down to the ice.

"What's all this, sir?"

"I believe this is where Oswald is hiding. Or should I say has been hidden. See if you can find a pickaxe and a spade, Sergeant, we have a body to unearth."

Head heads off in earnest while I survey the scene. Bobby has stopped his scrabbling and is sitting down as if on guard duty while eyeing me through beseeching eyes. A few minutes later Head returns carrying a pick and spade.

"Any sign of anyone from the house?" asks I.

Solemnly he shakes his head. "All quiet, sir. But I sensed eyes were upon me when I went into the tack room and again when I come out with the tools."

I nod in reflection. "Right, Sergeant, start breaking up the ground around the edge of the indent *only* for now or I fear you may stick your pick in Oswald."

Head removes his hat, his coat and his jacket, he hands them to me and I chuck them on the ground. He rolls up his sleeves, picks up the pick and meets Bobby's sorrowful gaze.

"That dog knows, doesn't he sir?"

"He knows alright."

Head raises the pick above his shoulders and brings it down hard where the point connects with the ground in a dull thud while barely penetrating an inch of soil. It is that frozen. Several more goes returns better results and soon Head has marked all around the indent.

"It's getting easier," says he breathing hard.

Clumps of semi-frozen soil are now being dislodged and taking up the spade I go behind Head and shovel it away. Bobby begins to bark towards the rear of me. Turning around I am confronted by the Richardson sisters, both are dressed to go out riding in their black dresses, fancy little hats and white silk neck scarfs. Both have sucking on lemon faces.

"What on *earth* do you think you are doing?" demands Amelia while violently waving a riding crop in front of my nose. "How *dare* you just walk on to this property and start digging it up without so much as a by your leave?"

"Quite easily," says I snatching the crop from her hand and tossing it away. "We are searching for a missing person that I believe is buried *right* there." I point.

"Nonsense! The only thing buried there is Bobby's brother Sammy who died just before the cold weather set in."

Head by now has straightened up and is leaning on the pickaxe handle while giving Amelia the evil eye. Bobby brings the riding crop back to me and excitedly hopes I will wrestle it from his mouth and then throw it again.

"We shall have your hides for this," puts in Rebecca, while sneering at Head.

"And we shall see you both in prison for perverting the course of justice," sneers back Head. "After giving the pair of you a damn good caning across your backsides. Now clear off and get the kettle on before you really piss the pair of us off," adds he, touching the handle on his revolver.

"I shall be talking to your superiors," snaps Amelia, as she makes a grab for her crop. Only Bobby refuses to release his hold until Rebecca stings the dog across his back with her own crop. Bobby lets go of the crop with a yelp and Amelia falls back onto the edge of the muck heap where fresh horse dollop had obviously been dumped just before we arrived. I know it's fresh because it is still steaming.

I know I shouldn't, but as Rebecca reaches out a hand to help a whining Amelia, I give her a good shove on her back so she too can enjoy the experience of falling in the shit and *not* coming up with a new dress. The sisters are spitting blood once back on their feet. Their clothes are in disarray and stained with horse muck and no doubt they smell nice and stinky.

"You haven't heard the last of this," spits Amelia as she and her sister stomp off.

I remove my coat and hat and chuck them down on top of Head's so they don't get dirty. We carry on digging and shortly we have a three-foot-deep trench all around the indent.

"That's deep enough, Sergeant," says I. "Let us see if we can't peel the top layers away without damaging the body."

The liveryman comes into view.

"Miss Amelia says you're to vacate the property right now or I must throw you off it," says he nervously.

"Try it," growls Head.

"Go back and inform the snotty cow that Inspector Potter orders no one is allowed to leave the house until he says so. Is that clear?"

"Yes, sir."

"And fetch me and the Inspector a nice cup of tea. We're bloody parched we are."

"Shall I stop tacking up the sisters' horses?"

"Absolutely," smiles I. "The only thing they'll likely be riding on this day is a seat in the rear of a police wagon."

"And bring some biscuits," shouts out Head to the liveryman's fleeing back.

We start to carefully peel away the snow and ice from the indent. Once down to the soil, Head gently chips away at it with the pick and pauses so that I can scrape the pieces away with the spade. Despite the cold we are both working up a sweat while our breath steams out like Puffing Billies.

Ten minutes later and barely a foot down we reveal the body of a black labrador laid on its side.

"We've been had," grates Head straightening up. "It's just a mutt."

"Let's pull it out, Sergeant and then see what lays beneath it."

Head takes hold of the dog's back legs and I take the front legs. The body is stiff as a board, but it is thin and light and we easily lift it out. I can see frozen blood on its skull that tells me it was killed by a heavy implement. We chuck it on the muck heap for now and carry on excavating further.

A foot or so further down unveils a ghostly frozen face that stares up at us. Though somewhat distorted, it is definitely the face of Oswald Standridge Carter.

Head bends down and raps Oswald's forehead with his closed fist.

"Hard as bloody rock, sir."

"He's definitely dead then?" says I sardonically.

Straightening up he says, "Do we dig him right up now or have tea first?"

"We'll have tea first. If we dig him up and then go off and have tea someone might pinch him and run off with him. Fresh frozen like he is, he must be worth a small fortune to the body snatchers."

Instead of being invited inside for tea, the liveryman returns carrying a tray with tea and biscuits on. On seeing Oswald's face, he turns deathly white and appears about to drop the tray before running for it. I grab it from his shaking hands and tell him to go. He didn't need telling twice.

Bobby by now is licking at his master's icy face. It is a pitiful sight but we cannot have him thawing Oswald's face out and possibly licking away forensic evidence. I pass Head the tea tray and grabbing one of Bobby's balls that was close by I tease him into following me into the tack room where, once in, I shut him in.

On my return I find Head has put his jacket back on and is sat on a mound of dirt with the tray at his feet while pouring the tea.

"How's the dog, sir?"

Head's answer is Bobby setting up a mournful howling from inside the tack room.

"He'll quieten down," says I, reaching down and snatching the only chocolate biscuit on the tray before Head grabs it, only to see the unmistakable smear of chocolate on his bottom lip as he passes me my tea.

"Have you been eating the chocolate biscuits?" accuses I.

"No," he obviously lies.

"There's such a thing as rank you know, Sergeant."

"I know, sir," returns he even more accusingly. "But it's a bit sad when a senior officer pulls rank just to get his hands on the best biscuits."

"I didn't mean pull rank. What I meant was; is it or is it not a common courtesy to offer the biscuits around before scoffing the best ones for oneself?"

"Not in my case. If I'd have stood on ceremony as a kid with my ten siblings I'd never had got a biscuit or any bloody thing else and would have had only the crumbs to lick up like my little sister got. That's why to this day she's still as skinny as a rake."

I sit down beside Head and sip at my tea while gazing at Oswald and surmising who put him there. There is only one strong candidate; Sir Stanley.

"Are we going to dig him right up after tea, sir?"

I meet Head's eyes, "No, Sergeant. We have more important tasks to do such as questioning everyone in the house until we get the truth out of them. Guard the body while I put things in motion." Standing up I down my tea and put the cup back on the tray. "Back in a minute."

I go around to the front door and ring the bell. The door is immediately opened by Jim who looks at me through *very* worried eyes.

"Do you have a telephone?" asks I.

"No, Inspector. Sir Stanley is in the process of acquiring one."

"Can you have someone saddle up a horse and deliver a message for me to Scotland Yard?"

He nods. "I'll get Raymond onto it right away."

"Thank you. Once the forensic team arrives from the Yard my Sergeant and I will be coming to speak to you all. Until then no one else, except for this Raymond, must leave the house under pain of arrest. Is that clear?"

"Yes, Inspector."

I head back to the stables, aware that eyes are following my every step. Once there I take out my notebook and write two notes. I've just finished as the liveryman comes up to me.

"Raymond is it?"

"Yes, Inspector."

I hand him the first note. "Hand this note to the desk Sergeant at Scotland Yard, he will do the rest."

"Shall I wait for a reply?"

"No need, just get yourself back here." I hand him the second note. "On your way to the Yard give this note to the first uniformed policeman you see."

"Shall I wait for an answer?"

"No, just proceed to the Yard."

"May I ask, Inspector? Is that Master Oswald in that grave?"

"It is indeed. Now get going Raymond and do not tell a single soul the nature of your mission, just deliver the notes as instructed."

I leave him to it and go back to find Head has put his coat and hat back on.

Donning my own hat and coat I realise there is nothing else to do except wait.

Jim comes around to pick up the tray. "Miss Amelia wants to know if you require anything else, Inspector?"

"Not just now thank you. Unless…"

He pulls out a hip flask from inside his red coat and holds it out, "She filled this up for you both. It's whisky I think."

I thank him and he goes off with the tray.

"Cor," says Head. "She's changed her tune. There's hope for the dopey tart yet."

"I would think she and her sister along with everyone else in the house have just begun to realise the enormity of the situation they now find themselves in, Sergeant," says I, handing him the flask.

"I'll bet," says he, taking a slug from the flask and passing it back.

I take a long swallow. The Scotch is creamy and slips down like peppered jellied eels.

"Well, Sergeant. All we can do is relax and wait."

"We could let Bobby out and play ball with him. It would stop his howling and give us something to do to keep us warm."

It is a good idea. I cover Oswald's face with my bowler while Head goes and lets Bobby out. We are to spend the next thirty minutes playing catch before the first plod arrives shortly followed by another. Knowing the team from the Yard won't be arriving for at least another thirty minutes I leave the plods to play with Bobby's balls while keeping guard over Oswald.

Head and I go up to the house where Jim lets us in and takes our hats and coats. We wipe our feet as best we can but I am not taking off my walking boots. Needless to say, we leave a trail of dirty prints all the way down the hall and into the drawing room where the sisters are stood in front of the settee, having got cleaned up and changed into a blue dress for Amelia, and a red one for Rebecca. Having lost their lemon chewing expressions in exchange for ones of beaten curs they sit down and stare transfixed at us through wet eyes filled with terror.

We sit down opposite them.

"We didn't know Oswald was buried out there," implores Amelia while wringing her hands together. "We honestly believed he had run off somewhere. Please believe us."

I am not about to let them off the hook despite believing Amelia is telling the truth. The more frightened they are, the more likely they will answer our questions truthfully.

"Explain the charade you put the first police officer through when he called upon you?"

"It was Uncle Stanley's idea. He wanted to confuse the police investigations into who the flasher was."

"His own son of course."

"Yes."

"Did you know Oswald was the flasher?" asks Head.

"Yes, we did."

"When did you know?" asks I.

"Right from the start," puts in Rebecca.

Amelia shoots her sister a warning glare.

"It's no good, Amelia," pleads Rebecca. "We must tell the Inspector everything."

Amelia drops her gaze, when she lifts her head she meets my eyes with ridged resolve.

"It started as a silly bet, Inspector. We were out and about with Oswald one fine day a few weeks ago, we were all a little merry and began playing stupid dare games while walking in Hyde Park. Becks and I then bet Oswald ten pounds that he dares not flash his thing at a pair of doddery old ladies that where hobbling about. Oswald won the bet and we had a hoot over it. We never dreamed that Oswald would become addicted to flashing nor become infamously known as Jack the Flasher."

"Anyway," cuts in Rebecca. "Sir Stanley quickly realised that the descriptions of the flasher given by his victims in the press matched Oswald. So, he followed Oswald and actually caught him red-handed flashing a young maid in Berkeley Street where we live. He was furious beyond reasoning and threw Oswald out. But Oswald threatened to go to the press if Uncle didn't pay him a vast, and I mean vast, sum of money."

"How much is a vast sum?" asks Head.

"Ten thousand pounds."

"*How much?*"

"Ten thousand pounds."

"And of course," says I, "Sir Stanley led everyone to believe he paid up to ensure Oswald cleared off and did not go to the press while he also succeeded in maintaining the status quo?"

"That is what he told all of us," says Amelia. "He also said he couldn't trust Oswald to keep to their bargain. Or that the police wouldn't come calling anyway should they get a lead on Oswald being in the frame. Consequently, Uncle instructed us all on what we were to say should the police call. But first Becks and I were to report having been flashed while giving a description of the flasher far more removed from the ones they had had thus far so as too muddy the waters even further."

"And you thought that was also rather a hoot, didn't you?" demands I.

Both women momentarily drop their heads in shame, but it is Rebecca who answers first.

"It was all a game, Inspector. A bit of fun to lighten the day. We never dreamed it would end up with Oswald lying in a cold grave."

"The housekeeper? Tell me, did Oswald get her pregnant or was that all just part of the charade?"

"Part of the charade. Uncle Stanley was on the point of dismissing the butler and the housekeeper anyway because they'd been at it out of wedlock. But then the Oswald problem cropped up and Uncle seized on the opportunity to give an alibi as to why Oswald disappeared. The butler and the housekeeper did not hesitate to take up Uncle's offer, better that than ruin and the poor house."

"And all they had to do was follow the script," puts in I, "and have everyone believe that Oswald had taken advantage of a servant and then had been kicked out of the family home as a consequence by a father who had much higher values than his licentious son."

"Exactly. And with everyone singing the same song, who was not to believe it until you and your Sergeant turned up?"

"Why did you turn up when you did?" cuts in Amelia in a tone that says she has regained a good deal of her composure. "We couldn't believe it and thought after the first police visit we'd never be called upon again."

"That convincing, were you?" grates Head.

She shrugs and starts to sulk.

"We turned up because of information we had received from a gardener who was part of another charade implemented by a pair of rather clever relations of yours," says I.

"Those bloody old hags the Spencers," spits Amelia. "I'll bet it was them. But why? They weren't part of *our* charade."

"I haven't quite worked out the why as yet," says I. "But I have a good idea."

"Are we allowed to be privy to your idea?" asks Rebecca.

"Not at the moment. The Longs. Why were they drawn into the charade?"

"I have no idea," sulks Amelia. "In fact, I have no idea who the hell you're talking about."

"I've never heard of them either," adds Rebecca.

"Well thank you ladies," says I, standing up. "That will be all for now."

"All!" shouts Amelia. "That cannot be all! We don't know how Oswald ended up buried in the garden for one thing. We don't know what those old twats the Spencers have to do with anything, or these Long people. And worse what's going to happen to us?"

Time to make a Christmas bonus. Looking behind me to ensure none of the servants has crept in without my knowledge I go for the kill. "The thing is, you have fed us a pack of lies which could easily see you both jailed for perverting the course of justice."

"How long for?" squeaks Rebecca as the pair of them stare at me with horror in their wide-open eyes.

"Until old women's hairs start sprouting out of your chins," says Head, totally deadpan. "Your teeth start falling out, your tits hang down to your knees like razor strops and your toe nails look like tortoise shells."

"Oh God," they cry in unison.

In truth Head and I are being a bit worse than cruel, but they started it.

Amelia, tears in her eyes, asks in a hushed whisper, "Is there anything we could do to lessen our sentence?"

I thoughtfully rub a hand over my chin, as does Head.

"There is a way," says I, reeling them in.

"Well it might alleviate the situation," adds Head. "Even if it is only a small alleviation."

"Oh… I don't know Sergeant, it just might go a long way with a judge who's not only soft for a pretty face but is also resigned to see repentance and charity all mixed up in the same pot."

"Tell us what it is," demands Rebecca.

"A hefty donation into the Police Benevolence Fund will soften even the most hardened judge's heart. It may also go a long way towards my Sergeant and I putting in a few good words on your behalves to recommend you receive nothing more than a severe reprimand for your misguided shenanigans."

"No prison?" squeaks Rebecca.

"Quite possibly."

"How much should we donate?"

"A hundred at least."

"Pence?"

"Pounds."

"Pounds! That's a small fortune!"

I shrug. "What value do you put on your freedom?"

"One hundred pounds it shall be," sulks Amelia, her questioning eyes swimming in temper. "I shall fetch the money." Standing up she stomps out of the room and we wait in silence.

A few minutes later she returns with an envelope which she hands to me.

"It's all there," says she gazing down at me with suspicious eyes.

"Thank you," smiles I. "Fear not Ladies you shall not be going to prison this day or the next. Just make certain you do not ever do anything so stupid again."

"One other thing," puts in Head. "Don't go around bragging that you have donated a large sum to the fund as it may be construed as trying to bribe a policeman which carries an even longer sentence than perverting and stuff."

"We won't," they sulkily say in unison.

"Wonderful," says I, stuffing the envelope into my inside jacket pocket. "We will now interview Beryl Jones in the common room if that's alright with you."

"That's fine," says Amelia. "Do as you please."

We will, thinks I. "Good day ladies. And thank you for all your help."

Head and I leave the room and shut the door. I bob down and peep through the keyhole while Head sticks his ear to the door.

"They're hugging each other," says I.

"Sounds like they're sobbing as well sir."

I stand up. "I do believe they have learnt their lesson, Sergeant and we shall have no more trouble with them."

Jim appears and says, "Who do you wish to see now?"

"Beryl in the common room if you would kindly fetch her."

"And any chance of another pot of tea with biscuits?" asks Head.

"Of course, Sergeant. I will arrange it. Please follow me."

We follow him down the long hallway, he sees us into the common room before going off to fetch Beryl and order tea. We sit down and wait.

"You seem to have a terrible thirst on today, Sergeant, and a craving desire for biscuits, is anything wrong?"

"Chloe cooked up some bacon for a sandwich for my breakfast. It's only the second time she's cooked bacon. The first time she burnt it to an inedible crisp and this time she salted it."

I am incredulous, "She actually *salted* the bacon? But why?"

"Because she knows I love salt and thought that's what you do when you fry bacon."

"Obviously you ate the sandwich hence your raging thirst."

"I didn't want to upset her."

"And the biscuits?"

"They take the salty taste away for a while."

"Fear not, Richard. Once Betty has given Chloe a few lessons in the art of cooking her culinary talents will progress in leaps and bounds. Send Chloe around to mine on Christmas Eve and she can learn from Betty how to make sausage rolls and mince pies."

"Thank you, Gerald, that would be much appreciated."

It is a trembling with fear Beryl who steps cautiously into the common room, right behind her is the cook, Petunia Plum, carrying a tray with tea and biscuits on, she definitely is not trembling. The cook sets the tray down on the little table, straightens herself up and clashes eyes with me.

"I insist on being present while you interrogate Beryl," demands she. "We cannot allow a young girl to be left alone in a room with two men, even if they are policemen."

"Very well," says I. "But do not speak for the girl unless we ask you to. Is that clear to you?"

She nods.

"Good. Please sit and we shall begin."

The cook moves her chair to sit closer to the roaring fire but thankfully this time she doesn't hoist her skirts up to her neck. Beryl sits opposite me and Head. Head pours the tea for all four of us and then snatches a chocolate biscuit which disappears down his gob so fast it's like a pelican scoffing a minnow.

To ease into it gently and before I hit Beryl with the heavy stuff I reiterate all she has told us before. She relaxes a little, the cook relaxes and Head scoffs all the biscuits before I can grab a single one while refilling his cup and gulping it down until the pot is empty. At last he takes out his notebook and pencil ready to take notes.

"Now, Beryl," says I. "I want you to tell me what you know about Oswald's death."

"She doesn't know anything about Oswald's death," snaps Petunia.

"Madam. It is written all over her face."

"Well why don't you read what it says and leave her alone?"

Beryl drops her head, covers her face and starts to cry. Time to get tough.

"Mrs Plum if you do not keep your beak out I shall have you removed and locked up in a cupboard. Beryl! You can do this here or down the station from the comfort of a cell. Pull yourself together and start talking."

Petunia shifts her seat beside Beryl's and takes hold of her hand. Beryl lifts her head and meets my eyes. I hand her a handkerchief and she pat's away her tears.

Beryl sucks in air and shivers as if the devil itself was running a hand up her spine. "I…I saw Sir Stanley hit Master Oswald on the head with a spade," she gasps out.

"Tell me from the beginning, Beryl. Do not be afraid, you are not on trial. Just speak the truth and I promise you all will be well."

She collapses into a flood of body racking sobs. It is hopeless. Head looks at me with impatient eyes that suggest we get *really* tough with her. However, I reason that it would be futile to try and bully the girl. I change tack.

"Mrs Plum, it is obvious to me that you are the only person who Beryl has confided in and you are trying to protect her. That is commendable but will get us nowhere and may land you both in serious trouble for withholding evidence. *You* tell us what happened."

Petunia sits up rigidly straight and stares into my eyes. "Very well, Inspector. Beryl was upstairs making Oswald's bed. I was in the kitchen. Lady Sarah had gone off to one of her charity events. The rest of the servants were about their business when suddenly all hell broke loose. Sir Stanley began ranting and raving at Oswald in the drawing room. Everyone could hear what he was shouting out, but of course everyone kept out of the way by hurrying to the servants' hall and closing the door. All that is except Beryl who was too scared to leave Oswald's bedroom. You see, Inspector, Sir Stanley is a wonderful human being but he does have a fiery temper. Oswald ignited that temper and encouraged it to explode. Oswald's room looks out over the stables and as the dreadful row between Oswald and Sir Stanley spilled out of the house and around to the stables they came into Beryl's view."

"I'll tell it now," interrupts Beryl. "It's best I tell it to the policemen."

Petunia squeezes Beryl's hand really tight. "Go on my brave little thing."

"I went to the window. I saw Sir Stanley waving his hands around like a mad man. Master Oswald was laughing at him and then he saw me looking down at him. And do you know what 'e did? 'E got out 'is thing and stared right up at me. Then he kept pulling at it as if he was trying to pull it right off. I think 'e done it to annoy 'is father. The next thing, Sir Stanley went and hit him on the head with the spade an' Master Oswald collapsed on the ground. I darted back from the window hoping Sir Stanley hadn't seen me. When I dared to take another peek, they had both gone. I thought that perhaps they'd gone back into the house. I went downstairs because it was now all quiet but it seemed no one was about until Mrs Plum came out of the servants' hall and I fell into her arms and broke down."

Petunia takes over, "The poor girl was hysterical so I took her into the common room and gave her a drop of brandy. She told me everything she had seen and I told her not to tell anyone else. A short while after that Sir Stanley came back into the house and I went out to ask if he required anything. He looked deathly white and was rambling on about having just thrown Oswald off the property. But he had mud on his shoes and dirt on his hands. He saw me looking him over and told me that Sammy, Oswald's other dog, who was ailing anyway, got so upset having heard his masters shouting at each other he promptly died of a heart attack. Once Sir Stanley had physically shoved Oswald out through the gates he then went and buried Sammy behind the stables. Hence the mud on his shoes and the dirt on his hands."

"Where were the dogs before all this happened?"

"At that time of the morning, shut up in their kennels around the side of the barn. They would have heard everything but seen nothing."

"So, it would have been unlikely that Sir Stanley would have taken the trouble to go and see if the dogs were alright having just had a violent confrontation with his son."

"Exactly. At the time I thought it odd, but I took Sir Stanley at his word. But later when he went out, I asked Raymond to see if he could confirm that Sammy was buried behind the stables. Raymond returned and said he'd shovelled away some dirt and found that the dog was indeed buried where Sir Stanley had said. After that I believed, and so did everyone else, everything that Sir Stanley told us."

"Obviously no one saw Oswald actually being thrown off the property because he never left the property? But then as you say all the servants, except for Beryl, were sheltering in the servants' hall anyway and wouldn't have seen anything."

She shakes her head, "No one would have seen anything at all. When there are family rows Sir Stanley expects the servants to make themselves scarce and not pry or listen in so they don't spread gossip."

"And no one suspected any foul play regarding Oswald's disappearance?"

"No one."

"Beryl. Do you have anything to add to all this?"

"No, sir. It is the truth and the whole truth so 'elp me God."

"And you have not told a living soul other than Mrs Plum that you saw Sir Stanley hit Oswald over the head with a spade?"

"No one else, just Mrs Plum. What's goin' to 'appen to me now? Will I go to prison?"

"I shall be behind bars long before you, young lady," says I, being truthful. "Have no fear. You may well have to give evidence in a Coroner's Court and a Court of Law, but it is highly unlikely you will face any criminal charges whatsoever. Did you witness a murder? Perhaps? Certainly, you witnessed an assault but had no way of knowing if what you saw resulted in Oswald's death. And of course, the cause of death is yet to be clarified."

There is a knock on the door and Jim sticks his head in, "There's an Inspector Clump waiting in the hallway to see you, Inspector."

"Thank you. Please inform him that I will be there hencewith."

"Forth?"

"Yes, thank you."

Jim appears confused for some reason as he withdraws his face. Of course, I realise that I can sound confusing at times but so much is spinning around in my head I really don't know if I'm going, just arriving or haven't even left. I wind up the interview and Petunia asks who I want to interview next. I tell her no one as I truly believe no one in *this* household, except for Sir Stanley or his wife were they here, could add anything more to what we already know. Head and I head for the hallway.

Jim and Clump are stood to attention by the front door. Clump looks very smart having at last trimmed his beard back. He is wearing a long mid-grey coat with a black velvet collar, an Eton tie and highly polished black shoes you could see your face in. But it is the Davy Crocket hat on his head that really draws our attention.

"The bloody old hypocrite," hisses Head. "That's the same hat I was wearing yesterday."

"Say nothing," warns I.

"Well done lads," says Clump as we step up. "Where can we get a nice coffee while you fill me in."

"Please follow me," says Jim.

We do and shortly we are back in the now vacant common room. Jim bades us sit while he goes to fetch coffee.

"Now I know what you are thinking, Sergeant," says Clump. "But after you left last night I began to think. If furry hats are good enough for The Royal Canadian Mounted Police they are good enough for us considering how bleeding ball bag freezing it is. So, I thought I should at least give it a try. Anyway, enough of that. Uniform are uncovering the rest of the body as we speak and forensics are measuring up and taking photographs. I am astounded by your discovery lads. You shall be commended for this. Now, tell me all."

I relate the story to him from the discovery of the body to our interviewing the Richardson sisters. I am about to move on to the interview with Beryl and Petunia when Jim comes in with a pot of coffee, three mugs and a plate of fresh out of the oven mince pies. He sets them down on the little table and then goes over and fetches out the brandy from the sideboard.

"Help yourselves gentlemen," says he before taking his leave.

"Lovely," coos Clump. "Nothing better than hot mince pies and a coffee with a drop of brandy in it."

"There are six mince pies on that plate, Sergeant," says I. "That's two each."

"I do believe the Sergeant can count, Inspector," grates Clump.

"Not when it comes to sweet treats he can't," says I.

"Um… Point taken," says Clump. Standing up he removes his hat and coat, slings them on the back of his chair and sits back down. "Sergeant, pour the coffee. Inspector Potter, please continue."

I continue until there is nothing left to tell, for now.

"And you say you intend to interview these Spencer sisters on leaving here?" asks Clump.

"Most certainly, sir."

"Good. Give the old sods a roasting and find out what the hell they are about. These people may think their positions in life exempt them from the law but let me tell you, no one is exempt, not even the royals. Just look what happened to King Charles the First." He draws a finger across his throat.

"Or that Caesar bloke," adds Head, making a stabbing motion with the silver spoon he's just stirred the coffee with.

I sigh in recognition that the privileged do often get away with murder when the murdered are common people. They often get away with it when the murdered are one of their own and I sense Clump is about to confirm the fact.

"However, the thing is this, lads. Sir Stanley is without doubt one of the most respected men of his ilk in the world. The chances of getting him convicted of murdering his own son will be slim at best, and nigh on impossible at worst. The best we can hope for, should he not confess to murder, is that he confesses to manslaughter on the grounds of temporary insanity. Therefore getting off scot free."

"So, what's the point of arresting him when he returns to England in a couple of weeks or so?"

"Because, Inspector, he has committed criminal acts. He failed to notify the authorities of a dead person. He conducted an unlawful burial and he has perverted the course of justice. All of which he will get away with, with no more than a slap on the arse. But… the ensuing scandal, once the press gets on to it, will ruin his social standing and destroy his exalted position within the Church."

What Clump is saying without saying it, is make certain you give the press all the information they need to crucify Sir Stanley. I agree with him. No one should be above the law and if the law won't punish the wrongdoer than the press will. Not only that, Head and I will make a bomb selling the story, secretly of course. No names mentioned.

Clump settles back in his chair and lights up a cigar. Having downed a couple of mugs of coffee generously topped up with the brandy and eaten his share of the mince pies he looks ready to drop off. For me and Head it is time to leave and make for the Spencers.

Malcom the maid opens the door of the Spencer's house when Head and I eventually arrive.

"Can I help you?" asks she with a sneer.

I cannot believe the mad woman is going to go through the same routine as before.

"We wish to speak to Miss Delphinium Spencer and Miss Rosebud Spencer."

"For what reason?"

"We intend to torture then into admitting their part in perverting the course of justice," smiles I.

"I will see if they are in," sneers she and promptly slams the door in our faces.

"That lump of lard could do with a good kicking," grates Head. "Who the hell does she think she is?"

"Obviously the woman has ideas above her station, Sergeant. She needs a lesson in manners and how to conduct yourself when answering the door."

The door opens again and stepping aside Malcom arrogantly waves us in and slams the door.

"The ladies will see you right away. Once you have wiped your cruddy shoes."

We wipe our feet and hand her our hats and coats which she holds out at arm's length with a big smirk on her face before dropping them on the floor again. Enough is enough. I haul a set of handcuffs out of my jacket pocket and clamp one on Malcom's wrist before she can grasp what is happening and twist it around her back, Head wrenches her other wrist around and we cuff that one. Initial surprise over she intends shouting the odds but as she opens her big gob Head rams his snotty hanky into it before she has time to grunt. Now she puts up a fight, her huge body twists and bucks in an effort to break away from our hold, she tries kicking out at us but all to no avail. We have extensive experience in subduing the violent criminal and Malcom proves to be all bark and not much bite, she quickly concedes defeat by fainting onto the floor. Well I hope it's only a faint.

"What now, sir? She looks dead to me. We can't just leave her there with handcuffs on her, someone will accuse us of police brutality which led to her death."

"Let's get the cuffs off her, drag her away from the door, open it up and roll her away down the steps. That way whoever finds her will think she just slipped on the ice and had a heart attack. Plus, it would help if she cracks her head on the stone steps a few times."

"Understood. Good idea, sir," says he.

Bobbing down we manage, with supreme effort, to turn her on her side and remove the cuffs. Shoving her back we grab hold of a leg each and are just about to get pulling when a voice booms out.

"What on earth are you doing with my wife?"

Dropping Malcom's leg, I spin around and come face to face with a tall skinny man dressed in a black long-tailed jacket and cream coloured waist coat and with two strands of grey hair combed over a shiny bonce. The butler? He wasn't about yesterday.

"The lady has passed out, sir," says I. "We were putting her in the recovery position."

"By pulling at her legs?"

"The quickest way to pump air into her lungs," says Head dropping the other leg.

"She has a rag in her mouth," says he obviously utterly confused by it all.

"To prevent her from biting her tongue," says I.

He puts his hands together as if in prayer. "We need a doctor. Dear God she looks so white."

"Fear not, good sir," says I. "We are policemen and quite used to situations such as these. Trust me she will be fine in a moment or two."

"What shall I do?"

"Go and fetch a glass of water."

"Yes, water. I must fetch water."

"Quick, Sergeant," says I, as the butler hurries away.

Head yanks the hanky out of her mouth. "Wake up! Wake up!" he demands giving her face a few hard slaps as I pump away at her chest with my hands.

At last she omits a strangled groan and tries to push herself up into a sitting position. We grab her by an arm each to assist her.

"What happened?" moans she running a hand over her face.

"You passed away madam," says I.

"Oh God! I actually died! Are you saying I just dropped down dead?"

"Temporarily," says Head.

"But fear not madam, no long-term damage will come from this and you'll be back on your feet in no time."

She attempts to get up just as the butler returns. Bobbing down he holds the glass of water to her mouth and places a steadying hand around the back of her neck. She slurps away as Head and I sneak away and head towards the parlour, assuming that the sisters will be there.

"Ah… Inspector Potter and Sergeant Head," greets Delphinium as we step into the parlour. "So good of you to come. Please take a seat."

We sit down in the same seats as before and opposite the sisters. It is deja vu, they are dressed in the same outfits and looking as nutty as ever. With her back to us over by the sideboard stands Rolland polishing the silver. There now stands a highly decorated Christmas tree in one corner with a heap of presents beneath it. The fire is crackling and blazing away and must be burning the sisters' backs it is giving out so much heat. They'll probably burst into flames at any minute.

"What happened to that lazy slug Malcom?" demands Delphinium. "She didn't escort you in."

"She fell over in the hallway. Her husband is tending to her."

"There you are then," says Delphinium. "I warned her, didn't I Rosebud?"

"You did indeed dear."

"I warned her, Inspector, that if she didn't lose a few pounds her legs would collapse one day from carrying too much weight. Now I am proved right. Anyway, to the business in hand. Charley, coffee or something more warming?"

"Something warming please," says I. "Sergeant?"

"Anything wet please," says he a dry tongue flicking out over his even dryer lips.

Delphinium twists her scrawny neck around. "*Rolland*, leave that crap, bugger off and tell the cook to make a pot of Charley, a pot of coffee and to bung a few cakes on a tray and hurry up so you can dish up the booze."

Rolland stomps off while the sisters give Head and I eye to eye contact.

"Now then, Inspector," says Delphinium conspiratorially. "I take it you have found out where Oswald has been hiding."

"We have, madam."

"But before you tell me you will demand to know why we set you up in the first place."

"I will." I am not going to tell her Oswald is dead until I have all the answers I need from her. "Perhaps you might start at the beginning. And be aware that my Sergeant will be taking notes and you may even be facing criminal charges."

She smiles a smile of 'you've got no hope of charging us with anything ever' and I am beginning to realise I am dealing with a pair of very shrewd adversaries.

"I take it you know who we are, in relation to the Standridge Carters?"

"I do indeed."

"Right, Inspector, here goes. Cousin Sarah came to see us just before that prat of a husband of hers dragged her off to India. She was in a right state over Oswald. She told us everything; including admitting that Oswald was beyond doubt the flasher. And that Stanley had told her how he had thrown Oswald out from the family seat and warned him that he was never to return. Disinherited, all photographs of him destroyed, or so *he* thought. Wiped from the family archives as if he had never existed. However, Sarah could not so easily fall in with Stanley's wishes as he had expected. Oswald, you see, has always been a nuisance; he was always getting on the wrong side of his father and always in trouble over one thing or another, but Sarah loves him and we love him, don't we dear?"

"We do, dear," agrees Rosebud with a tear in her eye. "Such fun. He always made us laugh. Didn't he dear?"

"He certainly did, the scallywag. Even when he came to scrounge money from us he would make us laugh. We knew him far better than his own father knew him, Inspector. And one thing we knew above all else was if his father, as he'd often threatened, did eventually throw Oswald out the first place he would run to would be here. He never showed up. Sarah was frantic and we were very worried as to his whereabouts and she left for India having made us promise to find out what happened to Oswald. Had he joined the army as Stanley had demanded? Was he on a tramp steamer heading for Timbuctoo? Or was he simply hiding out and licking his wounds? It seemed the police where getting absolutely nowhere in solving the flasher crimes which meant that no one would be looking for Oswald either. So, I came up with a plan to ensure I would get one of the best detectives in the country onto the case."

This revelation throws me off my perch. "Thank you for the accolade, madam. But whatever makes you think it was you who got me and my Sergeant onto this case.

"I sent my nephew a note asking him to come and see me."

I nod my head in deference, "That nephew being Sir Robert Percy, our new Commissioner?"

"Our youngest sister's son. You are very astute, Inspector. Robert said if anyone on the force can track Oswald down you can. So, he put you two wonderful men on the case and assisted us in honing our plan which was to name the flasher and spread further confusion to undermine the charade that Stanley had implemented. When we sent a message to Scotland Yard stating that we had new evidence we knew it wouldn't be long before you came calling. We also knew you were nobody's fool and would quickly see through us, but you were still duty bound to follow up with what our gardener had been primed to tell you. He, incidentally, being a gossip, told Malcom all that his friend, this Long chap fellow, had told *him*. Malcom subsequently told us as she is unable to keep a secret. So, you see we were well primed and only had to light the fuse."

"You could have simply told me of your worries about Oswald and that he was the flasher. It would have saved my Sergeant and I an awful lot of senseless investigating while leaving you utterly blameless of wasting police time."

"True. But what if you had subsequently believed all that you no doubt were told by those snooty Richardson girls and Stanley's servants? You may well have given up on the case. After all it wasn't exactly your forte now was it? You would have decided that without Oswald you had nothing worth proceeding with. You needed Oswald so you could put him in an identification line up to be picked out should he not confess. But was it worth the cost and all the effort to investigate and search for an upper class spoilt fool who had simply shagged the housekeeper and may, or not be the flasher? And who would care if he was then kicked out of his home by one of the most respected knights in the country? Gossip from a smelly gardener and a pair of dotty old women who presented you with a sketch of a new suspect may have seemed like a load of old crap, but it was enough to set you on the trail towards the truth. We knew, from what Robert told us; the more you were pissed about and led astray the more determined you'd be to find Oswald and put an end to it all. Because that is your forte, Inspector, you cannot give up and cannot stand to be made a fool of by anyone, especially those who believe they are your superiors."

Rolland comes in with a large tray of beverages and cakes. She sets them down and goes over to the drinks cabinet to fetch the hard stuff.

"We're on the scotch, Inspector. As it's brass monkeys. Rolland, get pouring."

Rolland pours good measures into four cut glass tumblers and hands them around. She then asks who wants tea or coffee. I plump for coffee; the sisters decline and Head goes for the tea.

"What's up with that slug Malcom and her drip of a husband?" demands Delphinium of Rolland.

"They have retired to their apartment Mistress."

"Retired! Bloody retired? What on earth do you mean?"

"Cook told me that Malcom is unwell and Mervin took her back to their apartment for a rest."

"Bloody cheek. I don't pay the buggers to rest. I pay them to work. I'll bet they're not resting anyway. The sods will be up to rumpy pumpy I've no doubt. *And* at my expense. If it wasn't for Christmas, I'd throw the bleeders out on the streets and see how they like *that?*"

"Will there be anything else, Mistress Delphinium?" asks Rolland with a heavy sigh.

"No thank you Rolland. Bugger off and get your lunch."

She curtsies and leaves.

"Where were we, Inspector?" asks Delphinium.

After that tirade I have completely lost the thread. However, I have all the information I require. "I think we shall leave it there, madam."

"Ah… No doubt you can work the rest out for yourself and have no further need to hear my ramblings."

I couldn't have put it better. I am about to hit her with the tragic news regarding Oswald when there is a sharp rap on the door.

"Come!" bellows Delphinium.

The butler comes in, marches over to us and stands to attention. "Madam. My wife is unwell and I fear I cannot leave her on her own. May I have the rest of the day off to tend to her?"

"Do you think I'm running a ruddy hospital, Mervin?"

"No, madam, I do not."

"Good. I'm glad that much is clear to you. Very well, bugger off for the day but don't expect to get paid."

"No, madam," says he shooting me an accusing glare before turning around and marching off.

"Well, cheers, Inspector," says Delphinium raising her glass.

"Cheers, Sergeant," says Rosebud clinking glasses with Head.

We all do the clinking glasses bit. I down half my scotch and brace myself to tell them that Oswald is dead. Maybe they have already considered the possibility but somehow, I doubt it. The sisters portray an image of a pair of tyrannical old eccentrics who couldn't give a damn about anyone or anything. I am about to test that image.

Rosebud is the one who picks up on my sudden melancholy. "Tell us about Oswald, Inspector. Where did you find him? Have you arrested him? Has he been locked away or set free pending further investigations?"

I can tell by the look in both their eyes they are expecting the worst but hoping for the best. I falter for a moment and it is Delphinium who spills the beans.

"He is dead, isn't he?"

"Yes. I am afraid he is. My Sergeant and I discovered his body this morning. I am so sorry to have to bring you such sad tidings, ladies. Please except our sincere condolences."

Delphinium smiles wanly while Rosebud lowers her head as teardrops fall and plink into her scotch.

"Was it murder or misadventure?"

"I am not at liberty to say as yet, madam, pending further investigation. All I will say is that Oswald's death is currently being treated as suspicious."

"Did the poor lamb suffer?" says Rosebud.

I shake my head, "No, apparently not."

"You would say that, though wouldn't you?" says Delphinium.

"Of course, I would. But in this case, it appears to be the truth. Oswald's death was quick and painless."

"Oh dear," cries Rosebud. "Poor Sarah. This news will break her heart. We must send a telegram to India immediately. Can you send telegrams to India?"

"I'm sure you can," says I. "But you will not attempt to contact your cousin without getting permission from us first. You may hamper our investigations, madam. If this does turn into a murder inquiry we cannot have the papers or anyone else spreading it all around the world before the body has even been formally identified by a close family member. And who on earth would want to hear about the death of a loved one by telegram. Until the Standridge Carters return to England you will keep this to yourselves no matter how difficult the task. Is that clear to you both?"

"It is, Inspector," sighs Delphinium. "Especially as you suspect that Stanley may well be responsible for Oswald's death. I am right, am I not?"

Having said very little, Head thankfully answers for me, "We are sorry, madam, but any further attempts to wheedle information from us will be met with silence. We cannot and will not divulge anything more before Oswald's nearest and dearest have been informed. Nothing will appear in the press at least this side of Christmas and cruel as it is, think yourselves fortunate that we came here to tell you about Oswald in the first place from the kindness of our hearts when we didn't have to tell you anything at all."

"We apologise to you fine gentlemen," says Delphinium. "Thank you for coming here and setting us straight. It was very kind of you."

Apart from furthering our investigations the real reason we came was because we were hoping to get another sizable donation for the Police Benevolence Fund, minus our commission of course, but with the sister's nephew being our bloody commissioner that one's off the cards. Still the scotch is wonderful, the cakes delicious, we're nice and warm and the company is nutty but entertaining and there's no point in trying to escape too early.

Two hours later we are all as pissed as frogs and on first name terms. I finally remembered to give Rosebud back her sketchpad which sets her off. She keeps badgering Head to strip off so she can immortalise him as her version of Michel Angelo's David, but he is having none of it. She even offered him twenty pounds, but *still* he turned her down. Such is life, I would have done it for a fiver. Delphinium then asks me to go to bed with her as she'd like to try it out before she is too old. Politely I decline but agree to giving her a kiss under the mistletoe.

She stands up and limping around the table she holds up a sprig of mistletoe bends down and gives me a smacker on my lips before limping back to her seat.

"As you can no doubt deduce, Inspector," smiles she. "I have a leg missing and wear a wooden one. But what you couldn't possibly deduce I am sure is how some bastard managed to steal the new leg I had treated myself to for Christmas even before it was delivered to me."

"I'm sure I couldn't," says I. "But if you give me the details of the theft, I will try my best to track the culprit down."

She waves away my offer. "You have more important things to see to, Inspector."

That much is certain, thinks I, sighing with relief.

On a visit to the lavatory I run into Rolland and ask her why she keeps working for the sisters while having to suffer so much derision from them. She tells me that despite their outward nastiness towards their servants they are in fact kind and considerate in many other ways, plus they are happy to accommodate couples provided they work. They pay way over the amount that any other employer pays, including the Queen, and there is a queue of domestics on the sisters' waiting list hoping for employment. Not only that, they hand out money to various charities like confetti.

At last I think it best we went home and for the tenth time I order Head to get his shoes on as he keeps spreading his cheese around the room. Eventually, in between giggling like a girl, he manages to get them on but can't do up his laces and Rosebud, despite swaying around like a sailor in a tempest, has a go and somehow manages the task.

We say goodbye, but before we leave we are presented with a beautifully wrapped large square boxed present each. There is a card stuck on each one that carries our name. They obviously had them all ready for us even before we arrived. How foresighted was that?

Rolland shows us to the door where we don our coats and hats. Just before she opens it she produces a piece of mistletoe from behind her back. I oblige her, not because she is attractive, but because it is tradition. Head though goes for it and five minutes later I finally manage to prise them apart and bundle him out the door.

We head off home in excellent spirits sure in the knowledge that having spent the afternoon with the Police Commissioner's aunts there'll be no recriminations to answer to. Conversation is limited as we walk because neither of us can string a sensible sentence together and we both keep falling or slipping over. It is dark, it is bloody freezing and it starts to snow. However, the inner glow keeps us warm plus the fact we've had so much piss we are practically anesthetised. The trouble is we end up getting lost and have to go into a pub to find our bearings, top up on alcohol, get warmed up and take a long pee.

How on earth I managed to wake up the next morning in my own bed I have no idea. What is clear is that I am seriously in the dog house. I forgot to get the chocolates and am not fit enough to get out of bed, let alone go to work. One thing though is *absolutely* certain, Betty *won't* be playing nurse maid. Apart from struggling to the bathroom for the usual I spend the entire day in bed mostly sleeping or drinking copious amounts of water. The very thought of booze makes me feel ill but, I am sure I will recover in time for Christmas Day.

The next morning, I awake to the aroma of sausage rolls and mince pies wafting up the stairs. It is Christmas Eve and Betty is already baking for the big day. Despite still feeling fragile I know I must get up and go to work or Clump will have my head. Talking about Head I wonder if he survived the other night, as he was in a worse state than I was. Vaguely I remember waving goodbye to him and seeing him stagger across the road towards the area where he lives. After that I don't remember a thing.

Suddenly there comes a resounding bang on the front door. Swinging my legs out of the bed I wobble over to the window and peer down but cannot see who it is. I hear Betty open the door and exchange words with whoever has come calling but can't quite hear clearly enough to ascertain who it is. I wobble back to bed, sit up and pull the covers up to my chin.

"You have a visitor, Detective Inspector," yells up Betty.

"Who is it?" croaks back I.

"I'm sending him up."

I hear heavy footsteps lumping up the stairs. It must be Head? The door opens and to my horror Clump steps in.

"Season's greetings, Inspector," grates he. "I see you are at least a bit more alive than your colleague."

"Am I?" says I, hoping I appear to him as crap as I feel.

"You are, just." He grabs the chair by the wall, swings it over close to the bed and sits down. "Sergeant Head looks like he's recently spent time as an inmate in a bloody morgue he's that grey. But at least he managed to stagger into work this morning and throw up on my office floor. I sent him home once he had spun the most ridiculous made up story to escape retribution that any officer in my entire career has had the nerve to imagine I would be even remotely resigned to believe a single word of. So here I am to hear your version of events."

"Um… Honestly, sir I cannot remember anything much after we left the Spencers house."

"Now that sounds much more likely than the pair of you chasing a shadowy figure all around the Eastend who you believed may have been Jack the Ripper and who had returned to rekindle his murderous murders." Taking out a cigar he sticks it in his mouth and sets it alight. "The next time you down enough booze to comatose yourself and are incapable of coming into work as a consequence, do *not* get that lovely wife of yours to tramp to the station and feed me with the, 'He's got the collywobbles' rubbish. The poor woman was embarrassed beyond belief and obviously telling porkies. As was Head's partner who arrived separately to inform the Desk Sergeant that Sergeant Head was incapacitated because of exhaustion through chasing after criminals throughout the night."

He blows out a cloud of smoke. "Do you have an ashtray?"

"No, sir. But you could use the chamber pot. We don't use it anymore so it is clean."

"I should hope it is," grates he. Bending forwards, he reaches down beside the bed and comes back up with my bowler hat in his hand. "An unusual looking potty, Inspector," says he before he flicks his ash into it.

I hear Betty coming up the stairs and know she will have a tray with drinks and hot sausage rolls on it. Lovely, I am feeling thirsty and not a little hungry. She comes in and sets the tray down on the bedside cabinet close to Clump. There is a plate with *just* two sausage rolls on the tray beside a *single* mug of steaming coffee. Perhaps Clump doesn't want anything?

"Enjoy Chief Inspector," says she shooting me a 'please die' glare before she flounces out.

"Still in the doghouse, are we?" grins Clump as he stubs his cigar out in my bowler and sets it down on the floor before picking up a sausage roll and munching away at it. "Delicious. Your good lady makes better sausage rolls than Mrs Clump," says he smacking his lips together. I have to watch as he devours both sausage rolls with tormenting gusto before slowly drinking his coffee and then relighting his cigar.

At last he says, "Now, down to business, Inspector, as to the real reason I am here. Lady Sarah Standridge Carter returned home early yesterday morning *without* her husband. She sent her liveryman to the Yard with a message requesting you and the Sergeant call on her forthwith. But of course, you couldn't attend as you were both still too inebriated to even fart straight. I went in place. Lady Sarah informed me that her husband had confessed to hitting their son Oswald on the head with a spade and killing him outright. He then hit the dog called Sammy on the head with the same spade in order to use the dog's body to assist him in covering up the crime. He told Lady Sarah that he did not mean to kill Oswald and did so through diminished responsibilities because of the disgusting act her son had carried out in front of him. Lady Sarah then said that Sir Stanley told her to go home early and inform Scotland Yard of his confession. He then walked off and was last seen sailing down the Ganges in a leaking boat. She believes he intended to sail off to his death. Where are we now with all this? Well, I do not believe the bastard had any intentions of killing himself and will in fact carry on living the good life out in India with no intention of returning home and facing the music within the near future."

"Surely he could be arrested out there and forcibly brought back to England?"

"Of course, he could. But you know and I know it will never happen unless the Prime Minister himself orders he be brought back. Which he won't, after all Sir Stanley may well have killed his own son, but in doing so he has also committed a great service to his country by ridding it of the pervert known, amongst others as Jack the Stripper. Should such have happened over Jack the Ripper we would *all* be now hailing Sir Stanley as the ultimate hero. Agreed?"

I nod my agreement. In short it will be the usual whitewash to maintain the status quo.

Clump continues, "Without the testimony of the investigating officers into the case the press will not dare spread a smear campaign against the Standridge Carters and gradually the entire sorry saga will fade into oblivion. No, Inspector, Sir Stanley will never be prosecuted for a single thing or suffer a scandal. Once time has passed Sir Stanley will come back home and life will carry on as ever it did. Except?"

"For Lady Sarah. Her life cannot possible be the same after what has happened."

"It will not. She made it abundantly clear to me, Inspector, that her marriage is over in every way except in name. She will never forgive her husband for what he has done nor forgive a selfish son she loved who after all has destroyed her life *and* her marriage. If anything at all, Inspector, we owe it to a fine Lady to protect her from suffering any more than she already has. On top of that Lady Sarah has donated a large sum of money to the Police Benevolence Fund."

"How much?"

"Five thousand pounds."

"How much!" gasps I sitting bolt upright. Christ I should have screwed a lot more money out of the snotty Richardson sisters.

"You heard," says he stubbing out his cigar again in my hat before setting it down on the floor. Standing up he makes for the door but pauses as he grabs hold of the brass knob. "Talking about donations, Inspector, I also spoke to a delightful pair of very pretty young ladies at Lady Sarah's home. Amelia and Rebecca, they said their names were. They asked me, with a smirk I may add, was the Inspector and the Sergeant content with their one hundred pound donation or should they give more to ensure they didn't end up in prison?"

The rotten bitches! grates I inwardly. In truth up until now I had completely forgotten about the donation and pray that I haven't lost it. But bollocks to it all. If I am to lose my share of the donation, plus any money I may have secured from the press for 'selling my story' I may as well give up and become an honest copper, therefore being the only one in all of London.

"They are lying through their teeth, sir", says I with conviction. "They actually donated fifty pounds not one hundred."

"I can carry that lie around with me for ever, Inspector. Just be sure to pay the Sergeant his *ten* percent *equal* share and hand me over the other eighty percent. Is that clear?"

"As ice," sulks I. But I suppose ten pounds is better than nothing even though I will have to swallow the fact that Clump will undoubtedly pocket the eighty pounds for himself.

"Good man," smiles he like a snake who's just poisoned his prey. "Have a lovely Christmas, Inspector. I shall expect to see you in my office first thing after Boxing Day."

Clump leaves and closes the door. All said and done it could have been worse and at least he's sanctioned me having today off with pay, even though he didn't say as much. I listen to him wishing Betty all the season's best before I hear the front door close. All I have to do now is go downstairs and seduce Betty into forgiving me and joining me in bed for a cuddle. She shouts up the stairs.

"Don't you dare come down here and try to creep around me, Detective Inspector. I haven't even remotely forgiven you as yet."

That's that idea totally buggered, thinks I. I may as well go back to sleep and dream how I can get back at the Richardsons. I am about to slip into dream land when there is another knock on the door. This time there is no mistaking the sound of Head's and Chloe's voices. Obviously, they have turned up for Betty to teach Chloe the art of baking fine pastries. Not that I'm going to get any of the results. I should get up, but I haven't the willpower and feel myself drifting off again.

I open my eyes to find Head gazing down at me, his cheeks look like a pair of pig's testicles, all pink and bulging. His eyes are so bloodshot he appears demonic and you can't define his pupils. In short, he looks terrible.

"You look bloody awful, Sergeant," says I.

"Have you looked in the mirror lately?" groans he as he comes over to the bed and lays down beside me. That's on top of the quilt and not under it, as that wouldn't be right.

"What's wrong with your cheeks? asks I.

"God knows? I had a shave and ten minutes later they just puffed up and turned all pink."

"Too much alcohol I suppose. Clump actually came to see me."

"He said he would," yawns he.

Laughter drifts up from the kitchen. Obviously, Betty and Chloe are having a good time of it despite knowing how poorly Head and I feel. Talk about being ignored.

"Are you in the doghouse, Richard?"

"Chloe spoke to me in bed this morning to tell me to remove my hand or else?"

"Or else what?"

"She'd punch me where it would really hurt."

"Betty's been sleeping in the spare room the past two nights. She's spoken to me a few times but only to tell me off."

He cranks himself up on one elbow. "Bloody hell, Gerald. All we do for them. We go off the rails once in a blue moon and have to suffer all this crap. Christ, don't they know what we have to go through just to put bread on the table?"

"We should assert our authority," grates I, "and tell them in no uncertain terms that we are men and they are merely women. What we say goes and if we decide to go on the booze and drink ourselves into oblivion it is our absolute right."

"Agreed. Why don't you get dressed and then we'll go downstairs together and put them in their place?"

"That sounds like a plan," says I, swinging my legs out of the bed. "Wait for me here, Richard. I shall wash, shave and dress and then we will confront them."

"Excellent. While you're doing that, I'll just have forty winks."

I pad into the chilly bathroom and reluctantly take off my nightgown. There's only cold water in the jug to wash and shave in so I contemplate yelling downstairs and ordering Betty to run up with a kettle of hot water. Strike while the iron's hot. Chickening out I wash and shave in a bowl of cold water as best I can. With a towel wrapped around me I go back into the bedroom to get dressed. Then I empty Clump's cigar butt from my bowler out the window while being resolved to carry it downstairs and hang it on the hall rack. Head is snoring away like an old boar while hugging Betty's pillow to his chest. It makes me realise just how much I adore cuddling up to Betty in bed, especially when it's cold. Even so I am not to be moved and I am determined to put her in her place once and for all.

Once dressed in corduroy trousers, woolly Christmas socks and a thick high-necked jumper I slip on my carpet slippers then give Head a good shaking.

"Are you ready to sort these women out, Richard?"

He yawns, "As ever I'll be."

I rub my hands together, "Right, let's get at them."

We step out on the landing and pause.

"As the senior officer, sir, you should go first."

"No, Sergeant. You must go first."

"Why?"

"Because I am ordering you to."

He fists his hips. "You're too scared to go first, aren't you?"

"No, I'm not!"

"Yes, you are!"

"So are you," sneers I.

"No, I'm not."

"Right let's toss for it." Digging out a penny from my pocket I demand, "Heads or tails?"

"I always go Heads, obviously. You should know that."

"Alright. No need to get waspy." I flick the coin in the air, catch it, then slap it over on the other hand. "It's tails," I cry gleefully.

"Just a minute," growls he grabbing me by the wrist before I can slip the coin back in my pocket. "Let me see that coin."

"No. It is my coin and I am not about to allow you to peruse it," snaps I, clenching my fist and wrenching it from his grip.

"Show me that coin or I'll…"

"You'll what?" demands I, putting on my mean face.

"I'll… I'll tell Betty you slept with Lady Hervington."

"I'll tell Chloe you were trying to kiss Rolland's face off while hugging *him* so tightly to your body you were practically glued together!"

"Don't you dare you shit-bag!"

"Nor you."

"Just show me the coin."

"Very well." I open my hand, Head takes the coin and turns it over.

"Oh… Sorry, sir I thought you had used your tails on both sides coin."

"As if I would cheat you, Sergeant."

"It's never stopped you before."

We are in dire danger of seriously falling out when Betty yells up.

"Hurry up you two, your teas are getting cold."

"What teas?" asks I of Head.

"I was sent up to tell you tea and hot pastries will be served in five minutes."

"That must have been at least fifteen minutes ago."

He shrugs. "I can't remember."

"Do you know what this means, Richard? We are forgiven and all is back to normal."

"I wouldn't bet on it, Gerald. They'll keep making us pay for this for ages."

I shake my head. "Betty doesn't sulk for long and I'm sure that Chloe doesn't either. Let's join them and test the soup."

"Water."

"Yes, water only, no booze until tomorrow."

For some reason he gives me an odd look before taking the lead downstairs where I hang up the bowler and we head for the kitchen.

We find the women sat at the table looking rosy cheeked with eyes sparkling. Sherry glasses in hand they raise them up and toast us.

"To the men in our lives," salutes Betty. "They may be useless at times but they are ours and we love them."

"We love them," giggles Chloe.

I wonder how much booze they've had already, it isn't even noon yet. "Does this mean we are forgiven?" says I, putting on the sorry little boy look.

"No," grins Betty. "Let's just say hostilities are at an end because we're half cut and can't be bothered to keep pecking at you. Anyway, we think you've suffered enough."

"So do we," groans Head as he flops down in a chair opposite the women. "Never again."

I sit down beside him and reach for one of the mugs of tea in front of me. Head picks up the other mug. "Cheers," says I. We do the cheers bit and then Head and I start tucking into a plate of still warm sausage rolls.

"Lovely," says I catching the twinkle in Betty's eyes that tells me we'll be in for an early night only to remember we always go to midnight carols on Christmas Eve.

"Don't get too comfortable," smiles Betty as she tops hers and Chloe's glasses up. "You still have a bit more penance to do. You two can trudge off to the butchers and pick up the meat. Then there's the grocers, the confectionary shop, the chemist and only heaven knows where else we need you to go to."

"Um…" I am about to say that's her job but think better of it. I know when I'm beaten.

"The air will do you both good," smiles Betty. Standing up she hands me the shopping list along with a very large wicker shopping basket, before handing a sulking looking Head another basket, plus a couple of cotton bags. I scan the shopping list. It is terrifyingly long.

Betty gives me a peck on the cheeks and Head also receives one from Chloe. Following that we are allowed to don hats and coats before being gently but firmly pushed out the door.

"And don't you dare even think of going to the pub," orders Betty before slamming the door.

"You've still got your carpet slippers on," says Head gazing down at my feet.

I am about to knock on the door as I haven't got my keys when it is suddenly opens a crack, my shoes are thrown out and the door is slammed shut again.

"I think we're still in the doghouse, Gerald," says Head as I slip into my shoes and leave my slippers on the step.

"I think you are correct in your assumption, Richard," grates I as we set off swinging our shopping bags. "We should have put them in their places as we said we would."

We pause and face each other.

"We could still do it. Let's go back and confront them," growls Head.

"You go first."

"No, as senior…"

"Don't let's start all that again, Richard. Let us just admit defeat and suffer our punishment like the men we are."

"Agreed, Gerald."

As we walk on I change the subject, "Did Clump tell you those Richardsons screwed us up?"

"He did, and he enjoyed it. Never mind Gerald, we have been more than compensated by the Spencer sisters."

"We have?"

"I opened the present they gave me. No doubt you've got the same in yours as I got in mine."

"They say opening a present early can bring you bad luck."

We pause to face each other.

"Not in this case," grins he. "Inside I found a gilt framed water colour of me. Brilliant it is. A bottle of cognac. A new cutthroat razor with my name engraved on it and best of all, twenty quid in fivers, no less. And I'll bet money you've got exactly the same."

"Marvellous," smiles I. "Richard this is going to be the best Christmas ever. I just know it."

"It is indeed, Gerald."

Thinking about money I reach inside my coat and dig out the envelope containing the money from the Richardsons. I give Head my shopping bag to hold while I open the envelope, extract the money and count it. I have to count it twice before realising it isn't short it's an over pay.

"That Amelia can't count," says I gleefully. "There's twenty quid too much in here."

"Marvellous," smiles he. "That's eighty for Clump and twenty each for us."

We walk on until our way is blocked by Honest Mick pushing a brand-new wheelbarrow.

"Out shoppin' are we," smirks he. "Doin' what the ol' woman told ya are ya?"

"We are," admits I. "Do you still have that wooden leg for sale?"

His eyes light up. "I do."

"How much?"

"A quid."

"Ten shillings."

"Seven and six."

"Done."

"I'll make it up to a pound if you'll deliver it for me."

Suspiciously he asks, "Where to? I don't deliver outside London."

Taking out my notebook and pencil I write down the Spencer's address, tear out the page and hand it to him. "Leave it on the doorstep, ring the bell and then clear off. If challenged do not say who payed you to deliver it."

"Do I look that stupid?"

"Yes," say Head and I in unison.

"You *can* read?" asks I.

"Look copper, an entranapere, an entrapinor. A business man in my position *has* to be able to read."

"It is a distinct advantage in life," says I. "Well bugger off and don't spare the horses."

He trots off whistling and we walk on. Once in the High Street and at the butcher's we find the queue stretching half way to hell.

"Bloody hell!" gasps Head. "We'll be here all bloody day."

"Good grief. Half of London must shop at this butchers. Fear not, Richard. I am sure the queue will quickly go down."

"Well I'm not standing here freezing me balls off. Let's get all the other stuff and come back later."

"Good idea."

We set off and over the next two hours manage to pick up everything else on the list. Arriving back at the butcher's we find the queue has increased not decreased. Those at the front of the queue look frozen solid. Even the butcher standing outside and leant back against a shop window looks frozen solid. But then I realise he is actually an advertising statue.

"Bloody hell," moans Head. "I can't stand here like a prize prick. Let's go and have a beer and come back later."

"I don't think that is a good idea, Richard. The women will go mad if we go back reeking of booze."

"They won't notice anyway. The way they were chucking it down earlier they wouldn't notice if we came back smelling like a barmaid's armpit. Are we men or mouse's?"

"Mice. Mice or men."

"Whatever, Gerald. This shopping's heavier than a bag of horse shit. My feet ache and I'm bloody frozen. I need sustenance and the Brewers Arms which just happens to be across the road. Take a gander, doesn't it look just like an advertisement for heaven."

I gaze over. It does indeed appear a mirage of enticing entrapment.

"Sod it," sods I. "If we wish to have a beer despite being ordered not too we *shall* have a beer. Or even two or three if it takes our fancy."

"If we wish it so we may well stay until the butcher's queue has subsided while drinking the pub dry."

"We may even partake of the odd glass or two of scotch."

"Or even a bottle or two," grins Head.

"We shall do as we please, Richard. For are we not *real* men? Such men as we are feared yet respected by the criminal fraternity. There are those who hate us and those who would do us serious harm if they could, including the odd copper who we've upset over the years. How they would laugh at us if they could see us now burdened down with shopping."

"Why they'd call us a pair of henpecked old women."

"Well so they might, Richard. It would be water off an elephant's ear. They can all go to hell and laugh all they want. For we are more than a match for any of the bastards. Especially after a few beers."

"My sentiments exactly, Gerald."

"Having said all that which one of us will actually be brave enough to admit to being the instigator of our ragged state when we finally make it home to be confronted by the women?"

"You should be as you're in charge."

"But you suggested it, and you're the one who keeps moaning about the queue. I am more than content to wait in the queue even if I do get freezer burn on my balls."

"Do you mean frost bite in your balls?"

"I do, I think. Look, Richard, what's wrong isn't that we are bored, cold and feeling less than the real men we are because of the way the women have belittled us. We richly deserved to be belittled. What is wrong with us is, we need a good old murder to *really* get our teeth into."

"You are right, sir. Well there's bound to be a few committed over Christmas so with luck we'll go back to work and be up to our necks in blood and gore in no time."

"And as such will be back to normal moaning about how dangerous our lot is."

"Exactly," smiles he. "But for now?"

"We best stay in the queue until it's our turn because if we cock this shopping expedition up and go home without the Christmas meat our lives won't be worth a donkey's dollop."

"Agreed," sighs he just as a pair of urchins sidle up to us.

"Do ya want ta sponsor a kid for Christmas?" says the eldest who happens to be wearing a Davy Crocket hat.

"How much is it?" asks I.

"Two bob a week. An' for that ya get regular updates on the kid's progress, plus no one will throw horse dung at ya for a month."

"And if we don't sponsor a kid?"

"You'll get seriously pelted with rock solid frozen dung balls by our mates," grins he flicking a glance behind us.

I take a look to see a small gang of mixed sex urchins wielding buckets of dung balls ready to throw. Being hit by a fresh ball of dung is never good, being hit with frozen ones will no doubt be a mind numbing new experience.

"Let us make a deal," says I as a plan forms in my mind.

"That was a cracking idea, sir," says Head as ten minutes later we head home having picked up the meat. "But I did feel sorry for all those poor sods who got hit."

"So did I, Sergeant. Still it did the trick, only cost a few shillings and got us to the very front of the queue in no time."

"And didn't those urchins run for it once they'd run out of balls to throw and the shoppers charged at them."

"They did. But at least it warmed everyone up a bit I should think."

"It did indeed. Anyway, Gerald. I think this will be the best Christmas ever for my Chloe. Not to mention me own self."

"I am certain it will be, Richard. For all of us. Let's put a spurt on and get home before it gets dark. There's a bottle of scotch waiting for us along with mince pies and sausage rolls."

"Lovely," smiles Head just before a frozen dung ball knocks his bowler off followed by another that lays him out cold.

The Blue Diamond

Head and I have been called out to attend a murder scene in Cow Lane just off Tannery Street. Having taken a cab, we are minutes away.

The cobbled lane consists of early Victorian two-up two-down terraces in reasonable condition with very few holes in the rooves. They have no frontage and open up straight onto the lane and number just twenty houses in all. That's ten on one side and ten on the other.

The cab pulls up outside Number Five where a plod is standing guard. Getting out of the cab I pay the driver and step up to the plod and realise I have had dealings with the moronic moron in the not so distant past.

"Morning, Inspector. Sergeant," greets he, with a salute.

"Constable Roberts," says I. "What's amiss?"

"It is a female not yet married, sir."

The man truly is an idiot but at least he can hear what I am saying unlike the last time I encountered him. "Do we have a body, Constable?"

"Yes, sir. You both do."

I am losing the plot already and it is only just gone eight in the morning. "Not our bodies! snaps I. "A murdered body."

"Oh, that one. It's around back in the privy. Do you wish me to show you where it is, sir?"

"If it isn't too much trouble, Constable," sighs I.

"No trouble, sir. Please follow me."

We follow the nutcase to the end terrace, around the back and along a narrow alleyway that is flanked by five feet high wooden fencing and cuts between the backyards of Cow Lane and the similar terraces from Pig Avenue. On entering through the back gate for Number Five, which is hanging from its hinges, we find Constable Jones standing guard.

After exchanging greetings, I take a quick reconnoitre of the narrow yard. It runs from a small vegetable patch full of weeds for about fifteen feet onto brick paving a further twenty feet up to the kitchen door. Butted on to the terrace is the single storey outhouse with its coal house, privy and shed. The privy isn't on the sewer system so the waste has to be taken away by the shit collectors. There is a four feet high rotting picket fence separating this yard from the neighbours. We all step up to the open door of the privy. Sat on the hole cut into the wooden seat with his trousers and drawers around his ankles is a big man in a grubby vest with a carving knife stuck in his chest. His head is right back to display his stubbled neck while mallet fists cover his private area. It is a grisly sight, but what is even worse is the stink and the bluebottles buzzing around.

Holding his nose Head bravely steps forwards, grabs hold of the victim's mop of grey hair and pulls his head up. A fifty odd year-old face with a boxer's nose and sagging bristly cheeks stares back at me through bloodshot, accusing blue eyes, yet strangely there is a smile on his face.

I look at Roberts. "You best go back out front, Constable. The meat waggon will be here shortly along with forensics. When they arrive show them around here."

"You won't get a waggon around back, sir."

"Really? Never mind have them leave it on the lane. Off you go." Before I kill you, I grate to myself.

"The man's got a brain of solid bone," grates Head once Roberts had gone. "But at least he no longer has trouble hearing us."

"He had his ears cleaned out," puts in Jones.

"What with, a blow pipe?" grins Head. "Did they stick it in one ear and then blow the wax straight out the other?"

"No, they used a syringe."

"Who cares," says I. "Let us forget Roberts' earholes and go back to the matter in hand."

"Well, suicide it ain't," says Head.

I shake my head. "Killing someone is one thing. But in broad daylight while they're having a shit really pans the depths of depravity."

"It's crap," agrees Head. "Still, at least he died with a smile on his face so he must have been having a good one."

"Looking at the size of his gut Sergeant, I'd say the man probably struggled to pass his waste until the killer scared him so much it loosened his bowels and brought that smile to his lips."

"A two-edged sword then, sir," says Jones.

"Indeed. Who found the body?"

"The victim's wife, sir. Mrs Edna Dunn. She's inside being comforted by a neighbour."

"We shall take a quick look up the alleyway and then go and interview her. You best remain here Constable until the others arrive."

"Very good, sir. But do you mind if I stand away from the stink and the flies."

"I would say it is imperative, Constable."

Head and I go out the gate and take a look around. The amount of footprints on the dusty ground tell me that the alleyway is well frequented, but there are signs of larger prints riding over the rest, going in and coming out of the yard. If they are the footprints of our killer then he is either a small man with big feet or a large man with big feet or somewhere in between. We trail off around to the front of the house to find Roberts standing to attention in front of the door.

"We shall interview this Edna Dunn, Constable," says I.

"Do you wish me to come in with you, sir?"

"No. Keep watch on the meat waggon once the forensics have arrived and gone around back. Make sure no one drives off with that waggon without my express permission."

"Very good, sir."

I knock on the door. Presently it is opened by a shrew-faced little old woman in a flower-patterned dress.

"We don't want it!" spits she and goes to slam the door but I put my foot against it.

"Madam, we are police officers. Are you Mrs Edna Dunn?"

"No. I is 'er neighbour. Mrs Ethel Spall."

"Kindly show us to Mrs Dunn, we wish to speak to her."

"What about?"

"The murder of her husband."

"Oh! You ain't come about the burglary then?"

"We know nothing much about anything at the moment, madam. So kindly let us in before my Sergeant arrests you for obstruction."

"All right don't get blousy. Follow me."

We follow her down a narrow bare-floored hallway with pealing rose-patterned papered walls and into a very small parlour, where sat on a rocking chair in front of a blackened range is another small woman in a grey dress and whitish apron nursing a glass of brown liquid that has a drunken wasp swimming around in it.

"Coppers come ta see ya," says Ethel plonking herself down on the only other chair in the room ensuring that Head and I have to remain standing.

"Is it about the burglary?" asks Edna to no one in particular.

"No, madam. It is about your husband's murder."

She fixes me with watery eyes and I imagine she has been crying.

"Bloody typical! I gets burgled three days back when I was out. The bastards wrecked the place. They turned out me draws, ripped up me floorboards and emptied me biscuits from the tin all over the floor. Not a single bloody copper comes to see me. But 'im," she stabs a finger towards the small window that looks out on the yard, "that useless lump, he goes and gets 'imself murdered an' you lot are around like flies on a turd."

Obviously, the woman hadn't been crying except possibly for herself. Now that she is without a provider she may well be facing financial problems and the threat of the workhouse.

"Here," she says brightening up. "As 'e's been murdered will I get any compensation?"

"Quite possibly, madam. There are charitable funds available for those who find themselves in difficult positions because of someone else's criminal act."

"What's that mean in English?"

"You will get to bury him for free and may be entitled to a pay-out."

"Cor, you lucky cow," puts in Ethel. "I wish someone would kill my ol' man so I can get a few bob."

"No doubt he feels the same about you," grates Head which sees Ethel drop her eyes and shut up.

"Now, Mrs Dunn," says I. "Apparently you found the body. Is that correct?"

She nods and then takes a long swallow of her drink, taking the wasp with it.

"Can you take me through the events? What happened leading up to your discovery of the body?"

"Well, Bert went off for a clear out about six just after breakfast like he always does. I was clearing up the plates an' makin' more tea. About an hour later I thought he best 'urry up or 'e'll be late for work."

I am incredulous. "An entire hour went by before you began to worry what was taking him so long?"

"I weren't bloody worried about the ol' bastard. He can take forever to push it out, can Bert. He'd sit on the pan all bloody day if he could while looking through the newspaper cuttings pretending he could read. Useless bastard! Anyway, I thought 'e'd probably dropped off as usual. I went out to tell 'im to get 'is finger out of 'is arse an' that's when I saw 'im sat there with a dirty great knife stuck in 'im."

"Was the door open or did you open it?"

"It was open. Bert always sat there with the door open to let out the stink. He believed a man could get gassed if the door was shut."

"Did you see anyone about? Any strangers? Anyone at all?"

She shakes her head and is so nonchalant I am wondering if she killed her husband.

"Do you know if anyone had a grudge against your husband?" asks Head as he takes notes. At least I hope he's taking notes and not merely doodling to pass the time.

Edna screws up her nose and takes another drink before answering. "His mother hated 'is guts but she died a year or so back. Other than that, I can't think of no one who actually hated him or 'ad a grudge against 'im except for me."

"Ol' Joe Simpson 'ated 'im," puts in Ethel.

"For what reason?" says I.

"Bert gave Joe's ol' woman one a few times around the back of Joe's chicken hut down the allotment."

"I never knew that!" gasps Edna sitting bolt upright. "The dirty rotten bastard. Fancy doin' it with that scabby ol' bag."

"She weren't scabby back then. Besides it was before you an' Bert was married," says Ethel. "Well before."

"How long were you and Bert married, Mrs Dunn?"

"About five years."

"Where might I find this Joe Simpson?"

"In the ground at St Mary's," cackles Ethel as she throws Head a 'stuff you' look.

I am losing the plot again. "Do either of you know anyone living who may have had a grudge against Bert?"

They both shake their heads and I change tack. "Mrs Dunn, had you seen the knife used to kill your husband before now?"

"No. But can I 'ave it once you've done as I could use a good carving knife."

"No. It is evidence. Now, how much was your husband worth?"

"I told you, he was useless which means he wasn't worth piss all. Now he's less than worthless 'aving got 'imself murdered."

"Was his life insured? Be warned, madam, we shall check up on your answer, so do not lie."

"Edna don't tell lies," puts in Ethel, giving me the evil eye.

"Insured?" scoffs Edna. "He weren't insured. I ain't insured. Nothing's bloody insured. We ain't got nothing and unless I get compensation or a new man bloody quick I'll be chucked out and end up on the streets back on the game."

'Good luck with that,' grates I to myself. "How many children do you have and where are they?"

"Him an' me didn't 'ave any together. I got three from me previous marriage but I don't know where they are. He had several from his previous marriages, but how many I don't know. I know he's got a son in prison and another in Australia. He's also got the little elfin one who's in the circus."

"Elfin one? What do you mean elfin one?"

"She means the dwarf one," butts in Ethel. "Billy Dunn is 'is name an' he's working for Billy Star's Circus over on Blackheath, but he don't come around here."

"Thank you, Mrs Spall. Anyone else you can think of Mrs Dunn?"

"Bert's got a girl called Sally. She comes around now an' again." She points to a photograph on the mantel piece. "That's her in that photo with Bert."

I take a look. The girl is pretty with light long hair that is probably blond. She appears to be quite tall and slender. "May I borrow this photograph, Mrs Dunn?"

"Borrow it? Keep the bloody thing so long as you leave the frame behind."

I take the photograph from its frame and slip it into my pocket.

"She's alright is Sally," says Ethel.

"Yeah," smiles Edna in reflection. "Always brings me an' Bert something when she comes around like a bottle of something so we can get sloshed and drown our miseries."

"Can you give me her full name? Is she married?"

"Sally Ann Dunn an' she ain't been married yet."

"She oughta get hitched soon or she'll get left on the bleedin' shelf," moans Ethel.

"I told her that," says Edna. "I said…"

"Madam, my Sergeant and I haven't got all day to listen to your claptrap. Where might I find this Sally?"

She screws up her face again. "Don't know where she lives but she works in a pub."

"What pub?"

"I think it's called the Twisted Neck. Or was it the Breakers Neck?"

Head shoots me a look of alarm which I return.

"I know what it was called," cries Ethel. "It's called…"

"The Neck Breakers Arms!" cuts in Head.

"That's it," smiles Edna.

I do not smile and neither does Head.

My thoughts are interrupted by a loud banging on the door.

"That'll be the lads," says Head and goes off to answer the door. I hear him speaking to Roberts and then he returns. "Roberts has sent them all around the back, sir."

"At least he got that bit right. We shall speak to you further Mrs Dunn before we leave and keep you informed of any progress."

"You won't," sulks she. "Bert was a nobody. Once you've taken your pictures an' nosed about a bit you'll all piss off never to be seen again. It'll be in the papers for a bit an' that will be that. Meanwhile…"

"Oh. One more thing," says I, to shut up her ramblings. "Where did Bert work?"

"On the docks for MacFarlane and Sons the chandlers."

"Doing what?"

She shrugs. "Odd jobs. Cleaning. He didn't 'ave any skills like I said…"

"He was useless," cuts in Head.

"Exactly."

We leave via the back door to find the photographer has already set up his tripod and is taking photographs of Bert. Dr Shelley, bag in hand, stands patiently to one side and accompanying him are two forensics. All are dressed in civilian attire. Constable Jones is down by the gate while several faces, mostly urchins are nosing over the back fence by obviously standing on the backs of other urchins.

Shelley turns his head as we approach. "Good morning, Gerald," says he. "And to you, Richard."

We shake hands. "What are your thoughts, Doctor?"

"Difficult. I may know more once I have investigated, but I doubt it. Whoever did this was probably in and out very quickly and subsequently has left nothing of any worth behind which might help with your investigations."

"They obviously came in the back gate Doctor and took the victim by surprise, lunged the knife in and just left without, quite possibly, anyone seeing him or them."

"Um…" ums he. "I assume this Bert Dunn was a creature of habit and his killer knew he would be on the pan at such a time."

"Which means it was someone he knew or someone who was well informed about Bert's habits."

The photographer moves away to take a panoramic view all around the yard, probably following on down the alley and then out front. The two forensic officers begin searching the area while Shelley moves in to examine the body.

Head and I, as always, are transfixed watching the good Doctor go about his business. Setting his bag down on the ground he opens it, extracts a large magnifying glass and scans it all over the knife's handle. He tuts a bit and frowns markedly. "No prints," says he, more to himself than anyone else. "Wiped clean." Going back to his bag he takes out a rolled-up piece of leather which he unrolls on the ground to use as a table top. Taking out a pair of tweezers he scans the knife handle again and then picks away at it with the tweezers. Straightening up he turns to us. "A few strands of cotton. After stabbing the victim, the killer wiped the handle clean with a cotton cloth leaving a few strands behind. This is someone, Gerald, who appreciates that although fingerprint evidence in itself won't be used in court to convict him it could still add weight towards a conviction."

Setting down the tweezers he starts to scan all over the body with his magnifying glass. Splaying out Bert's hands he scrupulously studies them for a while before setting down the magnifying glass. Taking out a notebook and pen, again from his bag, he straightens right up and writes down his notes.

"I confirm that our assassin thrust the knife in with considerable force. They would have had to stand side on to ensure the knife was tilted side on to ensure it went through the ribcage and into the heart." He demonstrates by clenching his hand around his pen and bending his elbow to bring his forearm back to his chest and then ramming it towards the body, stopping abruptly before the point end pierces the body. "Death would have been instantaneous. The victim shows no signs of trauma and no signs he put up any kind of a fight. In short, he did not know what hit him. I will know more once I have done an autopsy."

"So, no clues there then?" says I.

"Not necessarily. Something small with pointed edges has left an indelible mark in his left palm. Something that he was fiercely gripping on to. It may be nothing but I recommend we at least try to find out what it was."

"By…?" puzzles I.

"By emptying the bucket of shit he's sat over and searching through it to see if our victim dropped anything into it."

"Such as?"

"No idea, Gerald."

"Do you want him loaded up?"

"Not yet. Allow the officers time to search the area while I ponder over the scene."

"Tea?"

"That would be nice."

"Sergeant, see if you can get Mrs Dunn to make a brew." I fish around in my trouser pocket and find a sixpence. "Give her this."

Head goes off and Shelley says, "Not much to go on, Gerald."

"No. We shall ask around to see if anyone saw anything. All the usual." I flick an eye over to next door's kitchen window where I catch sight of a tattered curtain twitching. "Starting with the neighbour."

Shelley and I go and sit on a rickety bench that's propped against the end of the outbuilding and make small talk until Head comes over carrying a tray with half a dozen mixed cups and mugs that are well chipped and missing a few handles. Setting the tray on the ground he shouts out, "Slurp up."

Everyone stops what they're doing, grabs a tea and relaxes. The photographer lights up a pipe, one of forensics takes a pinch of snuff and an urchin shouts out over the fence that he wouldn't mind a cup of Rosy Lee if there's any more going.

"Clear off," yells Head, "unless you've got any information about the crime."

"I could make somethin' up, copper," replies he in expectation before he's obviously yanked from his place and replaced by someone else.

Once tea is over forensics continue their search. They bag up bits and pieces they have found but it is unlikely they have found anything of worth. Head and Jones go into the alley to question the 'spectators' whose numbers have now more than doubled, but at least they are fairly quiet. I go and knock on the neighbour's backdoor.

It is quickly opened by a spindly old woman with long starchy grey hair, a wizened face and a moustache. She is propped up by a walking stick and fixes me with a wonky eye and a one-toothed smile.

I introduce myself and she invites me into the kitchen. The room is Spartan and smells of damp. There is a small round table covered with a stained white cloth and a bowl of half-eaten soup with a wooden spoon in it. A scabby, vicious looking tabby cat stands on a stall beside the unlit range staring up at me with curiosity before arching its back and hissing.

"Your cat appears to be unfriendly, madam," says I while contemplating taking out my revolver and blowing its head off.

"Don't worry 'bout 'im," she sniffs. "'e's just pissed off 'cause I won't give 'im any of me soup."

She sits down in front of her soup and I take the only other chair opposite her. She tells me her name is Maud and she lives here with two of her five sons.

I ask her if she or her sons saw anything untoward first thing this morning.

"Me boys had gone off to work by five thirty to the slaughter'ouse. Bert comes out 'bout six for his mornin' dump. I saw 'im drop 'is drawers an' sit down. He don't never close the door so you see it all. But at my age it don't bovver me none. Besides it gives me something ta nose at. Anyway, in no time, Bert's gruntin' away an' looks about ta drop off when the gate opens an' in marches this big bastard who goes right up to the shit'ouse. He's got a big knife in his 'and behind 'is back. I can't see much then 'cause he blocks me view, but when he goes off I see he's left the knife behind stuck in Bert's chest. That's it."

"Did you not try and alert someone?"

"What for?"

"Madam, you had just witnessed a murder! The very least you could have done was to raise the alarm."

She spoons soup into her mouth before answering, "I was goin' ta rap on the window with me stick but thought I might break the glass so I decided it was best if I kept out of it. I didn't want no trouble."

I shake my head in frustration. Where on earth do these people come from?

"Can you tell me what that 'big bastard' looked like and what he was wearing?"

Wiping soup off her moustache she says, "My eyesight ain't so good anymore. He had on a dark felt 'at pulled down over his eyes. I think his suit was brown an' he 'ad big fists like a docker. That's all I noticed. Besides, I went into a panic. What if he comes for me? He might ravish me, cut my throat and ransack the 'ouse!"

The cat suddenly jumps up on the table to sniff at Maud's soup. She brushes it away, saying. "If Tiddles could talk he'd tell ya a few things I reason."

"I expect he would," grates I as the mangy thing gives me another hiss. Standing up I take my leave and show myself out to find Bert has been loaded up on a stretcher, the knife still sticking out of his chest.

"We are ready to leave," says Shelley covering Bert with a sheet. "I shall carve him up back at the mortuary and get back to you as soon as is possible."

"Thank you, Doctor."

From his bag he takes out a pair of black rubber gloves and hands them to me.

"For whatever poor soul gets the shit job," he all but grins.

I put them in my pocket and watch the two forensics convey the stretcher away. Shelley goes in front of them to open the gate while the photographer brings up the rear. I follow on to see how Head and Jones have been getting on but am accosted by several urchins.

"Oi, mister," barks a tall one with a big scab on his nose, "Now Bert's finished with his bucket of shit can I 'ave it?"

"No. It is evidence."

"Evidence! Fuckin' evidence!" he spins his head around to address the rest of the urchins. "'Ear that lads. The coppers want ta keep Bert's shit because it's fuckin' evidence."

"More like he wants to sell it an' rob us of a penny," spits a short brat with crinkled up ears. "Them coppers want it all."

I shut the gate and put on my sternest look. "I have no wish whatsoever to go back to the station carrying a bucket of shit even if it is worth a whole penny to a 'pure' collector. Now back off before I have you all arrested."

Shoving his thumbs under his armpits and flapping his bent arms like a chicken, Scab Nose starts strutting around like a peacock with haemorrhoids. "M'lud. Gentlemen of the jury," he calls out in a posh voice to the delight of the other urchins. "Members of the Public Gallery. Ladies, gentlemen and common riff raff. You may wish to take a deep breath and plug up your nose holes for the prosecution council is about to present to the court, Exhibit A. I call upon my esteemed colleague, Sir Henry Sewerage to bring forth Exhibit A. Thank you Sir Henry Sewerage. Please hand M'lud a stick for stirring and allow him to inspect the evidence first and then pass the bucket and stick along to the defence council. Thank you again, Sir Henry Sewerage. Now, gentlemen of the jury, please pass Exhibit A and the stick amongst you and try not spill any of the vital contents."

He pauses from his rendition to bask in the giggling adulation from the urchins. Scab Nose is an entertainer, that much is certain, and I give him credit for brightening up the day.

He continues, "As the court can see; before you is…, a bucket of shit. But, this is no ordinary bucket of shit, by God. This bucket of shit contains the final passings of a man's life and is evidence of the utmost importance in proving that the defendant did indeed carry out the heinous crime of murder while his victim was sat on that very bucket," he points to an imaginary bucket. "Bothering no one the hapless victim had been quite happy to just enjoy emptying his guts while listening to the sweet twittering sounds of the dawn chorus and the soothing rhythmic buzzing of the local bluebottles. When…"

Scab Nose's piece of theatre is rudely interrupted by the return of Head and Jones. Pushing their way through the urchins, Head gives Scab Nose a ringer around his ear and orders him and his 'tribe' to back off. They do so and retreat a few yards up the alley. But I know for certain they'll be back the second we leave. I ask Head and Jones how they got on.

"One urchin said he saw a big man in a floppy hat and brown suit turn into the alleyway about six this morning. He said the man had a big bulge in his trousers like he was tooled up."

"If he had a big bulge in the front of his trousers then it could have been anything and not necessarily a weapon."

"The bulge was pushing the man's jacket out at the back, sir. The urchin believes it was a long knife stuck down the back of the man's trousers. But it wasn't there when the man came back again barely a couple of minutes later."

"Did he hear anything?"

Jones shakes his head.

"Anything else?"

"Nothing," says Head.

I tell them what Maud told me and we realise we have nothing much to go on with at all.

"We'll do a bit of door knocking," says I. "While we're doing that, Constable Roberts can remain in the yard doing something of vital importance."

"Not being funny, sir," says Jones, "you can't trust Roberts with anything of the remotest importance. The only thing he's good for is standing guard and masturbating."

We are interrupted by Shelley coming back down the alley, he has a face like thunder and his cheeks are blood red through rage. "Gerald. Will you please come and sort that maniac Roberts out before I am forced to forget my Hippocratic oath and slit the idiot's throat."

Leaving Head to guard the gate we tramp around front to find Roberts has hold of one of the two horses' nose strap while violently waving his truncheon around. The prat has obviously taken my earlier order to the extreme and won't allow anyone to drive away the waggon without my say so first.

"Constable Roberts," says I stepping up. "You can safely release the care of the waggon into these gentlemen's professional hands."

"Very good, sir. Only obeying orders. There was no need for that doctor fellow to get his nuts in a knot."

"No indeed," soothes I placing a friendly hand on his shoulder as the waggon pulls away. "Constable Roberts you are to be commended for following orders to the letter. Well done."

He appears to be utterly amazed by my praise while Jones appears to be utterly horrified by it, but Jones has no idea what's coming next. I continue, "Constable Roberts, because of your unselfish devotion to your duty I have come to see you as a man of integrity. You are a shining example of dedication, stalwartness and bravery. An exemplary officer who would face any task, no matter how distasteful it might be if it furthered the course of a criminal investigation, which in turn may well lead to an arrest. We have a killer at large who is so brazen he not only committed murder in broad daylight and out in the open air, he did not care in the least who may or may not have seen him. This man is so dangerous he must be caught as quickly as possible no matter how distasteful the process is. Now, are you ready for anything?"

"Rely on me, sir," says he snapping to attention. "Archibald Roberts is as reliable as the aristocracy and as unmovable as Buckingham Palace."

"Good man. Follow me."

And he does, back to the alleyway, into the yard and up to the privy. With Head and Jones lining up alongside Roberts I step into the privy and holding my breath take a peep into the pan. It is close to overflowing with several dozen meaty flies buzzing around or enjoying a feast. Stepping back, I point towards the pan. "To further our investigation, I require a brave soul to empty that bucket in search of evidence." I face Roberts. "Constable, are you up for such an important task?"

"Rely on me, sir. I shall leave no turd unturned."

"Marvellous." I gaze around the yard. "Your best bet would be to empty the contents onto the ground and go through it with a fine-toothed comb."

"Do you have such a comb, sir?"

"I am afraid not. Sergeant, do you have such a comb?"

"I am afraid not, sir. I could ask the women inside the house if they have such a comb."

"Do not trouble them, Sergeant. Constable Roberts, use a stick or something."

"What about using my truncheon, sir?"

"Good idea, Constable. Once you have finished, bury the waste and wash everything you have used. There is a water butt on the end of the outhouse with no doubt all the tools you'll require in the shed. Help yourself."

"Very good, sir. Just one more question. What am I searching for?"

"I have no idea. The victim had something small in his hand that he may well have dropped into the shit, according to forensics. It may be something or nothing but it will be small, so keep a sharp eye out. Whatever it is we need to find it to either eliminate it from our enquiries or use it for… motive… evidence… whatever. While you are doing that we shall go knocking on doors to see if anyone saw or heard anything. Any more questions?"

"May I put a handkerchief over my nose to combat the smell?"

"Of course. Whatever you wish and be sure not to swallow any flies."

"No, sir. Indeed, I won't."

"Good man. And Constable I am glad that you got your hearing sorted out."

"That was down to you, sir," smiles he. "I took your advice and went to the doctor who syringed my ears out. Ever since then I've been able to hear my wife farting in bed."

"Marvellous." I hand him the gloves. "Use these rubber gloves but be sure to return them nice and clean."

He salutes. "Yes, sir. Um… what are they for exactly?"

"To protect your hands of course," grates Head. "You don't want hands smelling of Bert's arsehole, do you?"

He shakes his head.

"Anything you find Constable, however insignificant you may think it is, clean it up and place it in this cloth bag." I hand him the bag.

"Will do, sir."

"Wonderful. Right, get to it Constable Roberts and good luck."

"Luck doesn't come into it, sir, when Archibald Roberts is on the case."

"Glad to hear it, Constable. We shall see you later."

"Good hunting, gentlemen."

We set off to knock on doors. Jones takes one side of the road; Head and I take the other. As we are not so well known around the area as Jones it is safer to keep together. The area has a reputation for being dangerous but is nowhere near as bad as it was prior to the mass suicides from the Tannery Street case.

The lane is surprisingly quiet, but then almost everyone would either be at work or out begging or stealing. No one has set up any costermongers' stalls as there aren't enough people who frequent the area. Usually, even the urchins wouldn't be around because of the lack of opportunities to make a penny or two.

One hour later, having learnt nothing at all we head back to Number Five where we find a couple of hackneys are now parked outside, plus a hansom that I recognise as belonging to the Daily Star. Jones is nowhere to be seen. Going into the alleyway we come across a queue of people from God knows where, all obviously waiting to go and snout at the crime scene. We are accosted by a wiry, six-foot-tall shaven headed urchin.

"Mornin' gents. Join the queue if ya want ta view the murder scene. Entrance fee one penny. Guided tour of the house as well for another penny."

I meet his sharp eyes. "We are policemen investigating the crime. Now, either you disperse this crowd of ghouls or I shall arrest the lot of you for invading the scene of a crime and destroying possible evidence, not to mention racketeering and being ugly."

"I know ya game, copper," snarls he narrowing his eyes. "Ya want a share of me takings don't ya? Well ya can bugger off 'cause Micky Flynn don't share nothin' with no one unless they're partners."

"And who exactly is your partner?"

"Me Aunt Edna of course. This is 'er 'ouse now that useless prat has gone."

I ponder over the situation and know that even if I clear the area now it will quickly be invaded again the second we have gone. Besides, I can't blame Edna for trying to make a few bob, "Very well, carry on, but keep it low key."

"What's that mean?"

"Keep the noise down. A man has been murdered, so have some respect."

"Will do, gov'."

Stepping into the yard we find there is a small crowd over by the privy listening to an urchin giving out a rendition about the murder. The weedy area is free of people except for Roberts who, having removed his helmet and uniformed jacket and rolled up his sleeves, is busy filling in the hole he obviously dug to bury the waste. As we step up to him he straightens himself up and wipes the sweat from his brow with the back of his hand and rams the spade into the ground.

"Phew… Am I glad that is all over with, sir," says he flaring his nostrils. "That was the smelliest job any soul could ever have to undertake. And isn't it hot for early May?"

"It is indeed, Constable," says I. "Have you unearthed anything of interest?"

"I did, sir," says he, proudly. "There was mostly shit in the bucket but also a lot of peas."

"Well there would be," grates Head. "people don't just dump in the pan they pee in it as well."

"Not urine pees, Sergeant. Pea, peas. You know. Food peas. There were lots of them in there."

"He must have liked peas then," says I. "But obviously he didn't chew them properly so they went straight through him and came out whole."

"That's the trouble with peas," says Head. "They say they're good for getting your guts moving but you have to mash them up in your mouth before you swallow them or the fibre can't do its work properly. That's why I prefer mushy peas over whole ones."

"I don't touch them," says Roberts wiping his brow again. "They give me too much flatulence. Fart all day I can after a plate of peas."

We are interrupted by the urchin entertaining the crowd as he raises his voice to obviously drown us out.

"An' then 'e thrust in the knife like this." Cue stabbing action. "Stabbing poor ol' Bert through the 'eart an' killing 'im instantly. They say the killer would 'ave gone on to butcher Ol' Bert, Ripper style, cutting out 'is kidneys, 'is 'eart an' 'is liver, rippin' out 'is guts an' gouging out 'is balls. Only 'e 'adn't bargained with the brave Mrs Edna Dunn who, 'avin' 'eard Bert's screaming, 'ad rushed out to confront the assassin with 'er rollin' pin. The killer couldn't get 'is knife out from Bert's ribs 'cause 'e'd rammed it in so 'ard it got stuck. So 'e ran for it with the 'eroic Mrs Edna Dunn chasin' after 'im. But 'er poor ol' legs gave up on 'er an' the killer got clean away. Now, anyone got any questions?"

"I tried to get them all out, sir," pleads Roberts. "Only they refused to leave. Then Mrs Dunn came over to me and made it clear she wanted them to remain. 'I don't care if the queue stretches to London bleedin' Bridge,' she swore. 'The more the merrier.' I believe she is earning money from all this, sir."

"She is indeed, Constable. Do not remonstrate with yourself you have done well. Now, did you find anything of worth?"

With a self-satisfied nod he takes out the evidence bag from his trouser pocket and hands it to me. I gander inside it. There is a knotted-up sheath complete with contents, lots of peas, a couple of stones, and what looks like several rat bones and a cork.

"Not much for your efforts, Constable," sighs I.

"Ah…" smirks he touching his nose in a gesture of am I going to surprise you. Fishing around in his pocket again he retracts his now clenched fist and offers it to me. "There's this little item, sir."

I open my hand and he drops what looks like a small diamond onto my palm.

"I think it may only be glass, sir. It looks like something a woman would have inserted into her ring."

I am no expert but as I hold it up to the sun and peruse it I am certain it isn't glass. It has a distinct blue tinge to it; the light reflects magnificently from it and it feels right. I pass it to Head to peruse.

"It is definitely the real thing," grins he passing it back.

"Constable Roberts I commend you this day. You have conducted yourself in an exceptional way and gone beyond the call of duty by uncovering a piece of evidence that may well prove to have considerable importance in the solving of this case."

"Um… Thank you, sir, but can you put that in laymen's terms?"

"Certainly, Constable. Fucking well done."

A broad smile crinkles up his cheeks. "Thank you, sir."

"You are welcome. Right, hang around here for a couple more hours until it's all died down then wrap it up and get yourself down to the nearest pub, you will have earnt a few soothing pints by then." I fish out a half crown and hand it to him. "My treat. Take Constable Jones with you as well."

Just at that moment, Jones steps into the yard.

"Anything, Constable?" asks I as he steps right up to us.

Shaking his head, he says, "A waste of boot leather, sir. Sorry I've been so long I got chatting to an old lady friend."

"As you do," grins I noticing his fly buttons are undone. "Our search was also fruitless but Constable Roberts here had much more success." I show him the diamond.

"Is this the real thing, sir?"

"It is. I am certain of the fact."

"It's definitely not glass then?" queries Roberts.

I shake my head. "This little bauble is probably worth as much as my wages for an entire month."

"Not so much then," grates Head.

I continue, "I request that you all keep this news entirely to yourselves for now until my Sergeant and I have had time to investigate further. Talking of news, has the press not turned up as yet?"

"They turned up just after you left, sir," says Roberts. "They took a lot of photographs, even of me sifting through the shit and asked me lots of questions but I refused to speak to them. They called me a moron, swore a lot and then went inside the house. I haven't seen them since."

"Such is the press," says I. "Gentlemen, we must leave you to it I am afraid and head back to the Yard."

"That diamond turning up throws up a few ideas," ponders Head once we're out of earshot from the ghoul queue. "I'd say

Edna's burglars ransacked her dump for the sole purpose of looking for it."

Coming to a halt at the end of the alleyway we face each other.

"I agree, Sergeant. Why burgle a place that has nothing of worth anyway? Unless you know exactly what you are looking for."

"I'd say this Sally Dunn purloined it from somewhere and gave it to Bert to hold on to."

"But somehow the burglars found out or guessed that Sally had given it to Bert. When they couldn't find it, they sent the killer around to threaten Bert into handing it over."

"The killer confronted Bert while he was on the pan and demanded he hand over the diamond or else. Bert said, 'You want it get it yourself,' and opening his hand he dropped the diamond in the shit. This infuriated the killer so much he thrust the knife into Bert's heart and then just walked away."

"Which tells us what, Sergeant?"

"He'd rather lose the diamond than have to fish around in a bucket of shit for it."

"Exactly. Which also tells us that whoever the killer is, he isn't poor. Your average slum dweller would quarrel over a bucket of shit just for its 'pure' value. If they believed a diamond was swimming around in it they'd fight like hell over it."

"Even kill each other for it."

"Most certainly. Only our killer simply walked away."

"So, we are looking for someone not only hard enough to casually kill a man who was having a shit at the time but wealthy enough to walk away and leave a valuable diamond behind."

"Quite possibly. I am also thinking that the killing was as much about sending a message than recovering the diamond."

"Where do we go from here, sir?"

"We'll have to report back to Clump first. Then I suggest we search the archives for any unsolved diamond thefts and see if we can link our diamond to any of them. After that we will try and track this Sally down by visiting the Neck Breakers Arms."

"I'd rather steer clear of that place," grates Head.

"You and me both."

We tramp around to the front of the houses to find the lane is now jammed up with hackneys, private carriages and several horses being held by urchins. The front door of Number Five is wide open and all walks of life are squashing into the house to get their pennies' worth.

"News travels fast," says Head.

"Indeed, it does," agrees I as I notice that no one is guarding the Daily Star's hansom. "Do you want to drive or shall I?"

"I'll drive, sir," grins he. "You're too reckless."

I climb into the passenger seat and settle down while Head takes the reins and off we go.

Twenty minutes later and barely a street away from the Yard we abandon the hansom and walk the remainder of the way.

On entering the station, we log in with the Desk Sergeant and then head for Clump's office where we find his door is open and he's sat behind his desk with his feet up while filing his nails. It really is alright for some.

"Ah… Lads. Take a seat," says he putting down his file and sitting up. "How did it go?"

The drawer is opened and out comes the usual.

"Early days, sir," says I. I start to fill him in on everything we know thus far while he fills up the glasses before lighting up a cigar.

"Brutal! Bloody brutal," growls he blowing more smoke than usual all over us.

Head, obviously annoyed by it, waves the smoke away from his face.

"Sorry, lads. You have brought in a rotten stink with you that smells worse than some baby's soiled nappy. I am smoking you out to lessen the smell."

"Well it must have permeated into our clothes, sir," grates I. "We haven't touched any shit."

"Have you checked your shoes?"

We check our shoes, mine are clean but Head must have stood in some.

"Bastard!" curses he. "I'll have to go and scrub it off now."

"Get to it, Sergeant," says Clump. "We can't have the Yard stunk out."

Head sort of stomps off leaning on one foot while tiptoeing on the other one.

"I think he has invented a new kind of dance," grins Clump settling back and drawing on his cigar. "Right, Inspector. Show me this diamond."

"Yes, of course, sir."

Taking out the bag I hand it over. Clump tips the contents out on his desk and grimaces at the sight of the sheath, while several peas roll off his desk onto the floor.

"There appears to be an awful amount of sperm in that sheath, Inspector. Did it come from a horse?"

"I'd say not, sir. It hasn't been stretched enough for a horse."

"Um…" ums he. "Just seems rather full for just one man."

"Perhaps there's more than one load in there, sir."

His eyebrows shoot up. "Really? Do you think he was sharing the sheath with others? You know, passing it around?"

"Perhaps. Obviously, it has had repeated use."

"Probably to save money," he muses. "But you would think they'd at least wash it out before reusing it, wouldn't you?"

"I suppose," shrugs I. "Having never had to use one I can't really comment, sir?"

"Lucky you, Inspector. Having had to wrestle with putting the things on repeatedly over the years I would liken the act to trying to stretch an inflexible thick rubber balloon over a fence post. Anyway, enough of these shenanigans. Let us get on. I do not believe the sheath, the cork or anything else in this bag, except of course for the diamond, has anything whatsoever to do with this Bert Dunn's murder." Resting his cigar on the edge of the table he picks up the diamond and peruses it. "I am no expert, but I would say although small this is a serious diamond."

Putting it back in the bag he hands it back to me, picks up his waste bin and scoops the rest of the 'evidence' into the bin. "Waste of bloody time that lot. This has to do with the diamond, Inspector.

Get searching the records for unsolved diamond thefts and see if anything turns up."

"Right, sir." Downing my scotch, I get to my feet and turn to leave.

"One more thing, Inspector," says he just as I reach the door. I swing my head around. "Don't forget to log the diamond in front of a witness before it goes into the safe."

"I won't, sir."

Head and I spend the next three hours going through unsolved thefts that included small diamonds that may be a match to our diamond, which sits on my desk glinting in the sunlight filtering in through the window, as if to say; you can't have me. That much I do know. We have at last exhausted all possibilities and must choose one of the more likely candidates to further our investigations.

"The theft of twenty small diamonds two years back from this Lord Harley's place seems the most likely," says Head. "And this insurance photograph of the diamonds shows marked similarities to our diamond."

"Plus, it states the diamonds were considered to be 'blue' diamonds. We shall put this Lord Harley top of the list followed by this Dame Wisler, whoever she might be. Her insurance policy states 'one dozen small diamonds weighing two carats' but says nothing about their colour."

"So, next job, go and see this Lord Harley."

"We could, Sergeant, but my inner ear is telling me we had best try and find Sally Dunn, first. Which means…"

"A visit to the Neck Breakers Arms," groans Head.

"Exactly."

"Well I'm sorry, sir I will not venture into that place again without suitable back up or permission to use my firearm."

"Time has passed, Sergeant. I have no doubt that even if the same landlord is still running the place he will have learnt his lesson and will ensure our safety rather than cross swords with us again."

"I think you're being far too optimistic, sir. That bastard will never learn his lesson. He's far too arrogant and believes he is untouchable."

"We shall see," sighs I, while admitting to myself that I too have serious reservations about returning to the Neck Breakers.

We tidy up the files and return them to records. Witnessed by the Duty Sergeant, I register the diamond then Head and I head off.

"Some rotten thief has pinched our hansom," amazes Head as we around the corner where we left it.

"Typical," grates I. "You can't leave anything lying around if you don't want it pinched."

We grab a cab, settle back and enjoy the hustle and bustle going on in the streets we pass through until at last we reach the Neck Breakers Arms.

Head checks his revolver is fully loaded. Spins the drum then returns it to its holster. He then checks his short truncheon, knuckle dusters, handcuffs and flick knife.

"I'm not taking any chances, sir. If they start a ruckus I'm going to leave that bastard's solid wooden floor swamped in blood and his big head full of bleeding holes."

"You do not intend taking the softly, softly approach then, Sergeant?"

"No, I bloody well don't," snarls he. "And if that bastard who booted me in the balls comes at me again I'll cut his off and wear them around my neck like a scarf."

I pay the driver and Head and I alight. On entering the bar, we find it surprisingly quiet with just half a dozen dockers enjoying pints alongside a pair of aged fishermen eating herrings with crusty buttered bread. Apart from the odd cursory glance no one takes any real notice of us as we step up to the unmanned bar and ting the bell.

Sure enough the same landlord as before saunters in from out back looking as hard as ever with his sleeves rolled up to display his muscular tattooed arms.

"Well, well. Inspector Potter and Sergeant Head. Long time no see," drawls he.

"Not long enough for me," glares Head.

The landlord's eyebrows go up and his fixes me with glinting mocking eyes.

"What can I do for you, gentlemen?"

"We require a few minutes of your time," says I, in my pleasantest tone. "But first a couple of pints of bitter would be nice. And are you still serving food?"

"We are," he smiles. "What would you like?"

"Bacon and eggs with chunky buttered bread, please. Sergeant?"

"The same for me, please."

"Would you like mushrooms and beans with your bacon, eggs and crusty buttered bread?"

"I don't, thank you. Sergeant?"

"A few beans would be nice, thank you," coos Head.

"Take a seat, gentlemen. I shall order your lunch, pour your beers and bring them over to you."

We go over and sit at a table in the corner that affords us a clear view around the barroom while keeping our backs to the wall.

"It's quiet enough," says Head scanning suspicious eyes all around. "I can't see us having any trouble, sir. But that landlord is as cocky and as slippery as ever he was."

"That much is clear, Sergeant. Let's just hope he truly has learnt his lesson and like us doesn't want any trouble."

"I wouldn't bet on it, sir."

The landlord comes over with our beers, sits down opposite us and folds his arms.

"What's this all about then, Inspector?"

Taking out the photograph I hand it to him. "Do you recognise the man or the girl in this photograph?"

Sitting up straight he peruses it and nods. "I know them both. The girl is Sally Dunn and the man is her father, Bert Dunn."

"Do you know where I might find this Sally Dunn."

"Well usually you would have found her here. She works for me and has done so for a couple of months or more but she failed to turn up for her shift on the Tuesday before last and I haven't seen her since."

"Do you know where she lives?"

"She was living with another girl in a flat down Fish Bone Alley, above a pawn broker."

"Is the pawn broker called Bray Waunepcy?"

"I believe it is. In fact, I'm sure it is," says he handing back the photograph.

"And Bert Dunn. What do you know about him?"

"He's in here after work most days for an hour or two. Likes his beer. Quiet type, doesn't say much but gets on well with his daughter. If we're not too busy I'll let Sally go sit with him for a while. What's this all about, Inspector?"

I ignore his question as I believe he is being just a bit too casual in the way he is answering me. "Where were you this morning between say five-thirty and six-thirty?"

He didn't flinch at all at my question and I sense he has fully prepared himself well in advance in case he received a visit from the police. The man is as guilty as sin, but what of exactly?

"I was in bed," grins he.

"Can anyone confirm this?"

We are interrupted by the arrival of the barmaid carrying a large tray with our meals on it. She is the same one who served us before but appears to have dropped her limping leg act.

"Who's got the beans?" she asks, smiling at Head as he raises his arm.

Leaning across the table she passes Head his plate while deliberately displaying most of her cleavage. She then takes my plate and unceremoniously dumps it in front of me. I do not get a smile or a cleavage display and realise the woman really doesn't like me, though only God knows why. Perhaps it is because I wear a wedding ring.

Once the barmaid has set down the bread and butter dish, knives, forks and accompaniments the landlord grabs her by the wrist.

"Sadie. Tell the Inspector and his Sergeant exactly where I was between five-thirty and six-thirty this morning."

Tossing her hair, she laughs, "Why between my legs of course."

"Can anyone else confirm that?" demands Head.

"Obviously I can," frowns the landlord.

"Anyone else other than you I meant," grates Head.

Getting to his feet the landlord goes over to the bar and bellows out, "Jenny! Get out here for a minute. I need a word."

Returning to his seat he pulls Sadie onto his lap and wraps an arm around her waist and she cosies up to him, which I can see by his icy stare doesn't go down too well with Head. A few seconds later a tall dark-haired beauty in a white pinafore comes over.

"Is something wrong with the food?" she demands hands on hips while fixing me with a frosty glare. What is it with the females in this place when it comes to me?

"It looks wonderful, madam," says I, "and I have no doubt will taste just as good."

"Jenny," says the landlord. "Kindly tell the good policemen where you were between five-thirty and six-thirty this morning?"

She stabs a finger at her chest, "You know where I was."

The landlord points at me, "But he doesn't and he wants to know."

With a shrug she says matter of fact, "I was with you and Sadie."

"Doing what?" demands Head.

Her eyes beseech the landlord, "Do I have to answer that?"

"If you don't mind," he smiles.

"Well I do mind! But if I must," she glares at Head. "It! We was doin' it."

"So, were all three of you doing it together or were you doing it in turns?" demands Head.

She puts a hand on Sadie's bare shoulder and gives it a squeeze, "What do you think?" she sneers.

I am becoming somewhat peeved with Head's stupid questions. It is obvious all three will swear they were at it like rabbits even if they weren't and to keep questioning them about it is fruitless. Plus, my eggs will be getting cold and I can't abide having to dip my bread into cold yolks.

"Thank you, Jenny, you may go," says I.

She flounces off, Sadie gets up from the landlord's lap and swinging the tray in her hand also flounces off.

"Just to confirm," goes on Head staring into the landlord's eyes. "You, Sadie and Jenny were all together in the same bed between five-thirty and six-thirty this morning, doing it?"

"We were indeed," smirks he. "Is there a law against it, Sergeant?"

"There must be. It's not right two women doing it together" says Head.

"Let's just say I was between the girls throughout and their bodies never touched. How would that suit you?"

I have truly had enough of this farce, "Thank you landlord for your time. We, well at least I, get the picture."

"That's it then?"

"It is."

Standing up he saunters away and I pick up my knife and fork to begin cutting into my bacon. I sense Head waiting for me to have a go at him but it can wait until I have finished my meal. While we eat laughter comes from the kitchen and echoes around the barroom, attracting the attention of the dockers, two of which gather up all the dockers' glasses and go up to the bar. The fishermen have left while a pair of aged prostitutes come in and also go up to the bar and ting the bell.

Grinning broadly the landlord comes out and sets to filling up the dockers' glasses while obviously sharing a joke or two that is undoubtedly at our expense. The landlord then pours gin into tall glasses for the prostitutes who converse quietly with him for a minute or two before breaking out into ribald laughter they shoot mocking glances over in our direction as they go and sit down on a table adjacent to the dockers.

Head moans, "One of my yolks is hard."

"Never mind, Sergeant. I suspect it is nowhere near as hard as your brain matter."

"So, you believed all that three in a bed rubbish?"

Scathingly I meet his eyes. "Can we disprove it? Three people have stated they were all in bed together between five-thirty and six-thirty this morning. Giving all three alibies and more importantly giving the landlord a rock-hard alibi." I set down my knife and fork. "I am sorry, Sergeant, but you have made a right prat of yourself. Whatever possessed you to ask such stupid questions?"

"Because I couldn't bear that arrogant twat getting one over on us."

"That arrogant twat, may or may not have gotten one over on us, but what he has achieved is you, yes you, making us both appear utter fools!"

"Has he really? Well, sir, for once I will educate you… I asked those questions for a reason. Now, when I asked that Jenny what she'd been up to she gave the answer, 'It. We were doing it,' Implying all three of them were at it. The landlord's eyes were dancing with a 'aren't you, jealous look', but that Sadie's face said it all. She may have been happy to lie that she was spreading her legs for her boss at the time but the look of horror on her face when Jenny inferred that she was also doing it with her as well, was too much for Sadie."

You clever boy, thinks I allowing him his moment of glory.

He goes on, "I was clandestinely watching that Sadie's face and eyes. They said it all, 'I will lie for my boss and don't mind if everyone thinks I am letting him poke me, but I'm not happy for anyone to think I'm also doing it with a bloody woman.'"

"Thank you, Sergeant for that brilliant piece of physiognomy on Sadie's features."

"You what?" he frowns.

"You truly are a student of life Sergeant and I take my hat off to you." And I do so, placing it on the table. "I apologise unreservedly for not only doubting your ability as a detective but also for being bloody rude about it. Please accept my sincere apologies."

"No need to go overboard," says he giving me the confused look. "Apology accepted."

We polish off our food, down our beers, and I go up to the bar to pay.

"Do you also want to pay for the money you stole from me as well?" sneers the landlord.

"No. Do you wish to confess to murdering Bert Dunn?"

"Not really," grins he.

Leaving it at that, Head and I head off.

"Where to now, sir?"

"As it's barely a ten-minute walk away I suggest we go and visit Bert's place of work and see if we can find out a bit more about Bert himself."

Presently we arrive at Macfarlane and Sons, chandlers. It is a large store that overlooks the busy docks and we enter to find several customers browsing around just about anything on earth that seafarers could possibly want. We go up to the counter where an assistant offers to help. Introducing us I ask to speak to the manager. He goes off, comes back and then takes us to the rear of the store and the manager's office where we are introduced to a Mr Michael Macfarlane, the owner himself. He is a portly, grey-haired man in a pinstriped suit sat behind a huge desk smoking a large cigar.

"Sit down, gentlemen," says he gesturing. "How may I help you?"

Head and I sit down opposite him on green leathered bucket chairs.

"We understand, Mr Macfarlane that you have a Bert Dunn working for you?" says I.

He nods, "We do indeed. But if you wish to speak to him I am afraid he isn't here. He did not turn up for work today."

"That's because he's dead," says Head, deadpan.

Macfarlane sits up straight and sets his cigar down in an ashtray. "Dead? As in dead, dead?"

"Murdered early this morning," says I.

"No wonder he didn't turn up today," smiles he. "As excuses go I don't suppose you could beat that one?"

"You do not appear to be overly upset, sir," says I.

"Sorry, Inspector, I don't mean to sound callous, but Bert dying means I do not have to sack him."

"You were about to sack him? For what reason?"

"He was lazy and bloody useless, that's why. Bert spent half his time sneaking out back and smoking when he should have been working. If you sent him on an errand he'd take twice as long as anyone else. Last in, first out and forever stretching his lunch break."

"You allow your workers to have lunch breaks?" amazes Head.

"We do, Sergeant. Macfarlane and Sons believe it is good practice to look after the welfare of our staff. Providing of course they do not take advantage of the fact."

"Or take the piss," says Head.

"Do you know if Bert was in any kind of trouble, sir?" says I.

He shakes his head and picks up his cigar. "He suffered from constipation a great deal, but apart from that, no, he did not seem to have any real problems."

"Do you know of anyone who might have wanted him dead?"

"His wife comes to mind. Otherwise, no. Bert got on with his colleagues and in truth, apart from being useless, no one had any real problems with him."

"Has anyone visited him at work lately? A stranger perhaps?"

Macfarlane takes a long draw on his cigar before he answers, "His son visited him a week or so back. The little fellow from the circus. They chatted for a while, on my bloody time I might add…"

"Why didn't you tell them to save it until after work?" asks Head.

"Because at the time I thought the little fellow was a customer."

"Do you know what they talked about?" asks I.

"No idea, Inspector. What I do know is Bert had rather a smug look on his face after his son's visit. The kind of look that says things are looking up."

"In what way?"

"Well, every time I threatened to sack him, Bert would start to panic and plead his case. I would relent and Bert would work his socks off for a while before drifting back into his old habits. This time was different, I told him, after the incident with his son, that he was finished. He merely shrugged and said, 'Who cares.' What do you make of that, Inspector?"

"A lot, sir. But I cannot at this moment in time comment further." I get to my feet. "Thank you for your time Mr Macfarlane, we shall leave you in peace."

"Where to now, sir?" asks Head as we tramp away from the docks.

"Let us see if we can't find this Sally Dunn first before we go looking for Billy Dunn."

Head flags down a passing hackney and we climb aboard.

"Fish Bone Alley, please driver," says I.

"I'd say the landlord is up to his thick neck in this," says Head as we trot along. "His alibi is a load of old rubbish which has me asking why make up an alibi to cover yourself unless you are guilty of at least something."

"Very true, Sergeant. It doesn't make sense to involve his staff in his pack of lies when all he had to say was; 'I was still in bed'. Being that he would not have gone to bed until the early hours, such is the life of a landlord, it is quite feasible that he would lay in bed the next morning and who could really question the fact. No, I think it more likely that someone he knew spotted him out and about near the scene of the murder and he panicked in case that someone should inform us of his whereabouts. And that is the real reason he connived to make up his alibi."

"That being the case the man is as guilty as sin. Either he was in on the original robbery of Lord Harley's diamonds, or he somehow ended up with them?"

"This Sally Dunn then foolishly helped herself to one, maybe even more than one, and passed one on to Bert for safe keeping, but somehow the landlord found out…"

"Of course, he did," butts in Head. "And as…"

"I haven't finished yet," butts in I.

"Sorry, please continue."

"Thank you. Now, where was I?"

"No idea, sir."

I shoot him my creased eyebrow look. "I think you do, Sergeant. I think you know exactly where I was up to."

"No, I don't! How on earth could I know? All I was about to say was the landlord must have either caught Sally red-handed stealing from him or he suspected her. He then tortured her to reveal where she had hidden the diamond…"

"Possibly."

"Can you please stop interrupting me…"

"No! I am the senior officer and if I wish to interrupt you I shall do so at my discretion. Is that clear, Sergeant Head?"

"I was merely saying…"

"Well don't. Anyway, what if it was Billy who gave Bert the diamond when he visited him at the chandlers?"

Appearing to be a bit sulky he says, "How on earth would Billy have gotten hold of one of the landlord's diamonds?"

"Perhaps Sally gave it to Billy. Other than that, I have no real idea at present."

"There you go then," sneers he throwing up his arms in apparent despair. "It is obvious to me, Inspector Potter, that you have no real idea about anything much at all."

This really rattles my cage. "I have more idea than you do."

He shrugs. "Really? What makes you think that?"

"Because I am an Inspector and you are a mere Sergeant."

"It doesn't mean you are cleverer than me."

"No, it doesn't," concedes I. "But it does mean I can pull rank whenever I like."

"Pull whatever you like and if it comes to it make sure you don't pull back on your punches either because I certainly won't."

"That's it. Driver!" I yell. "Stop the cab."

The horse comes to a halt. I jump out one side and Head jumps out the other. We are on a rough made-up lane, flanked by brick warehouses, that appears deserted except for a dead cat being devoured by a mangy dog. Why it should have come to this between Head and I, I have no idea. I take off my jacket and lay it on the cab seat, placing my revolver on top. Head does likewise before coming around to my side to face me. We roll up our sleeves and start staring each other out. I do not intend to back down; however, I cannot say I am that confident in getting the better of the Sergeant when it comes to a punch up.

After what seems like an age the driver growls out, "Oi, you couple of bloody Nancies goin' to get to it or you just goin' to stare each other to death?"

"What's it to you?" demands Head.

"I ain't got all bloody day to fart around while you two ponce around. I got a business to run."

"Are we or are we not paying you?" demands I.

"You are. But the longer you hold me up, the less customers I'll get and the less tips I'll get. So, get on with it before I bugger off and leave you here."

"Just you try it!" roars Head.

"That didn't quite work, Richard," says I as we tramp on.

"Well at least we still have our hats on to keep the sun off our heads," smiles he.

"True. But our jackets, complete with our notepads and everything else including my wallet are still in the cab."

"Plus, our bleeding revolvers!" gasps he. "Christ we'll cop it from Clump if he finds out."

"We must find that cab driver, Richard, and fast."

"Do you know how many cab drivers there are in London, Gerald."

We stop to face each other. "No, do you?"

"No. I thought if anyone would know you would."

"Well I am sorry to disappoint you, Sergeant but I do not know everything."

"Good," smiles he. "I am pleased you have finally admitted the fact."

Half an hour later and by now, hot, sweaty and dying for a drink, we arrive outside Bray Waunepcy's pawn shop to not only question him about Sally Dunn but also to warn him that our stuff has been stolen and he may well be approached by the thief. We enter the shop to the clang of a ship's bell that has been fixed above the door. Head slams the door behind him so hard the bell drops off which has Waunepcy jumping out of his skin. As usual he is behind his junked-up counter and stares up at us with a mixture of utter surprise and pure hatred.

"I don't bleedin' believe it," spits he. "You two again… This is police harassment."

"We haven't spoken to you or been in this flea-pit for months," grates Head. "So, keep your mouth shut or you'll lose a few teeth."

We go right up to the counter. "Sally Dunn," says I. "I understand she's been living in a flat above this very shop."

He nods.

"Is she in at the moment?"

He shakes his head.

"Do you know where she is?"

He shrugs.

"Are you being funny, Waunepcy?"

He shakes his head.

"Answer the Inspector properly or I'll knock your teeth out," demands Head.

Waunepcy's arms shoot dramatically up into the air. "Make ya bloody mind up copper. You just told me not to open me gob under the threat of knocking me teeth out. Now you're sayin' if I don't open me gob you'll knock me teeth out anyway. What's it to be, gob shut or open?"

"Open," says I. "Now, tell me, do you or do you not know where I might find Sally Dunn?"

"No, I don't," he sneers. "She cleared out ten days ago."

"For what reason?"

"She was behind with her rent and I threatened to confiscate all she owned if she didn't settle up, either in cash or in kind, by the end of the week."

"What kind of kind?"

"You know?"

"The sex kind," says Head. "As if a young woman like her would prostitute herself for a dirty, flea-bitten, stinking old goat like you."

"Why not? Plenty of 'em do. But that little cow just packed her stuff an' done a moonlight flip."

"And you have no idea where she went?"

He sticks a dirty, part-gloved finger, up his nose and roots around a bit before he answers. "No."

"Sally had a roommate I believe? Where is she?"

"At work and won't be back until about six."

"Where does she work?"

"Same place as Sally. Pub near the docks called…"

"The Neck Breakers Arms," cuts in Head appearing as surprised as I feel. "And her name's Sadie?"

"It is. Look what's this all about? I'm a very busy man an' I ain't got time for idle prattle. So, say ya piece and fuck off."

"Sally's father, one Bert Dunn was brutally murdered this morning. We believe Sally may be in mortal danger and we need to find her as quickly as possible."

"So why are you wastin' ya time here then?"

"Because we like tormenting you," grins I. "What do you know about the theft of a load of diamonds some time back from a Lord Harley?"

"What's that got to do with, Sally?"

"Maybe nothing. Just answer the question."

"Don't know nothin' about the theft." He scratches thoughtfully at his wiry beard. "Except lately there's been a few diamonds doin' the rounds. I was offered a couple. Nice too. Nice an' blue. But I didn't buy 'em, still too bloody hot. Always hard to fence anythin' stolen from the aristocrats because you never know if you're tryin' ta sell one of the prats their own stuff back."

"You get a lot of aristocrats come into your austere establishment, do you?" mocks I.

"The odd one or two," he sneers. "Well I had one come in last year looking for dirty books." He points a finger at me. "But I don't stock that kind of stuff. Now, is that all?"

"Nearly. Once you hand us back everything we've had stolen from us a half hour or so back we shall leave you in peace."

"What stolen stuff?" croaks he as what little you can see of his face turns bright red.

"Our jackets and contents therein. Plus, our revolvers of course."

Waunepcy bobs down behind his counter while muttering and cursing, the revolvers are then banged down on the counter followed by our jackets. Putting on our jackets we go through the pockets.

"All there," smiles Head in relief.

"I only just bought that bleedin' lot," groans Waunepcy. "How the hell was I to know it belonged to you couple of twats! I mean, how the hell was I to even know they was stolen goods?"

"Check your wallet, Sergeant," says I, as I go through my own wallet.

"Empty!" growls Head, waving it in Waunepcy's face. "There was close on five pounds in there."

"Ya bleedin' liar, more like five-shillings."

"My wallet is also empty," says I. "That's ten pounds you'll need to recompense me for."

"Piss off," says he in exasperation while throwing his arms up and down. "You're a pair of bloody crooks you are. You couldn't lay straight even if you was on the bleedin' rack. I'll give ya a fiver between ya and that's it! Take it or leave it."

"We shall take it," says I, giving him my best evil look.

Waunepcy hands over a five-pound note but is very reluctant to let go of it and I have to yank it from his grip.

"I'm well out of pocket now," whines Waunepcy. "Carry on like this an' I'll be in the bloody workhouse by Christmas. Now, if that's your lot kindly bugger off so I can cut me throat in peace."

"Nearly done," smiles I. "We wish to look around Sadie's room."

"Got a search warrant for it?"

"We have," growls Head, clenching his fist. "It's called a punch between the eyes warrant."

"Follow me," mumbles Waunepcy.

We follow the stinky old reprobate into a back room that is even more junked up than his shop, you can't see more than an inch of bare wall and heaven only knows what's buried beneath the piles of books, stacks of clothes and assorted oddments, but there is a distinct odour of vermin.

"Up here," sulks he, and leads the way up a rotting, winding stair that cracks so loudly you fear your feet will go through the sagging steps.

At the top we squash up on the tiny landing, Waunepcy is so close to me I can smell the dead lice under his armpits.

Pointing into a small room he says, "In there."

Head and I go in. There are two single beds barely a foot apart. A wood-wormed dressing table come washstand, a single stool and a small wardrobe with no door. The walls have the faded remnants of a flower-patterned paper and the creaking floorboards are bare. At least the candlewick quilts on the beds appear reasonably clean and the room has a pleasant scent of dried lavender from a small dish on the tiny window-sill, that woman's touch. Very little light filters in through the tiny, very dirty window, but it is enough to see what we are doing as we go through Sadie's things. There isn't much to see, a few clothes, clean but tatty and a pair of scuffed black shoes. It takes just a few moments to reach the conclusion that Sadie is as poor as a church mouse, if she was sleeping with the landlord I have no doubt she'd own a lot more than we see before us.

"Nothing," says Head in reflection. "No clues here, sir."

We creak our way back downstairs to find Waunepcy busily hiding something beneath his counter, whatever it is I doubt it's of any real importance, but I look anyway.

"What is it with you, Jerry Pot?" moans he once I've pushed him aside and stuck my head beneath the counter.

"It's me being a copper," says I. Standing up and opening his ledger book on the counter I start to go through the recent entries of sales in and sales out.

He starts to panic and tries to grab the book. "You leave that be, it ain't nothin' to do with you."

"Back off," warns Head as he physically yanks Waunepcy back a couple of feet.

Running my eyes down the past month's recordings I note that ten days previous, Waunepcy purchased a small piece of 'ice' for two pounds. The following page records: Piece of ice stolen.

"Explain these two entries," demands I, stabbing a finger from one date to another. "And do not lie or I shall arrest you for handling stolen goods."

"All right, all right," snaps he. "I bought a small diamond from Sally ten days ago when she got back from work. 'Cause, I knew it was stolen. I mean bar wenches don't usually get to own diamonds, do they? Anyway, I didn't pay 'er, I payed meself the two quid instead in lieu of 'er rent. She got stroppy about it and flounced off to 'er room. That night she did 'er flip having somehow got into one of me safes an' stole back the diamond along with a small bag of silver. I ain't seen nor heard of 'er since, but I've got people lookin' out for her. The rotten bitch! All I did for 'er an' she thieves from me." He points a finger at me again. "No one steals from Bray Waunepcy if they know what's good for 'em."

"So, I have heard," returns I caustically. "You find that girl and harm her in anyway and you'll have me and my Sergeant to deal with. Find her and bring her to us and I give you my word we'll, shall we say, turn a bit more of a blind eye to your activities."

"Promise," scowls he, crossing his heart.

I cross my heart. "I promise."

This brings a smile to his mouth. "One thing I know about you, Jerry Pot, you keep ya word and I will keep mine. I find her and you'll be the first ta know. Now, is that it?"

I shake my head and he drops his in exasperation.

"Do you know where I might find that cab driver who stole our things?"

"I do…" smirks he. "And I shall tell ya, but only if ya promise to get back the fi… ten pounds I gave him for your stuff."

I cross my heart again.

"Try the Skinners Arms and The Black Dog, he'll definitely be in one or the other at this time of day. His name's Cecil somethin' or other."

"I am thinking, Sergeant," says I as we tramp towards the Skinners Arms. "that this Sally is well practiced in the art of thieving. Not only has she almost certainly stolen from the landlord of the Neck Breakers but she has in fact stolen from Waunepcy. The landlord would have kept the diamonds in a safe but somehow Sally managed to get into his safe and to also get into Waunepcy's."

"And now she has disappeared," muses Head. "But to where?"

"Who knows? What we shall do is to find Andy my informant and instruct him to put the feelers out. What with his and Waunepcy's contacts looking for her it shouldn't be too long before someone finds her."

"Unless the landlord gets to her first," warns Head.

"Indeed," ponders I. "I believe that bastard murdered Bert but we do not have any tangible evidence to corroborate the fact."

"Which leaves us where exactly?"

"Nowhere much as yet. When all is said and done his bravado and bullshit might just be his warped idea of having a laugh at our expense."

"It might, sir. But I'm betting it isn't. He's as guilty as sin but is so arrogant he can't help himself from goading us."

As we plod on in silence, I have a sickly feeling in my stomach that this case is going to turn even nastier before it is done with. What with Waunepcy and the landlord both out for vengeance Sally hasn't a hope unless we get to her first. Whatever Waunepcy promised me back in his shop I know he will renege on as he can't afford to lose face or be seen to be assisting the police in any way shape or form in case the criminal classes he deals with should turn on him.

We reach The Skinners Arms to find several cabs parked outside while a dozen or so laughing cabbies are sat out enjoying their break and the sunshine while drinking themselves silly. Head and I look around to see if 'Cecil' is amongst them. He isn't, but we recognise his cab. We go inside while feeling questioning eyes burning into our backs as we go up to the bar and order two pints.

"Can't see him anywhere," says Head gazing around the near empty barroom.

"Let's try the lavatory," suggests I.

Crossing the bar, we go down a narrow hallway and out back where the smell from the lavatory block assaults our senses. Head leads the way in, there is a half full piss encrusted metal trough and a closed door to the actual toilet. Quietly bobbing down Head tilts his head and peers under the door before recoiling in apparent shock.

Standing up he whispers in my ear. "There's four feet in there. Two male feet stood up on the pan, toes pointing outwards, trousers and drawers around the ankles. The other pair of feet are pointing inwards and belong to a female."

"Do you want to kick in the door or shall I?" whispers I.

Head grins and raising a leg kicks the door with such force it slams open and hits the female in the back causing her to jerk up straight before letting out a stream of obscenities which are mostly drowned out by a male voice screaming out even worse obscenities.

The woman attempts to shut the door again but Head pushes his way in and somehow manages to wrestle her around the door and push her out into my arms.

"Against the wall," demands I shoving her away. "And do not dare to move."

Glaring at me she moves back against the wall. She is young and tiny but hard eyed, and every bit the seasoned prostitute who knows the score when it comes to dealing with the likes of us.

"My bag's still in there," she spits. "Don't you get it all dirty."

"We shall try our best, madam," smiles I.

Head drags Cecil out by the scruff of his neck and shoves him back against the wall. He isn't happy at all; not only did he not get to finish his pleasure, it appears by the blood dripping from his member he came very close to getting the end bitten off.

"You bastards!" snarls Cecil hands clasped around his privates. "I could 'ave lost 'alf me knob there!"

"Yeah! An' I could 'ave swallowed the bugger!" gasps the girl looking suitably horrified. "Why didn't ya just knock like normal people do?"

"Because they ain't normal," groans Cecil doubling up in his agony. "They're stinkin' rotten coppers, that's what they are."

"All right then," says the girl, hands on hips. "You gonna arrest me or what?"

"Or what," says I. "Grab your bag and clear off."

She points a rigid finger at Cecil. "He ain't paid me yet an' I ain't leaving here until he does."

"How much does he owe?" asks Head obviously feeling sorry for her.

"Sixpence."

Head fishes around in his jacket pocket, pulling out a shilling he gives it to her.

"I ain't got no change," says she in hope.

"Keep it and get lost," orders Head.

With a shrug she weaves around us, fetches her bag and manages to give Head a saucy smile before flouncing out of the block.

"Right, Cecil," says I. "Kindly wrap something around your wound and pull up your trousers."

"I ain't got nothin'" pleads he.

Taking out a clean handkerchief from my jacket pocket I hand it to him. He quickly wraps it around his knob, pulls up his drawers and trousers, straightens up and glares at me.

"I'm gonna sue you bastards for assault," spits he. "Before I've done with you pair, you'll be pounding the beat again while forever lookin' over ya shoulders in fear of old Cecil runnin' over ya with his cab."

"Is that before we charge you for theft of government property, theft of personal property, indecent exposure and committing a licentious offence with a common prostitute in a public convenience?"

"Should receive at least five years, sir," grins Head.

"Especially if we add assaulting a police officer while in the execution of his duty, Sergeant."

"That'll add a couple of more years, sir. Do you want to punch me in the face or shall I punch you?"

"All right! All right! I get the picture," snaps Cecil. "What now?"

"You pay back the ten pounds you took from Waunepcy, plus five pounds compensation to the Police Benevolent Fund and we'll call it quits."

"I ain't payin' that crooked pawnbroker no ten pounds the thievin' bastard. He gets a fiver an' that's it."

"Fair enough."

"Pass me my bag then," snaps he pointing to the lavatory door.

Head steps into the toilet and comes back with a woman's small black handbag covered in green sequins and hands it to Cecil who takes hold of it with a look of abject horror.

"This ain't me bag," croaks he. "It's that friggin' tart's bag. Where's my bloody bag?"

"That was the only bag left in there," says Head. "Did your bag have a long brown leather strap attached to it that could be slung over your shoulder?"

"It did!"

"And did the bag's flap have a small photograph of the Queen stuck on it?"

"It did!"

"I fear, Cecil," says I. "That in this instance the 'tart' has run off with the Queen leaving the knave feeling very sore."

"Bastard! There was close on twelve quid in that bag, the biggest take I've had in years! What the hell am I gonna tell the ol' woman when I go home with no money?"

"And how the devil are you also going to explain the teeth marks on your knob?" asks Head.

"God knows."

"Never mind, Cecil," says I. "At least you have learnt something this day."

Incredulous he stares into my eyes, "Like bleedin' what?"

"Crime doesn't pay. Now, my Sergeant and I shall down our beers and then you will drive us around to wherever we must go."

He appears to brighten up. "And you'll pay me the goin' rate?"

"No. We shall knock it off what you owe us."

"Bastards!" snaps he tossing the bag in the piss trough.

"Thank you for that, Cecil. Come on, let us get on."

After downing our beers, we climb into the passenger seats and Cecil clicks the horse into a trot and we head off to where Andy can usually be found. One hour later and having instructed Andy on what I require we head for home.

"What now, sir?" asks Head.

"I think, Sergeant we shall take our good ladies to the circus tonight. That way we can enjoy the show courtesy of expenses and afterwards we shall question this Billy Dunn and find out if he knows anything about his sister's disappearance."

"Sounds like a plan, sir. What time does the circus start?"

"No idea. Cecil," yells I. "Do you know what time the circus over on Blackheath starts tonight?"

"Last show's at seven-thirty," he yells back before groaning out in pain as we thud into yet another pothole. "Bleedin' potholes they'll be the bleedin' death of me they will."

Cecil drops Head off first and ten minutes later I walk into my kitchen to find Betty rolling out pastry on the table for the steak pie she promised she'd make for dinner.

"You're home early, Detective Inspector," smiles she, wiping flour off her nose with the back of her hand.

"Home early but not yet finished for the day." says I going up behind her, wrapping my arms around her waist and gently squeezing her body into mine.

"I'm trying to make a pie," she giggles as I brush away her hair and kiss the back of her neck. "You're just taking advantage of my preoccupied position, Detective Inspector."

"You could leave the pastry and cover me in flour instead."

"I could but I won't. By the time I get back to finishing the pie the pastry will have gone dry and won't work so well."

"Rubbish."

She turns around and gazes up into my eyes. "And what do you know about pastry, Detective Inspector?"

"Um… Not much really. I know how to eat it."

"In other words; you know nothing at all."

"True. But I would like to learn."

"What, now?"

"Not right now. How about after we've tested the bed springs?"

"How about after I've put the pie in the oven? If you have to go back to work later, I best make sure you've been fed. Man cannot live on love alone you know, Detective Inspector."

"True, but isn't it an absolute pleasure trying to?"

She gives me a peck on the lips and turns back to her baking.

"Head and I have been investigating a man who was murdered while sat on the pan," says I going into the larder to fetch a bottle of beer.

"What sort of pan? A frying-pan, a saucepan?"

"No, a poo pan."

Pausing from her baking she throws me her 'is this is a joke' look.

"Honestly Betty, the poor fellow grunted his last when a carving knife was stuck through his ribs."

"That's disgusting! Why couldn't the killer wait until the poor man had finished his toilet?"

"I don't know as yet. Perhaps he was in a hurry and had a train to catch," smiles I going to sit down at the table opposite her.

"Sometimes, Detective Inspector, your cavalier attitude towards the cases you work on could be misconstrued by those who don't know you, as being callousness and indifference."

"True. However, you know and I know that the way we coppers cope with the blood, shit and gore we have to encounter on a daily basis is by looking at life from a different perspective." I take a swig of my beer straight from the bottle. "In short if we don't have a laugh now and then I fear our emotions will overpower us and we shall become ineffectual in our work. Anyway, all that aside, how would you like to go to the circus tonight with Richard and Chloe?"

"I would love to, but I thought you were working?"

"I am. But I see no reason why we can't mix business with pleasure my little pastry chef, especially when I can claim most of the cost on expenses."

"Lovely. Well I best get a move on," says she rolling her pastry at twice the usual speed. "There's dinner to serve and you to serve," she grins. "And most importantly there's a dress to choose."

"It's only the circus, Betty. Go exactly as you are, you look absolutely lovely."

"What complete with a grubby pinafore."

"Discard the pinny, sling on a shawl and Fanny's your aunt."

"I do not wish to have a Fanny for my aunt, Detective Inspector. I wish to look my best no matter where I go. So, don't think you can persuade me to go as I am just so you can get out of helping me decide what to wear."

I know when I'm beaten and slink off to the parlour to read the paper and top up on scotch. Two hours later, after a delicious pie, mash and gravy dinner, and a quick go at breaking the bed springs, I am washed, dressed for work complete with a nice clean white shirt and am sat on the bed trying not to drop off while Betty, wearing nothing bar her corset, goes through her wardrobe.

"The white or the red?" demands she at last holding up the chosen dresses, one in each hand.

Now, I need to be very careful here. If I say the white one when she's already more or less decided on the red one, or vice versa, then the entire business may well go back to scratch.

"Um… Which one do you prefer?"

"I don't prefer either of them. I love them both. I'm merely asking your opinion. Which one do you think is most suitable for a night out at the circus?"

'God knows,' says I to myself. "It is difficult my darling. Red enhances your femininity and your sexuality, whereas white enhances your inner purity and softness…"

"What a load of bunkum, Detective Inspector. Admit it you don't really like either of them, do you?"

"I do, my little wasp. I just don't know what one to pick as you will look ravishing in either. In short I am finding it impossible to pick a winner."

"Oh… Just pick one and be done with it, Detective Inspector, we are running out of time and I still have to choose what gloves, shoes, stockings, jewellery and coat, or shawl, to wear."

'Shoot me now,' groans I to myself.

"I heard that," she snaps.

"I didn't say anything!"

"You didn't have to. Last chance. Red or white?"

Sod it. Here goes. "Red."

"I knew it! And what's wrong with the white dress?"

"Nothing." Now I am really losing my patience, but then a spark of brilliance careers through my brain. "Why not cut them down the centre and wear the white half one side and the red on the other side."

"You're not taking this seriously, are you Detective Inspector?"

"I have never taken anything so seriously in my life my love. It's just that time's moving on and the carriage will be here in half an hour and you haven't even got your pantaloons on yet."

She throws the dresses on the bed beside me and adopts the hands-on-hips approach. "And who may I ask took them off in the first place."

"No comment," smiles I.

"Right, just go away and leave me to dress in peace if you're not willing to help."

Not requiring confirmation that I have been spared the trauma of further dress selecting, I make my way downstairs and pour a nice strong scotch and sit down to wait for the cab. Twenty or so minutes later, and to my utter amazement, Betty joins me wearing the red dress, a small dark blue hat with a big feather in it, white gloves and a light blue shawl over her shoulders. She does the twirling bit.

"Absolutely stunning," says I. "So, I did pick the right dress after all?"

"No, you did not. You merely stated that you preferred the red over the white."

Sometimes the logic of the female leaves me completely flummoxed; this is one of those occasions. Fortunately, I am excused further reverie thanks to the resounding rap on the front door announcing that the cab has arrived.

Betty leads the way out and climbs into the passenger seat beside Chloe and I squash in beside Head. We exchange the usual greetings before Cecil clicks the horse on. Dressed in a cream dress with little blue flowers dotted all over it and a bonnet to match, Chloe looks absolutely lovely and it is easy to sense how proud Head is to be seen out with her. That feeling is mutual judging by the way Chloe constantly flicks a smile his way. The girls are both very excited and chatter on endlessly while Head and I are content to merely sit back and enjoy the scenery.

Close on an hour later we have arrived at the circus. Cecil grudgingly signs my receipt for expenses incurred throughout the day, two pounds ten shillings no less, and hands over a further five pounds, thus releasing him of his debt to the Police Benevolent Fund; namely mine and Head's pockets. We head towards the big top; the show should be starting in fifteen minutes.

On entering the big top, we find it is half empty and there are plenty of seats to choose from. We select half way up and settle down to wait, Head and I are on the outsides and the girls are in the middle. I am immediately accosted by an urchin seated directly behind me.

"Oi, mate. You gonna remove that bloody great 'at of yours. I can't see?"

I swing my head around to find Andy sat there grinning at me. "Did you pay or sneak in?"

"I paid, honestly. An' thanks to you I brought me muvva and sibs. We're sat back up there," he points to the back of the tent. "Saw ya comin' an' skipped down ta see ya."

"Did you find out where Sally's hiding out?"

He dolefully shakes his head. "Not yet, but the rumour is she's hidin' out because Waunepcy and that Jacob Sparks…"

"Who's Jacob Sparks?" cuts in I.

"The bloody landlord from the Neck Breakers. Like you said, them two are after Sally for stealin' from them." His eyebrows go up for dramatic affect. "But that's only a part of it; apparently Sally knows somethin' that could get both the buggers hung."

"What is it?"

"I don't know."

"Why don't you know?"

"Because I ain't found out yet. Soon as I do I'll come an' tell ya. One thing I do know they definitely want her dead."

With that he hurries back to his family as the ringmaster has just stepped out to a rapturous applause and into the spotlight centre stage. Dressed in the traditional black boots, white trousers, black top hat and red-tailed coat he raises his long arms to acknowledge his audience.

"It's about to start," cries Betty, giving my hand an excited squeeze while I put Andy's revelations into the back of my mind.

The ringmaster goes through the usual rhetoric before announcing Act One: "Ladies and gentleman, a huge hand for the Three Mucky Tears, the funniest clowns in any circus from here to Istanbul."

The Mucky Tears are about as funny as a boil on your buttocks. The strong man who follows is so weedy I have seen more muscles on a mouse. Following him are three old nags who canter around the ring with female acrobats on their unsaddled backs. The acrobats do flip overs, stand on their hands and other 'death defying' acts, rounding it off with all three horses riding side by side and the outside riders changing places by diving right over the middle horse. One makes it but the other flies right over her horse to land head first in the sandy ring where she is duly carted off by the Three Mucky Tears dragging her away by her feet. But at least they get their first real laugh of the night.

After a few more so-so acts the ringmaster returns to announce the last act before the interval.

"The incredible. The lovable, hilariously funny yet unbelievably brave and death defying. Ladies and gentlemen, I give you the Seven Dwarfs."

On they come to deafening clapping, cheering and whistling. Seven little people all dressed in colourful elfin costumes and pushing in a gigantic grey painted wooden cannon.

"Surely they're not going to shoot one of those little people from that cannon?" gasps Betty wide-eyed.

"Perhaps all seven are going to be shot out one after the other," jokes I.

"Or, all at once," grins Head. "They'll be flying out in all directions I shouldn't wonder."

"Don't be so cruel," chides Chloe. "Poor little people. It's wicked using them as human cannonballs just for our entertainment."

"They love it," laughs Head slipping an arm over Chloe's shoulder. "Without the circus where would they be? Shoved up chimneys or down mines, so their employers can get around the child labour acts."

"Richard's right," says I. "At least in the circus they get looked up to instead of being looked down upon while being exploited a damnable lot more. They are stars in their own right. So, let us applaud them and celebrate their achievements."

The audience adore them, they run around tickling children's chins, sitting on adults' laps while sucking their thumbs and pretending to be babies. They perform acrobatic feats of tumbling along with walking on their hands, wheelbarrowing each other around and even comic attempts to play leap-frog with the three clowns who have entered into the fun. Thus far they are way out in front as the best act of the evening.

At last the sobering sound of drums' boom booming brings the panting dwarfs to a standstill, while also quietening down the audience. It is time for the human cannonball act.

The spotlight falls onto one of the male dwarfs, he raises his arms then spins around showing that he is the one chosen to be fired from the cannon. Silence by now fills the big top, Betty has a hand over her mouth, Chloe lets out a big sorrowful sigh and in truth I find it hard to swallow my apprehension. These acts are notorious for going wrong, people get seriously hurt or even killed. But with everyone in the place praying for the act to be a success I feel confident the little fellow will come through it all relatively unscathed and in one piece.

A ladder is propped up to rest on the cannon's exit hole and our little hero begins his ascent. The drums roll louder, the crowd falls into a deathly silence, our hero reaches the top of the ladder and waves to the audience. Then he disappears, slipping feet first down into the cannon.

The ring master, loud hailer cone in his hand, comes centre stage.

"Marcus Flambé will be fired from the cannon," he points towards a safety net some yards away and several yards up from the ground, "to land safely into the net. He will be travelling at over thirty miles per hour, so don't blink or you may miss him. If he misses the net he will almost certainly be killed. If the degree of pitch isn't exactly right he could suffer severe injury or even death. He must travel at exactly the right speed; too slow and he will crash to the ground, too fast and he could be shot straight through the big top and end up on the moon."

This brings a short burst of laughter from the audience.

"Ladies and gentlemen. Boys and girls," shouts the ring master waving his free arm around. "A huge round of applause for the incredibly brave Marcus Flambé."

One of the other dwarfs takes hold of a long piece of cord, steps back several feet and yanks hard on the cord. The audience hold their breath. Nothing happens. The dwarf pulls the cord again. The audience holds it breath. Nothing happens.

"Perhaps the gunpowder's damp?" says Head, matter of fact.

Suddenly there sounds the bang from hell, instantly followed by a tremendous flash of fire. My ears are punched with pain and I slam my hands over them, I can barely see a thing but can still make out that the cannon has split apart like a peeled banana. It's on fire and smoking. Marcus' head has landed safely in the net but where the rest of him went is anyone's guess. The audience go into total panic, screaming and cursing they fall over each other to flee from their seats and stampede towards the exit, while all manner of debris rains down upon them, from smouldering bits of cannon to no doubt bits of smouldering Marcus.

The other dwarfs have been knocked flat on the ground and covered in all sorts. The air stinks like burning chickens' feathers while a whirling cloud of grey-black smoke hovers over the scene like the end of the earth is nigh.

"We need to get out, Gerald," yells Head.

We do indeed thinks I, but the still screaming, cursing audience have caused so much panic between them they have blocked the exit as they fall over each other before trying to scramble over everyone in their way. The base of the big top is being lifted by several strong men to afford another escape route as people of all ages scramble under the tent and out into the open.

"Over there, Richard," points I.

Grabbing a dumbstruck Betty by the wrist I haul her to her feet and drag her towards the improvised exit. Head does the same with Chloe and within seconds we are outside in the evening air. Smoke is billowing out of the main exit and then fanning up into the sky. Several people are collapsed whimpering on the ground, more are wandering around in a state of confusion. Nearly everyone has smutty marks on their clothes and faces. A few are brushing smouldering bits from their clothes, several more are retching while others are being comforted by those who are more in control of their faculties.

"We must go back in, Richard, and help," says I. "Betty, pull yourself together. Take Chloe over to the beer tent and get yourselves a stiff brandy."

"Don't leave us," she pleads falling into my arms.

Gently I push her away. "We must. It is our duty. Come on, Sergeant."

We crawl back under the tent to find a portable fire engine has been brought in. Several circus hands are pumping away like mad, sending jets of water high in the air and fanning it all over the place to drench everything in its path including the still-burning cannon. Most of the smoke has rolled out of the now open flaps at the exit but debris is still whirling around. At least the big top itself does not appear to have caught fire. Through it all Marco's head hangs from the safety net like a watching, accusing ghoulish apparition.

The remaining dwarfs are being helped to their feet before being led away. We step up to the ring master who is bellowing out orders to the fire crew. He has lost his top hat, his face, hands and clothes are covered in smut and his waxed moustache has been well singed, other than that he appears uninjured. He meets our eyes with questioning confusion.

"Did you put too much gunpowder in?" asks Head.

"What?"

"I can answer that," says a voice behind us. Spinning around I meet no other than Mick O'Reilly's eyes.

"Mick! What the hell are you doing here?"

"I was enyoin' the bleedin' circus, so I was, like everyone else."

Grabbing me violently by the arm and no doubt causing me extensive bruising he leads me away with Head following.

"You'd best leave Billy Star to it," says Mick as he releases my arm and we come to a stop at the far reaches of the ring. "I'll tell ya all ya need to know. But first let's go and get us a drink."

"That is a good idea," agrees I. "Sergeant?"

"Well the girls should be over there, sir. The pile of bodies by the exit has cleared, the ring master seems to have everything in control, so we may as well go and get a drink."

"You're good men, so you are," grins Mick. "Especially as you're buyin'."

Following Mick outside I notice that half a dozen plods are already on the scene and are quickly restoring calm, order and a sense of security for the traumatised. Excusing myself I go over to speak to a Sergeant who appears to be in charge and introduce myself.

"What do you require us to do, sir?" asks he.

"No more than you already are for now, Sergeant. Once you have restored total calm can you move everyone as far away as is possible and place a guard on the big top until my return. I shall be in the beer tent liaising with my Sergeant and a member of the public who may well be able to explain what exactly happened."

He salutes me. "Very good, sir."

Leaving him to it, Head, Mick and I go into the beer tent to find it quite crowded but unusually quiet. Betty and Chloe are seated by a small table, one of only a few, along with three other women. Mick goes up to the bar while we go over to talk to the girls to find they are much calmer but still in shock. Gazing around it is easy to tell by the expressions on faces that most everyone is in a state of shock. We go and join Mick.

"Pay the man, Jerry me ol' darlin'," grins Mick pushing a pint my way.

I square up with the barman and the three of us go over to a quiet corner to talk. Head starts the conversation. "I suppose they put in too much gunpowder, Mick?"

Mick chucks down half his beer before he answers, "If you're thinkin' this was a careless accident you'd be very mistaken, Dick me ol' mucker. This was an act of cold-blooded murder. The only explosives used in the act are merely for effect, so they are."

"They don't use explosives to fire the man out of the cannon?" queries I.

Mick shakes his head, "No. Inside the cannon is a powerful spring, it's ratcheted down to load it and is held in place by four lugs…"

"What, ear lugs?" says Head.

"Not bloody ear lugs ya prat," grates Mick. "Metal lugs. Now don't keep interruptin' me. Where was I?"

"Ratcheting lugs," says I.

"So I was. Once loaded all you do is pull hard on the cord, the lugs go back and set the spring free to shoot ya man up in the air. The only gunpowder used is in the small row of fireworks that go off at the same time as the man shoots out to cause the illusion that the cannon's actually been fired. Now to cause an explosion of that magnitude you'd have to have packed a lot of powder into that cannon, powder or dynamite or more likely; nitro glycerine, set up somehow to go off when the spring was released."

"You seem to know a lot about this, Mick," says I with suspicion. "I hope you weren't involved in any this."

Mick gives me the evil eye. "To be sure I woke up this mornin' and said to meself; Mick me ol' darlin' what shall you do with yourself this day? I know, I'll go to the circus and see if I can't blow up a dwarf or two. Of course I didn't have anythin' ta do with it, Jerry an' you should know better than ta even think that Mick O'Reilly would do somethin' so bleedin' rotten."

"Well someone did, Mick. Someone with not one shred of conscience. That explosion could have killed a lot of people and I'm thinking that it is linked to the case we are on at present. The very reason we came to the circus in the first place."

Mick downs his beer, "Drink up me lucky lads, then you can buy me another while you fill me in on this case of yours."

By six o'clock the next morning I am in Clump's office having been up most of the night except for a couple of hours of snatched sleep in one of the caravans at the circus. I haven't been home and am close to dropping off, but at least Clump hasn't brought out the scotch as even he realises it is far too early to get sloshed.

"So," says he, "you ordered the Sergeant to escort the women home while you remained at the circus to coordinate operations while carrying out your investigations until Superintendent Mackenzie arrived at around midnight?"

"Correct, sir."

"Why then didn't you go home once Mackenzie had taken over?"

"Because, sir, I have discovered that the man who was blown up, one Marcus Flambé, wasn't the intended victim. Billy Dunn was the intended victim. Billy is the one who normally gets shot out of the cannon, but he twisted his knee the night before and wasn't quite sure if he would be fit enough. It was decided that should Billy pull out at the last minute, this Marcus would take his place. After playing leapfrog with the clowns Billy's knee had swollen badly enough for him to drop out, thus Marcus Flambé was murdered instead of Billy. Which means that whoever is out to get Billy will almost certainly try again."

"And you believe this is all related to the death of this Bert Dunn and stolen diamonds?"

"I am certain of the fact."

"And our old adversary the landlord of The Neck Breakers Arms, is in… what is that American phrase again?"

"Cahoots, sir."

"In cahoots with that foul-smelling, flea-ridden, decrepit ball-scratching little shitbag known as Waunepcy, the pawn broker from hell! Well, Inspector, if you are right then we must act fast as we know how ruthless those pair of bastards are. Let's get to it. Leave no clown unturned. Question everyone including the bearded lady."

"They do not have a bearded lady I'm afraid, sir."

"What? No bearded lady? Now that is a shame Inspector, I have always wanted to interview a bearded lady."

"They did have one but a pair of thugs broke into her caravan one night and shaved off her beard because she wouldn't tell them where she hid her money. She was so upset she went and hanged herself."

"Really? A bit drastic, Inspector. I can't say I would kill myself should someone shave off my beard. How about a fat lady, do they have one of those?"

"I am afraid not, sir."

"Damn it, never mind let us get on. Fetch forensics, Inspector and then we shall leave."

"Doctor Shelley won't be in for at least two hours, sir."

"We don't need him," scoffs Clump scraping back his chair and standing up. "He'll only waste time taking his stupid fingerprints anyway. We shall gather up as much of the dwarf's remains as is possible and bring them back here for Shelley to poke around with."

"Right, sir. I am ready to go."

"Good. One more thing, Inspector, we will also require an explosives expert to accompany us."

"In hand, sir. I have secured the services of an expert in the field."

"You appear shifty in the eyes, Inspector. Who exactly is this expert?"

"Mick O'Reilly, sir."

"What! That mad Irish bastard? I would rather employ Jack the bloody Ripper, it would be safer for all concerned."

"The Ripper wasn't available, Chief. But Mick is and what he doesn't know about explosives isn't worth knowing. Plus, when it comes to circus folk Mick speaks the same language. He'll get more out of them then we'd ever get."

Clump exhales dramatically before pulling open the drinks drawer and extracting a bottle of scotch. "If needs must," he sighs pulling off the cork and taking a long swallow before recorking and chucking the bottle back in the drawer and slamming it shut. "I am fortified. When can you get hold of O'Reilly?"

"He's in the canteen right now having his breakfast."

"Is he just?" growls Clump. "I don't suppose he's bloody paying for it either, is he?"

"On the house I told him."

"On the bloody house! Right, let's get to it."

"Bloody mad Mick 'The bloody Mauler' O' bloody Reilly," he mumbles as we head down the corridor.

Clump veers off to round up whoever's available from forensics while I go and fetch Mick. I find him polishing off his breakfast by running a thick wedge of bread around his plate before shoving it into his mouth to bulge out on one side of his cheeks. Pushing his plate away he sits back and fixes me with sparkling eyes. "By all that's holy," he grins patting his stomach. "Me sainted granny, God bless her rotten soul, couldn't 'ave cooked a man a finer breakfast. That Jerry Pot, me ol' darlin' is as good as it gets. If I'd known how well you buggers feast down here, why I'd have joined the police force the second I popped out into the world, by Jesus."

"It's not all bacon and eggs, Mick."

"So, it isn't I'm sure," says he picking up his mug of tea and chucking it down his throat. "Now then, how did the hairy bugger take it when you told him I was on board?"

"He wasn't that enthralled," grins I.

Mick gets to his feet and kicks back his chair. "Knew he wouldn't be. But if it helps you me ol' mucker and I get paid for it, the hairy bastard can go kiss his own backside, so he can."

"Let's get to it then," says I.

Mick follows me to forensics just as Clump is coming out followed by the photographer and just one forensic officer. It is inevitable that Clump and Mick will clash immediately they set eyes on each other.

"A top of the mornin' to ya, Arthur," grins Mick.

"It's Detective Chief Inspector to you, O' bloody Reilly. And don't you ever forget it."

"Sure, I'll try not to Arthur."

They square up to each other. "If I had my way O'Reilly, the last explosive you will ever see would be the stick of dynamite, with its very short fuse already lit, that I shove up your arse to send you to hell where you belong."

"Thank you for that, Detective Chief Inspector Clump. Your interest in my arse fills me with joy, so it does." Mick's eyes turn aggressive. "Now, do ya want me bloody help or not?"

Without answering, which is an answer in itself, Clump stomps off and we all follow. Once outside we find the sun is shining and the meat waggon waiting, but no other vehicle.

"Where's the carriage I ordered?" shouts out Clump to the driver.

"No one was available to drive it, sir," says the driver.

"Never mind," growls Clump promptly hauling himself up next to the driver and then pointing down at us. "You lot can get in the back."

Steering Mick into the back we sit down opposite the photographer and the forensic officer and settle down as the waggon moves off. Mick takes out a pack of small cigars and offers them around, the photographer happily takes one, the forensic and I decline.

"I don't think the hairy bastard will ever give me so much as an inch," says Mick as he lights his cigar and blows out a smoke ring. "Sure, the man's obsessed with doin' me down. Why I believe if I was a beautiful virginal nun and I offered meself to him the prat would rather cut his own throat then try and get into me habit."

Mick's imagining he is a virginal nun is like the devil believing he could take over from the pope should the popeship become available, it's that bizarre. I change the subject.

"Why were you at the circus, Mick?"

"I was there with Rosy me new lady and her mother, so I was. Rosy wanted to go so I took her, only her ol' woman tagged along as well to chaperone us, but she ain't a bad ol' bird. Now I'm thinkin' if I'm doin' what the mother wants and what Rosy wants, I could truly be in love."

"Mick you're always truly in love every time you find a new woman, until the next one."

He pats me on the thigh and winks. "Not this time Jerry Pot me ol' mucker. This time it's for real. I aim ta settle down and tread the good Christian path. Be more righteous, more forgivin' and a lot kindlier towards the rest of the human race."

"Does this mean no more breaking jaws and booting balls?"

"I wouldn't go that far," grins he, stretching out his legs and settling down.

I do the same, it could take an hour to get to Blackheath, I may as well close my eyes for a while.

A cloud of depression hangs over Billy Star's circus when we eventually arrive. That cloud is so dense it spiritually blocks out the sun. As we climb out the back of the waggon you can taste the doom and gloom. No one appears to be doing anything much except mooching around or sitting around drinking and smoking outside their caravans, it is so quiet it is eerie. Clump quickly shatters that quiet when he booms out, "I will commiserate with the owner and the dwarfs first. You'll come with me Inspector. You," he stabs a finger towards Mick, "go with forensics and start poking around, but don't bother with taking stupid fingerprints."

Clump and I head over towards where half a dozen traditional gypsy caravans and a few, much bigger, modern 'train carriage' style caravans are. The dwarfs sit outside one of the modern caravans. Two are sat on little chairs, the remaining four are sat on a large tartan blanket. There are several bottles lying around and you know they have been up all night. As we draw nearer, I note that the seated couple are the elder members of the troop; a middle-aged man in a floppy hat smoking a pipe bedside a woman of a similar age dressed all in black with matching bonnet, she too is smoking a pipe in between raising a pewter mug to her mouth with a heavily bandaged hand. Sat on the ground on the blanket are four younger dwarfs, two females and two males, all have drinks in their hands, all appear as miserable as sin, all have dark skin and black hair except one who is fair-haired and pale-skinned. Except for the fair-haired one they all have singed eyebrows and scorch marks on their hands and faces. They are lucky to have escaped with their lives.

"Good morning everyone," says Clump brightly as we come to a halt barely feet from the man in the chair. "I am Detective Chief Inspector Arthur Clump and this is Detective Inspector Gerald Potter." He waits for a response.

The man on the chair lifts tired wrinkled eyes to gaze forlornly into Clump's eyes and removes his pipe from his mouth. "It is not a good morning, Detective, it is a fuckin' shit morning. I am Shaun O'Connor, head of this household. What do you want?"

For once Clump appears somewhat flustered as he takes off his hat before answering, "Firstly Mr O'Connor I wish to commiserate with the famous seven dwarfs for their terrible loss…"

"You may have noticed, Detective that there are only six of us now. Try again."

"My apologies Mr O'Connor for the slip of the tongue. My sincere commiserations to all six of you. My colleague wishes to ask you some questions if you are up to it."

"We are," says he.

"Good," says Clump attempting to smile. "I shall go and speak to the owner Mr Billy Star."

"Good," says O'Connor and points his pipe over the green towards a large highly decorated caravan sat beside a steam engine. "You'll find him in there."

"Thank you," says Clump and slapping his hat back on his head he marches off as fast as his legs will carry him.

"Don't hurry back," calls out O'Connor to Clump's back.

I remove my bowler and find myself awkwardly standing there wondering what to say next.

"Ruby," says O'Connor fixing a stare onto one of the women on the blanket. "Go fetch the detective a chair and a glass."

She gets to her feet and hurries into the caravan, returning seconds later with a small chair in one hand and a tall glass in the other. She sets down the chair to face O'Connor. Going to sit down I misjudge the distance from the seat of my pants to the seat of the chair and fall back on the grass which brings sniggers from every one.

"Sure, the taller they are, the further they fall," laughs O'Connor. "Why, it works every time. You see detective your brain tells you the chair is so high, the height that you are used to, so you sit down as you always do without even thinking about it."

Standing up I straighten the chair and try again, this time I am successful, but it is an odd feeling sitting down so low with my knees forced up close to my chest.

Ruby hands me the glass with a grin on her face and sits back down. The short respite from their misery soon vanishes. One of males on the blanket pours beer into my glass and then offers me a cigarette which I decline.

"Now then," says O'Connor. "This is my wife, Mary. My girls," he points with his pipe, "Ruby and Catherine and my son Michael. The other lad is no relation so he can introduce himself.

"You are Billy Dunn I presume?" says I meeting a pair of sharp blue eyes.

"I am," says he sounding suitably surprised.

Turning my attention back to O'Connor I ask, "Marcus Flambé, was he related…"

"My eldest son," cuts in he, "Marcus Flambé is… was, his stage name. His real name is… was, simply Patrick Shaun O'Connor, and why the hell anyone would want to kill him I have no idea. Perhaps you can tell me, as I'm thinking that knowing Billy's name, you're also knowing a hell of a lot about what's really going on here."

I am astounded by not only O'Connor's lack of any accent but by his obvious intelligence. He is well-spoken, educated, and I have no doubt very shrewd.

"My investigations are at an early stage Mr O'Connor and it would be unprofessional of me to present anything less than the facts to you at this point. However, it may bring a small respite to you when I tell you I believe that Patrick wasn't the intended target…"

"But Billy was," cuts in he. "I said as much to my Mary. Didn't I Mary?"

She nods her agreement as a tear falls from her eye.

"I was the real target?" gasps Billy, looking suitably horrified. "But why?"

It comes to me that Billy has no idea that his father has been murdered. Perhaps he doesn't even know his sister Sally has disappeared. What intrigues me is why O'Connor assumes that Billy was the intended target.

"An educated guess," says O'Connor, picking up on my thoughts.

The look he gives me leads me to reason he wishes to speak to me without Billy being present. Taking a slow drink from my glass I play for time, who do I question first? If O'Connor has some kind of prejudice towards Billy it may have a detrimental effect on the way I question Billy. Draining my glass, I set it down on the ground and stand up. "Billy, I wish to speak to you alone. Is there somewhere we can go for a little privacy?"

"Use the van," says O'Connor. "We need to stretch our legs for a while." Pushing himself up from his chair he takes his wife by the hand and walks away towards the heath beyond the circus with the rest of his family trailing behind. I watch them go for a full minute while feeling their pain and reasoning that they are truly a wonderful family, utterly shattered by the loss of Patrick. I vow to bring the killer, or killers to justice or execute the bastards myself. I follow Billy into the caravan.

Inside the caravan it is classic gypsy, spotlessly clean, very tidy and fashionable with its made to measure teak furniture, array of glass-fronted cabinets stuffed full with carnival glass and treasured nick-knacks. Photographs in gleaming silver frames take up every available piece of space. The floor is of highly-polished dark oak with a Persian carpet to highlight the main sitting area. Billy goes and sits on a heavily cushioned white leather sofa that spreads around a large window that looks out towards the heathland where several, mixed coloured horses are tethered while busily grazing.

"Would you like a drink, Inspector?" asks Billy wanly.

"No thank you. This is truly a magnificent interior, Billy. Do you live here?"

"Nah, I bunk down in a tent with the roustabouts. Why would someone try and kill me?"

"We will get to that in a short while. I take it you haven't heard the news regarding your father as yet?"

"What's the useless ol' fool been up to now?" he half jokes.

"I regret to inform you Billy, your father is dead."

"Oh! As in not breathing dead?"

"Exactly. When did you last see your father?"

He spreads out his arms, "I don't know. Weeks ago, maybe months. We weren't very close, he didn't want much to do with me, me being a dwarf. How did he die?"

"He was murdered yesterday morning at his home."

"Oh… Who by?"

"We have no idea at present," lies I. "I was hoping you might shed some light on the matter."

He shakes his head. "Sorry, Inspector I have no idea."

"Your sister, Sally. When did you last see her?"

Exhaling dramatically, he says, "Weeks ago. She came to see the show escorted by a right Jack the lad. Smarmy type, full of himself he was. We had a brief conversation before my act and she left without coming to say goodbye. We didn't get on either, in much the same way as me and the ol' man. Has something happened to Sally as well?"

"She has disappeared. That is all I can tell you at this point in time."

With a shrug he turns his head to gaze out of the window and says in reflection, "Sally and me could have been close if it wasn't for that useless ol' bastard." He faces me. "I'll bet good money whatever was going on my ol' man was behind it. Knowing him, he probably borrowed, or stole money from the wrong people and got himself killed as a result while putting me an' Sally in mortal danger."

"Perhaps. The truth of the matter is we have only conjecture and supposition at the moment and the only reason I believe you may be in dire danger is the obvious link between you and your father. The big question is; what on earth has your father's murder even remotely got to do with you? Especially when you haven't clapped eyes on him for months."

"I honestly have no idea, Inspector. Maybe it doesn't have anything to do with me. It's common knowledge that Billy's circus is in financial trouble and that Joe Bassett from Bassett's circus has been trying to buy Billy out. What if he orchestrated the blowing up of the cannon to force Billy to sell up?"

"Thank you for that," smiles I. "I shall look into it. However, let us err on the side of caution, I suggest you keep vigilant while maintaining a low profile. Just make sure you let us know where to find you should you decide to move away from the circus. If you should hear from your sister let us know immediately for we fear her life may also be in danger."

"Very well, Inspector."

Getting to my feet I make my way outside with Billy following. Outside I spy the O'Connor family in the distance heading back just as Clump comes out of Billy Star's caravan with Billy himself, they shake hands before Clump heads over towards me. Billy Dunn makes himself scarce and walks away towards the grazing horses.

"How did you get on, Inspector?" asks Clump coming to stand right in front of me and breathing whisky breath in my face.

I glance behind me to check that Billy is well out of earshot. "I have just been lied to by that young man."

"Who is he?"

"Bert Dunn's son, Billy Dunn."

"And he lied, because…?"

"I don't know as yet, sir. He said he hadn't seen his father in months but I have a reliable witness who will swear he saw Billy talking with his father just a couple of weeks back. How did you get on?"

After a hiccup, burp and fart, he says, "Alright. I do not believe Billy Star has anything to do with this. He is so upset, Inspector he has decided to sell the business to a rival circus run by a Joe Barret."

"Bassett, sir."

"What is?"

"Joe Bassett, sir, not Joe Barret."

"Don't split hairs, Inspector. I know what I said." Scratching around his fuzzy beard he appears pensive for a moment before growling, "I want the bastards who committed this obscene act, Detective Inspector Potter. I want them so badly I hope to God they are taken alive so that I can beat the shit out of them before I see them strung up and swinging. Now, I shall go and check up on Mick O' bloody Reilly. What is your next step?"

"I shall question the O'Connors, sir before tackling the rest of the performers and workers. Did Billy Star say if anyone saw the cannon being tampered with?"

"He said he asked around first thing this morning, but no one admitted to seeing anything untoward, or any strangers about before the crowds turned up for the show. Now, where exactly has Sergeant Head got to?"

"I ordered him to go and put a bit of pressure on Bray Waunepcy before he comes here, to see if he couldn't unsettle him enough for the stinking reprobate to let something slip which might give us a clue to further our investigations."

"Waunepcy is more slippery than a bowl of snotty grease, Inspector and the chances of unsettling him are nil. Waste of time, trust me, the only way to get Waunepcy to open his mouth would be with a pair of pliers." He shoots a glance behind him before saying hurriedly, "The O'Connors are coming. I'll leave you to it, Inspector."

Why he seems almost afraid of Shaun O'Connor I have no idea, but I do intend to find out.

"Are you ready to talk to me now, Inspector?" asks Shaun as he steps up to me a minute later.

"I am, Mr O'Connor."

He gestures with his arm, "Then let us go inside and partake of a brandy."

Shaun follows me in, he takes out a bottle of brandy and two cut glass tumblers from a cabinet on the wall.

"Sit down, Inspector," says he, nodding towards the sofa. I sit down at one end of the sofa while he sits down the opposite end, that way we are almost facing each other. Shaun sets the brandy and glasses down on the coffee table and half fills the glasses. "This is a good brandy," says he obviously trying to smile. "You will not need to ruin it by adding something to it. Unless of course you do not partake of neat fine brandy?"

"Neat is the only way to drink fine brandy, sir," says I.

He passes me a glass, "To my Patrick. God bless him."

"God bless him," echoes I. We drink slowly to savour the silky-smooth taste. "Absolutely superb. Thank you."

"I will not dwell on my son, Inspector. We have a lifetime to do that. Let us talk about Billy. He has been a part of our troop for close on six years. He applied for the position from an advertisement I put in the papers. We were six dwarfs then, I reasoned that if we were to become seven that magical number could make all the difference to the way we were perceived by the public. I was right. People resonate with the number seven much more than the number six. Billy has been good for us, he is hard working, incredibly athletic for a dwarf and also quite fearless. However, he has a darker past that I am wondering may have come back to haunt him. I will explain. Billy took up with us just after he was released from two years in prison for attempted burglary. He was caught one night half-way up the drainpipe of a sumptuous house over Hampstead way by the owner and two of his servants, both armed with revolvers. Billy went easily, admitted his guilt in court and said that as he passed the house he saw an open window and tried his luck, a stupid spur of the moment act, that he was truly sorry for. He had acted alone."

"Only he didn't tell the truth, did he, Mr O'Connor?"

"He did not. Billy had willingly been involved in several burglaries previous to when he was caught until things turned sour and he wanted out, only the gang leader would not allow him to sever their relationship. A year or so before Billy got caught, the gang broke into a mansion house on the outskirts of Greenwich that turned really nasty. The owner confronted the gang, as they were coming in via a moonlit downstairs window, and began to shout out to raise the alarm. Billy said the leader of the gang bounded forwards and brutally coshed the owner on his skull three times. The first stunned the man, the second felled him to his knees and the third, resounding crack, finished him off. Billy and three more of the gang wanted to flee, but the leader and his second in command insisted, with threats, that they complete their mission. Silent and deadly the gang went through the house, taking anything of worth that was easily carried. The leader and his second in command took the master bedroom upstairs. Returning downstairs, Billy reasoned, over twenty minutes later where they ordered everyone out. The haul netted the gang priceless jewellery, various silver and gold artefacts along with a velvet-covered box of small diamonds. The next day the evening papers screamed the details of the brutal deaths of not only the owner but also of his wife. She was found strangled on her own bed with her night attire ripped wide open, she had been brutally raped, it is believed, after being forced to open the safe."

"Did Billy name names?"

"No. Still too terrified to unmask the brutes. I urged him to go to the police but he refused. As time went by it all faded into the background, we got on with the show, so to speak, and Billy never spoke of it again. Perhaps what happened then, has nothing to do with now? Perhaps it has nothing to do with Billy?"

"I believe it does, Billy's father has been murdered and his sister is missing. Did Billy tell you exactly when and the Greenwich murders took place, or who the victims where?"

O'Connor takes a long drink before answering, "He wouldn't say, but curiosity got the better of me at the time and I went to the national papers in order to find out. It didn't take long. If I recall correctly; the victims were a Sir Alfred Soanes and his wife Lady Patricia Soanes. For some reason I have never forgotten their names but I can't recall anything else."

"It is enough, thank you, Mr O' Connor." I try to recall the victims' names and the case but nothing comes to mind. "I will look into the case as soon as I am able to. Do you know if Billy has had any contact of late with his father or sister?"

"I do. Billy's father turned up out of the blue a couple of weeks or so back and according to Billy tried to beg money from him. Bert said he was in dire trouble and if Billy didn't help him he was done for. I saw them quarrelling over by the roustabout's tent, then Bert stormed off. The next night, Billy's sister turned up with a right Jack the lad on her arm. She seemed in a state of extreme anxiousness. We were about to go on but she held Billy back while imploring him to help her and their father. I told Billy to be quick and went into the big top to start our act, Billy joined us after a few minutes. Later that evening Billy confided in me; he said his sister and father had done something really stupid and had crossed some really bad men. I asked him to elaborate only he refused, saying; 'It's better that you don't know for they have done for me and I don't want you or your family involved because I love you all so much.' Following that nothing untoward occurred, Billy seemed settled enough, I asked him how things were with his family and he said, almost casually, that he had sorted everything out and not to worry. But then Bert turned up again two days back, I saw them quarrelling over by the horses, before Bert went off looking rather pleased with himself whereas Billy appeared to be very unhappy. I asked Billy what was wrong and he said it was nothing to worry about. Well how I wish I had bullied him into opening up a fuckin' lot further! Now my beloved Patrick is dead, Bert Dunn is dead and his daughter is missing, perhaps also dead and I have not a clue who is behind it all," his eyes turn really dark, you can see the fury in them and he fixes me with an iron stare, "I have been too stunned by events to interrogate Billy, but now I am ready to know the truth and if he does not start opening his mouth then he will be very sorry. I will not be responsible for my actions. The carnage reaped upon this circus has boiled up everyone's blood lust, Inspector, should they even remotely think that Billy could be behind it in some way they will tear him to pieces and I will be throwing his remains to the dogs."

"Say nothing to anyone for now and allow me to talk further with Billy, Mr O'Connor. If he is keeping something from us, trust me I will quickly find out. Now, this Jack the lad character, did you catch his name?"

"Sally addressed him as 'Sticks', obviously a nickname. He was tall and thin, pinched features, shifty eyes, thick black sideburns, no beard or moustache. He had a three-inch straight scar across his cheek. I'd say he'd been slashed by someone."

"Dress?"

"He wasn't wearing a dress."

"What was he wearing?"

"A top hat, black frock coat, they looked new, but his dark trousers and knee-high boots were old and tatty as was his green peacock design waistcoat. He acted the dandy, swaggering around as if he was someone of importance."

"Thank you, Mr O' Connor," says I. Getting to my feet I down the rest of my brandy. "I implore you not to do anything rash. I understand your sorrow and your desire for revenge, but you must leave this to us Mr O' Connor or you may find yourself in trouble. Is that fully understood?"

"It is, Inspector, but be advised I shall not leave it for too long before conducting my own investigations."

"Understood. I have decided to take Billy into custody for now for further questioning and his own safety. I shall keep you informed of our progress as much as is possible. Thank you for the brandy, Mr O'Connor, we shall speak further before I leave."

He stands up and holds out his hand, we shake and he nods in a way that says it all; for now, he will trust me to do the very best I can to track down the killer of his son.

Outside it has turned cloudy, there is the scent of rain in the air as I make my way over towards where the horses are. There is no sign of Billy Dunn as I scan probing eyes all round me and I have the sick feeling that Billy has made a run for it. Striding over to the big top's entrance I see forensics have put up a sign: 'No entry. Police only'. On entering I spot Clump standing talking to the photographer and go over to them.

"Have you seen Billy Dunn, sir?" asks I.

Clump shakes his head, "Should I have?"

"I think he has done a runner, sir."

He scratches at his beard, "Well he couldn't have gone far, his legs are too little."

"Not if they're over a saddle. There was a thoroughbred bay mare outside the last time I looked, but now it has gone."

"Shit! Come on, Inspector, let's saddle up and chase the bugger."

"Can you ride, sir?"

"Of course, I can bloody ride. Can you?"

"Donkeys on the beach in Southend as a child is about all. Well, one donkey, once."

"Well now is the time to learn, Inspector. Come on!"

One of the circus hands confirms having seen Billy ride off on the bay mare some ten minutes previously as he quickly saddles up two black and white, rather huge horses for us. Clump mounts deftly up, while I have to have a leg up by the circus hand.

"Hold on tight," bellows Clump before kicking his horse on in the direction that Billy apparently took.

I hold on, gripping with my legs so hard it is a wonder the pressure doesn't force the horse to fart bricks. Vice-like I hold the reins as, with a will of its own, my mount charges off in a different direction. Having no control whatsoever over the brute I am bucketed about like a child sat on a rampaging elephant, while my testicles experience the sensation of being repeatedly punched by a demented gorilla. Within seconds I have abandoned holding onto the reins in favour of falling forward on the brute's flowing mane while desperately trying to wrap my arms around its thick neck. My feet are out of the stirrups and the friction between my thighs and the saddle is as hot as a clothes iron, in fact I am convinced I shall burst into flames at any second. But it is my spine that is suffering the most as it is being constantly jarred by the horse's see-saw motions. At last, I feel the horse slowing down a tad. Lifting terrified eyes, I see we are heading towards a five barred gate nestling between curling masses of bramble bushes. Sighing with relief I manage to grab the reins and sit back up, the horse has slowed to a bouncy trot, obviously it intends to come to a final halt at the gate, thank the Lord. Suddenly it rears up and I hold on for dear life. It then whinnies so loudly it pierces my eardrums. The whinny is returned by whatever is behind that gate, my mount then takes off as if hell itself is biting its arse while snorting out snotty stuff that slaps into my face as he charges straight at the gate. The brute either intends to try and jump the gate or crash straight through it, either way I am sure that I will not be surviving.

Luckily or unluckily, I manage to somehow fly up in the air the second the brute takes off to clear the gate. Even more luckily, I come to earth with a thud on my front without hitting the gate or landing in the brambles.

Rolling over I sit up on a bum so numb I reason the nerves are dead. Struggling back on my feet I am aware that I am in one piece with no bones broken. I may have missed the hedge but have still got a long-since-dead length of brittle bramble embedded in my backside, even if at present it isn't hurting me. However, I know that I shall have extensive bruising, plus as I rip off the bramble branch, a good many thorns for Betty to pull out later on. As I go and lean on the gate I can see that at least my mount is blissfully happy giving one to what appears to be a very expensive racing filly. Oddly my revolver is still in its holster and a quick search around confirms that apart from my bowler I haven't lost anything other than my pride. To my chagrin, my mount, having had his oats, comes trotting over towards me. Taking out my revolver I consider shooting the brute, but it has such a genuinely sorry look in its eyes on reaching the gate I slip my revolver back in its holster. Lifting the latch, I swing open the gate enough for the horse to pass through and then shut it. The brute then drops its head, picks up my bowler with its teeth and then offers it to me complete with teeth marks in the rim. I reconsider shooting it but it is a hell of a long walk back to the circus.

It is a struggle trying to mount, but after the tenth attempt I am back in the saddle even if I have to stand in the stirrups, as life has returned to my bottom cheeks to give me the sensation of being stabbed by a thousand needles. We set off at a steady walk, the horse looks back behind it and whinnies as much to say; 'See you later,' and as females do she whinnies back as much to say; 'And don't you bloody dare leave it so long next time'.

A slow painful journey back to the circus accentuates my discomfort; my buttocks feel as if they are on fire while every muscle and bone in my body hurts like hell.

A circus hand comes up to take the reins as very gingerly I dismount and sigh with relief to feel solid ground beneath my feet again. I head over to the big top where I see Clump talking to the photographer again. Mick is still poking around what's left of the cannon. The forensic officer has laid out a small tarpaulin sheet on the ground upon which is a gruesome collection of 'evidence' including Patrick's head plus whatever else could be found of his remains. Clump swings his head around in my direction.

"So, you're back then, Inspector?" asks he with a grin.

"So, it would seem, sir," grates I.

"You have adopted an odd gait since your ride, Inspector. Can I assume that utter terror has invaded your stomach to subsequently take it over and demand it empty itself?"

"You assume wrong, sir. I fell off the horse. I am no doubt black and blue all over. My backside is full of thorns, but I have not shit myself."

"Good man, Inspector. We cannot have members of the force losing control of their bowels every time they face adversity, we would be a laughing stock should we all be seen adopting the same gait as you."

I change the subject, "Did you catch up with Billy?"

"A veritable carthorse chasing a thoroughbred. Not a hope, Inspector." He turns his attention to the photographer. "Go and rustle up some tea for everyone, Mr Blake."

"Go and see Mr O'Connor the victim's father," puts in I. "He will gladly brew up for us."

"Right," says he and heads off.

"I should go over and speak to O'Reilly, sir," says I.

Clump shakes his head, "Don't bother. I tried that and got sent off with a wasp in my ear."

"Don't you mean a flea, sir?"

"I know what I mean," snaps he and slaps a hand on my shoulder. "Come on, let's go outside for a while, Inspector. The stench of burnt flesh and acrid fumes is getting to me. We shall take a break while you tell me how you got on with Shaun O'Connor and Billy Dunn."

Once outside and away from the big top we sit down on the grass where I grit my teeth and try to ignore the thorns in my arse.

Clump lights up a cigar while I tell him everything I found out from Billy, which was nothing much. However, when I relate what Shaun told me his eyes open wide and I can sense his brain working overtime.

"It would be wise, Inspector," says he blowing smoke in my face, "to take seriously what O'Connor has told you. He is a very perceptive man, intelligent, shrewd and most of all a man of honour."

"Do you know him personally, sir?" asks I cagily.

"Oh, yes. We were both at Eton at the same time."

"That is a revelation, sir."

"In what way, Inspector? Did you think dwarfs were excluded from joining the ranks of the elite?"

"Not in the least, sir."

"Of course, you didn't. Not that it did O'Connor any good."

"Why so?"

"Prejudice, Inspector. A good many people see a dwarf and reason they must be a moron incapable of anything other than being a figure of fun. In Shaun's case the general census amongst the Eton elite was that Shaun was only allowed into Eton because strings were pulled. Although he is a bastard, Shaun is the bastard of an earl, no names mentioned. His mother was a gypsy who worked the fields on this earl's estate. They met when the earl was out riding and happened upon this beautiful gypsy girl bathing naked and alone in a brook, so the story goes. They instantly fell in love and had started a torrid affair before the earl was even out of his saddle."

"As you do," says I, imaging the scene in my mind's eye.

"I wish," sighs Clump. "Anyway, the result was Shaun. For reference the dwarfism came from the earl's side, not the gypsy's side. Of course, the affair scandalised the upper classes and the earl was pressurised into ending it. However, he did not forsake Shaun or his mother and sent regular sums of money to enable them to live comfortably. Shaun was brought up in a modest country house where his mother eventually married a local farmer who did not want Shaun around. Still funded by this earl, Shaun was sent off to Eton where he proved to be an excellent scholar. He was well-liked and popular with a small but loyal following of his peers. He would have gone on to Oxford had life not turned sour for him. His benefactor died and the new earl immediately stopped the payments to Shaun's mother. Shaun was fortunate enough to have a fair amount put away so he had no immediate money worries." He takes a long draw on his cigar and blows more smoke over me before continuing. "However, the worst of it was, with his mentor now deceased, Shaun had also lost his protector which culminated in the most disgusting display of outright snobbery and blatant cruelty I have ever witnessed. Determined to hound Shaun out of Eton by treating him as a figure of fun a group of over-privileged buffoons calling themselves the: Keep Up Noble Traditional Standards, the abbreviation of which is of course, grossly offensive, began their crusade by luring Shaun to an unsavoury inn with the sole intention of using him as entertainment for the evening. Having hired an upstairs room, they had also secured the services of a prostitute who was up for 'doing' it with a dwarf. Shaun of course refused to play ball and events turned very nasty very quickly. The instigator of the intended 'prank' demanded that Shaun be debagged and forced to perform with the prostitute. Shaun was manhandled onto a table where eager hands attempted to rip off his breeches. Shaun put up one devil of a fight, others joined in on his side and a full-blooded war broke out. Chairs were thrown along with bottles, glasses, oil lamps and anything that came to hand, even the prostitute got hurled across the room. It culminated with Shaun getting knocked unconscious via a chair leg where upon he was stripped naked. The landlord entered the affray but couldn't restore even a semblance of order. The curtains caught fire and everyone stampeded for the stairs to escape with two of Shaun's supporters dragging him downstairs and out of the inn where they laid him, still naked and unconscious, on the grass. The police arrived shortly after, randomly arrested a few lads including Shaun and carted them off to the station. The inn burnt to the ground and everyone else went home."

"I take it they covered Shaun up for dignity's sake?"

"Of course, they bundled him up in a big coat and threw him in the back of the paddy waggon as quickly as they could."

Cramp in my buttocks forces me to lean to one side to relieve the pressure.

"Do you intend breaking wind, Inspector?"

"Merely making myself more comfortable, sir. What happened to those who were arrested?"

"Strings were pulled in high places and nearly everyone was let off with nothing more than a slapped bottom."

I am incredulous. "The police slapped their bottoms?"

"Metaphorically Inspector. Metaphorically."

"And Shaun?"

"Ah…This is where the Keep Up Noble Traditional Standards brigade got their wish. Shaun was charged with causing a riot and being naked in a public place. Prison loomed before him unless he agreed to publicly admit his guilt, leave Eton and get back to where he belonged. He refused. They gave him six months hard labour which, apparently, he did standing on his head. Which must have been bloody uncomfortable."

"I don't follow you, sir."

He grins, "Have you ever tried standing on your head for six months, inspector?"

"Very droll, sir," sighs I.

"Anyway, once released from prison Shaun vanished and I have not clapped eyes on him since, until today."

"Yet you still feel guilty?"

He drops his eyes to stare at the grass and stubs out his cigar before meeting my questioning gaze. "You are as always very perceptive, Inspector. At the time I and many others could have spoken up for Shaun and protested his innocence. But we did not because we were cowards who were more worried about being expelled than upsetting the status quo. It has haunted me to this day."

"Why don't you take the bull by the balls? Just go over to Shaun's caravan, and simply tell him you are sorry for what happened back then. I am certain he will accommodate you."

"I doubt it. He'll more than likely tell me to fuck off."

"We can but try, sir."

The photographer returns carrying a large tray with a gleaming silver teapot on it along with everything else required, including biscuits on a silver plate.

"Wonderful," beams Clump clapping his hands together. "Set it down, Mr Blake. Set it down and then go and tell that mad Irish bugger and that other chap, it is tea time."

Blake sets the tray down on the grass right in front of the Chief before heading into the tent.

Clump pushes the tray closer to me, "You can be mother, Inspector. I shall be the fortifier." The whisky flask comes out from his jacket pocket, he waits for me to pour the tea and add the milk before he adds the whisky.

Mr Blake rejoins us along with Mick and the forensics officer.

Sometimes a short respite out beneath a clear, blue sky can do wonders for the equilibrium.

By the time we are ready to 'get back to it' we are focused, positive and determined to catch Patrick O'Connor's killer. The sympathy towards the O'Connor family is immeasurable and there is nothing we can do to ease their suffering other than ensure we do our duty to our utmost abilities.

We carry on; Clump slopes off to see Shaun, Mick and forensics head back into the big top and I take myself around the tents and caravans to question everyone I meet. No one it seems saw or heard anything leading up to the explosion. By one pm, six hours after arriving, Mick and the forensic officer are ready to deliver their findings. More tea and coffee are sent over from Shaun and Billy Star personally delivers a bottle of scotch. Sitting out on the grass again we form a circle and everyone helps themselves, which is a mistake when it comes to the scotch as Mick and Clump appear to be in competition over who can down the most fortified coffee the quickest, while practically fighting over the bottle. At last things settle down and Clump offers a toast.

"To success and the annihilation of the bastard or bastards who dared to commit such a heinous act while believing they would get away with it."

We toast and then Mick delivers his findings first.

"Briefly, Chief, the cannon works by way of a huge spring. Chains are fixed to the top rung of the spring with the other end onto a small metal drum. A crank handle is put into a hole on the outside of the cannon which when turned winds the chain around the drum, thus loading the spring which clicks into lugs to hold it in place. It is now ready to fire."

"What no gunpowder or dynamite?" queries Clump.

Mick shakes his head and takes a swig of his more scotch than coffee, before answering. "The only charges are small ones that go off once the spring is released. To be sure they are only for effect so it appears to the audience that the cannon has actually been fired like a real one. Our man is catapulted out of the cannon, the small charges go off with a flash, a bang and a good puff of smoke, then hopefully, if the projections are right our man lands safely in the net. Now, at the bottom of the cannon is a foot square maintenance door that is opened from the outside via a small lever. You can then check the workings, oil 'em up or even repair them if ya have too. I found the shattered fragments from more than one small bottle along with a piece of charred cord that was attached to what was left of the mangled spring. Painstaking as it was, I reconstructed a part of one bottle, especially what was left of the neck which also had a fragment of cord still attached to it. My conclusion is that someone tied two, maybe three, small bottles of nitro glycerine to the spring via the maintenance door. Now, that stuff is so volatile it could 'ave gone off at any time. Sure, it's a miracle it didn't go off when the dwarfs were pushing the cannon into the big top. Had it been the intention to kill all the little people in one go? They were all so close to the cannon at that point it would have almost certainly maimed or even killed the lot of 'em. That aside, once the spring was released the nitro bottles would have been seriously jolted, more than enough to set them off. Any questions?"

"Is the cannon made of metal?" asks Clump.

"No. This one was made of wood. It was put together in much the same way as a beer barrel, except it was also glued before having a few metal hoops hammered on to hold it firm."

"Did you find any clues that might provide a lead to whoever was behind this?" asks Clump.

"I did," grins Mick. "It ain't easy to legally get hold of nitro, Chief. And it's nigh on impossible to get hold of it illegally unless you have some serious underworld contacts." He holds up a small piece of glass between finger and thumb, "There's a tiny piece of label still on this bit of glass that tells me the name of the company that traded it."

"And is this company crooked?" asks I.

"Not as far as I know. The firm would have to log the full details of whoever bought the nitro along with the reasons why. Paying the firm who sold that nitro a visit to find out who bought it is now top of my list, so it is."

"You've done well, O'Reilly," says Clump with some reluctance.

"That's rare praise indeed coming from you, Arthur," grins Mick.

"Don't dine out on it just yet," growls Clump and fixes his now watery eyes on the forensic officer. "Did you discover anything of worth?"

He holds up a small square of white card, stuck on that card is a strip of sticky celluloid that covers black finger print powder with a clear impression of a thumb print from the left hand.

Clump slaps the palm of his hand onto his forehead. "A bloody fingerprint! How many times do I have to repeat myself? Finger printing is a waste of time and will never catch on. That being the case, pray enlighten me as to the reason you have bothered to present this specimen to me?"

"I have taken a good many fingerprints today, Chief. No doubt they will indeed prove to be a waste of time, but this one may not. It was taken from the metal handle used to close the maintenance door on the cannon. After I had taken it, I asked around the circus to ascertain who was the last person to touch that handle. It turns out that yesterday the circus's main maintenance man opened the door to check the workings and oil the spring. He then cleaned the cannon, giving it a buff up, you now a…"

"We know what a bloody buff up is. Just get on with it."

"Well, sir, he was adamant that he wiped the handle clean of any prints. I am thinking that this print may possibly belong to our killer."

"Fucking brilliant, whatever your name is…?" sneers Clump

"Parker, sir."

"Parker, did you check if the print belonged to the maintenance man?"

"I did and it did not. I also checked that it didn't belong to any of the dwarfs except possibly for Billy Dunn who'd done a runner by then."

"And Patrick O'Connor? Did you check his prints?"

"I did, sir. Luckily, I found one of his thumbs, it was the opposite one to the one I had taken a print of, but in truth it was far too small a thumb to come anywhere close to the thumbprint I had taken."

"Perhaps Patrick O'Connor had one thumb bigger than the other Mr Parker?" sneers Clump in his best reel them in tone of voice. "Did you also fingerprint all the uniformed officers who have been mooching around since last night while no doubt touching everything in reach, particularly the cannon? In fact, Mr Parker wouldn't it be prudent to go out and finger the entire population…?"

"Print, Chief," puts in Mick.

"Shut up O'Reilly. Do not interrupt me when I am fishing." Clump lets out a deep sigh. "Anything other than the print to report?"

"Nothing as yet, sir," says Parker turning bright red beneath Clump's scathing stare. "Dr Shelley may come up with something when he, um…, conducts his autopsy."

"Autopsy! Is there enough of the victim left on which to carry out an autopsy do you think, Mr Parker?"

"Oh yes, sir. It should be relatively easy for Dr Shelley to ascertain the cause of death."

Clump throws his arms up in exasperation. "We know the cause of death, Parker. The poor sod was blown to bits."

"But he may have died of a heart attack because of the trauma of being blown up, sir."

"Did you actually find his heart in one piece?"

"Um…"

"Exactly, let us move on. Mr Blake. Have you anything to report?"

"I have taken extensive photographs of everything and everything, Chief Inspector. I also took the trouble to walk all around the perimeter of the circus' encampment."

"For what reason?"

"To see if I might find where the killer entered the encampment."

Clump pours the last of the coffee into his cup and tops it up with the dregs from the bottle of scotch. He yawns in apparent boredom before saying, "And did you find said entry?"

"Yes, sir, I believe I did. Two distinct footprints from a large pair of feet, one, one side of the barbed wire fence that marks the heath's boundary, the other on the other side. Also, on the barbed wire I found a piece of tweed cloth, where whoever had straddled the wire obviously caught the seat of their trousers. Not only that, there was blood on one of the wire spikes. It is conceivable that the killer caught his hand on the fence. I took photographs of everything and then reported back to Mr Parker."

"Who said nothing about this a minute ago when I asked him what else he had come up with," grates Clump giving Parker the evil eye. "Why was that, Mr Parker?"

Parker shrugs, it is obvious the man has become so intimidated by Clump he wishes to say nothing and escape Clump's presence as quickly as is possible. "Um…"

Swallowing his coffee Clump's eyes soften a little and when he speaks it is with more professionalism, "What action did you take when told of Mr Blake's findings?"

"I took plaster casts of the footprints and scrapings of the blood, sir."

"What no fingerprints?"

"Not possible, sir."

"Good. Let us review this new piece of conjectural evidence. Anyone could have come into the circus encampment area as you put it, anyone. Top of the list would be thieves followed by those trying to sneak into the big top for free. Perhaps a member of the workforce who'd sneaked off to the local inn sought a way to return without being seen. He may have come in anywhere as there are no guards or vicious guard dogs to keep unwelcome intruders out. However, it is a noteworthy piece of detective work and evidence that is far more welcome than stupid fingerprints. Anything else? No? Good. Inspector Potter please inform the crew of your findings."

Relating the little I have found out takes no time at all. There are no questions and Clump takes over.

"Whether our killer acted alone or in collusion with others we do not know at this point in time. However, someone is calling the shots even if their own hands are clean, for that someone to go to such extremities to commit himself or engage others to murder for him tells us we are dealing with a very dangerous individual indeed. So be careful gentlemen, do not think you are untouchable just because you are on the side of law and order. O'Reilly, your priority is to try and find out who has obtained nitro glycerine of late, legally or illegally. Parker you will follow up on your stupid fingerprint, not that it will take you anywhere. There are the footprints and the blood scrapings and of course you will have to liaise with your senior, Dr Shelley," he pauses to reach into his jacket pocket. "Mr Blake. This is a photograph of the O'Connor family, with Billy Dunn also in the frame that I purloined from Billy Star. I want to see an emotional article in tomorrow morning's daily papers so tear jerking it would touch the heart of the devil himself, while also raising the anger of the masses. I want the papers saturated with pictures of the devastation wrecked on the circus and its people, especially the O'Connors. I also want the missing persons plastered all over the front pages. That's Sally Dunn, Billy Dunn and a shifty shit called 'Sticks'. Inspector Potter will have a police profile artist draw up a sketch of this 'Sticks' character for you to use and he also has a photograph of Sally Dunn. Put up a five-pound reward to anyone who can offer information as to where any or all of our missing persons are hiding out. And put up a twenty-pound reward for information that will lead to the arrest of whoever is behind these hideous murders. Inspector Potter, you will reopen the Soanes case. Go through the files and see if it leads anywhere. Right, gentlemen, let us pack up and head back to the Yard. I am in dire need of a good lunch."

And I am in dire need of having the thorns plucked out of my backside, groans I to myself. The pain of their presence has abated somewhat but they are now as itchy as an infestation of giant lice.

It takes another hour to finish off and tidy up. Patrick O'Connor's remains are put into a body sack and almost ceremoniously chucked into the back of the waggon. We all go and pay our respects to the O'Connors and Billy Star before we set off. Clump and I sit up with the driver and go over what we have learnt before the question of Head's whereabouts comes up again.

"I am thinking, Inspector," says Clump dolefully, "if Sergeant Head isn't back at the Yard by five we will call out a search, for I have a bad feeling in my stomach, along with the gas, that something isn't right."

"I agree, sir. Head should have turned up at least a couple of hours ago. It is rather worrying."

"It is, Inspector. Before I forget; I have to thank you for urging me to seek forgiveness from Shaun. We embraced, as men do I hasten to add, the past is water under the bridge and all that matters now is to find Patrick O'Connor's killer."

"That is the best news of the day, sir."

"It is indeed," he smiles before closing his eyes and dropping off.

We arrive back at the Yard just before four pm. There has been no sign of Head, he hasn't reported in and no messages from him have been received. It is truly worrying.

After a quick late lunch of cheese on toast in the canteen I settle down in my office to write up a rough draft of my notes, intent on writing them up in full later on. The Soanes case files are delivered to me and I start going through them. At most I have thirty minutes to familiarise myself with the case if we are to set off at five in search of Sergeant Head. To fully ingest the extensive records of the Soanes case will take hours and would best be done with Head's help. I just hope to God he doesn't end up with his own murder having to be put on file.

Dead on five o'clock, Clump musters half a dozen hardnosed uniform together and arms them with rifles. Four further detectives, armed with revolvers, are seconded and a Superintendent Rant volunteers to come along. Mick is handed a revolver by Clump with the warning; "Do not shoot people willy-nilly O'Reilly or you could find yourself up on a murder charge."

"Sure, I'll try not to, Chief," winks Mick pushing the weapon into his belt.

Clump addresses us, "Men, we are about to go on a mission. Sergeant Head has disappeared and we fear for his very life. First stop is the pawnbrokers in Fish Bone Alley run by one Bray Waunepcy. He is a decrepit, flea-ridden reprobate more slippery than a bowl of melted lard. We shall route him out and torture - I mean question him as to the whereabouts of the Sergeant should he not be found safe and sound at the shop. Failing that we will do door to door in pairs. Do not be afraid to stick the fear of God into all you come across. Knock out a few teeth and break a few noses if you have to but do not go too far, we do not want to start a riot leading up to a blood bath. Right let's get to it."

Outside we find a pair of open waggons, normally used for transporting goods, waiting for us, each drawn by a pair of heavy horses. Clump obviously wishes the entire world to see us out in force. We load up, the six uniform and the superintendent take one waggon, the rest of us climb onto the other with Clump sat up beside the driver. Clump raises his arm, shouts out, waggons roll and off we go with our waggon leading the way.

Once away from the Yard the horses are urged into a trot, their heavy hooves clattering loudly on the tarmacadam and even louder when they hit cobbles. The sight and sound of our small but noisy cavalcade scares everyone in our path to get out of the way. Urchins race alongside us while daring to hurl dung balls at us along with the odd dead cat and several rats, not all of which are actually dead. As we turn into Fish Bone Alley the urchins and half of anyone else who is about quickly disappear down narrow alleyways, flee indoors or skip behind anything that will shield them from our searching eyes. They have no idea of what we are about but as the majority will be wanted for something or other, out of sight is out of mind.

"Pull up here," bellows Clump as the pawnbrokers' sign comes into view.

The horses are reined in and come to a halt right outside the shop and the handbrake is applied. Waggon two comes to a halt just as Clump jumps down ready to address everyone as they jump out and form an arc in front of him.

"Listen in men. Uniform, you will remain on guard outside as there will not be enough room to manoeuvre inside this junked up little shithole if we all go in at once. I and my detectives shall go in first making enough noise to wake the dead in Scotland. If, we meet any resistance resulting in exchanges of gunfire then you will follow Superintendent Rant's instructions. Is that clear?"

Everyone nods.

"Good. Detectives draw your weapons and follow me."

Clump steps up to the shop door and raises one of his size twelves. With the force of a bull he kicks in the door so hard it flies right off its rusted hinges to crash six feet in onto the floor, while the bell above the door clangs away like it's being rung by a demented campanologist and Clump's bowler falls off to be caught by yours truly. Clump takes one step inside and bellows out, "Armed Police". The metal bell suddenly falls from its hook, dongs on his head and then falls to clang on his foot. "Bastard!" curses he before kicking it away to roll across the floor in a series of clangs and dongs. I hand him his hat over his shoulder.

"Armed Police," yells he slapping his bowler back on. "Come out into the open right now or suffer the consequences."

Nothing happens. Clump cautiously moves further inside. We all trail in and I realise then that Mick is alongside me. Fanning out while waving our revolvers around we scan wary eyes around the shop.

Mick hisses out, "What's that sound?"

A deathly silence invades the shop as seven pairs of ears strain to listen. A grunting sound is heard, followed by a loud snort and a rattled breathing sound.

"It sounds like it's coming from upstairs," ventures I.

"It sounds like some kind of animal chomping on something," says one of the detectives wide-eyed. "A wart hog, or maybe a hippopotamus."

"More like a pig," scoffs Clump. "Knowing that stinking reprobate Waunepcy he's probably keeping one upstairs so he has something even uglier than himself to sleep with, the poor bastard. That's the pig not Waunepcy."

"Sure, it might be a dangerous wild beast, chief," puts in Mick. "Ya never know what some of these animal lovers will keep in their homes."

"I knew a bloke who kept a giant snake in his shed once," says a detective. "He brought it back from the Far East when he was in the merchant navy. Course it didn't live long."

"Did he not feed it right?" asks Mick.

"I don't know. Apparently, it did well until the winter frosts set…"

"Will you all shut up and listen," hisses Clump.

We listen.

"Silent as the grave, so it is," shudders Mick.

The superintendent sticks his head in, "What's happening, Chief Inspector?"

"We may have a wild beast of some kind upstairs, Superintendent."

"Really! Well I hope it isn't eating your missing Sergeant's body."

"There's only one way to find out," growls Clump and stepping around the counter he leads the way towards the stairs where he pauses to listen by the open door. A distinct snoring sound bounces down the stairs and momentarily picks up tempo before fading away with the sound of exhaling air.

"That's a man snoring," says Mick.

"Isn't it just," growls Clump thumping angrily up the creaking stairs. He pauses at the open bedroom door and then leaps inside while fanning his revolver all around. "Holster your weapons, men. We have nothing to fear other than Sergeant Head's bloody snoring."

We pile into the room. Head is sound asleep on one of the single beds totally oblivious to our presence.

Bending down Clump sniffs around Head's mouth, "The prat is pissed out of his head." Straightening up he looks worse than furious. "Here we all are, worried out of our minds as to what has happened to one of our own and all the time, he's having a jolly siesta while no doubt dreaming of laying on a tropical beach with a big fat cigar in one hand and a brown-eyed near-naked beauty in the other. Well that's what I would be dreaming of. Right, let's see if this will shatter his dream?" Grabbing the water jug from the wash stand he hurls the contents into Head's face, which has no effect whatsoever other than enrage Clump even further. "Wake up you, drunken bastard!" He shakes a fist at him. "I shall have your guts for this. You will be put on a charge, demoted and pounding the streets back in uniform by tomorrow morning. Do I make myself clear?"

"I can't say he's listening, Chief," says Mick pushing himself forwards. "Do ya mind if I takes me a look?"

Mick goes over and lifts one of Head's eyelids to expose an eye so vacant it is more akin to a dead man's. "Sure, the man's been drugged."

"Bloody drugged!" growls Clump. "Not drunk?"

"To be sure, Chief. The man's in cuckoo land, so he is."

"Where's that?"

"Somewhere between nowhere and nowhere."

Scratching at his beard Clump turns to two detectives hovering by the door obviously ready to run for it should the need have arisen. "You two get the Sergeant downstairs I want him on my waggon, now!"

He turns to me, "What the hell's been going on here, Inspector?"

"Well, sir, see the wardrobe," I point, "it is empty. Waunepcy is nowhere to be seen so I would guess he and the girl fled after somehow managing to administer some kind of sleep inducing drug to the Sergeant."

"Just what I was thinking, Inspector," lies he. "What girl?"

"The girl who worked with and shared a room with Sally Dunn before she disappeared. Her name is Sadie Calver."

"Right. Search the place."

Head is dragged downstairs while the rest of us search the place. Waunepcy has indeed run off; both of his safes are empty along with a wardrobe in the only other bedroom. Draws have been left open in a chest of draws telling us that Waunepcy quickly took what he wanted and left the remainder behind.

"A hasty exit," says Clump scanning his eyes around the room. "Uniform will remain here and ask around while we get back to the Yard, Inspector. You can sit up with me on the waggon so we can liaise as to where we are with all of this."

"So, how many potential missing persons do we have now?" asks Clump as the horses trot along and we exit Fish Bone Alley.

"Five, sir if you count this 'Sticks' fellow."

"Ah…" ahs he. "Sally Dunn and her brother Billy. Bray Waunepcy and this Sadie Calver who works for Sparks."

"I am assuming that as she's done a runner she no longer works for Sparks, sir."

"The question is, Inspector, why did she run?" Removing his hat, he sweeps his scruffy hair back in frustration. "We are nowhere with this and we will continue to be nowhere until we catch up with at least one of our missing persons."

"Perhaps one of my snouts will turn something up in due course."

"And once the missing persons' mugs are plastered all over the papers along with the offer of a reward we should hopefully receive a quick response. I think tomorrow, Inspector, you and Sergeant Head, assuming he has recovered by then, will take a trip to see Sparks. Lean on him heavily enough and he might just let something slip."

"He won't, sir. Trust me the man is as impenetrable as a rock. Besides we really do not have a shred of evidence that he has anything to do with all this. Plus, he has an alibi when Bert Dunn was murdered, it is undoubtedly a false alibi but until we can disprove it…"

"We must continue to treat him as innocent. However, the man is as bent as a kipper and has gotten away with all manner of criminal activities over the years, mostly because of who he knows. I want to see him pulled right off his arrogant perch. I am already convinced that he is our man and this time no amount of 'friends in high places' will stop me putting a noose around his balls and hanging him out for the entire world to see."

"The Sergeant may have some information once he comes around," says I flicking a glance behind me to check that Head is still snoring happily away in the back of the waggon.

"Let us hope so. I shall have the doctor examine him when we get back at the Yard and then we shall question him the second he is coherent enough."

Head's condition over the next three hours failed to change. The police doctor who examined him assured us his heartbeat was regular and there was nothing to do except allow him to sleep it off. Clump arranged for Head to be taken home, still snoring, and also for a message to be delivered to Betty informing her that I was fine but wouldn't be home until late.

I finally arrive home at ten o'clock expecting to find Betty in a right state despite having been told I was alright. Stepping into the parlour I find her curled up and snoring on the sofa. On the coffee table sits a half empty bottle of sherry, one glass and her latest read; A Lovers Lament. Bending down I give her a peck on her cheek and a gentle shake to her shoulder.

"Oh… Detective Inspector, at last," she groans rubbing her eyes and struggling to sit up. "Where on earth have you been?"

Sitting down beside her I yawn out a sigh of relief to be home, followed by a grimace as the thorns in my buttocks decide to torture me further.

"What you need is a stiff drink, Detective Inspector," says she wobbling to her feet. "Something to eat followed by a nice bath and then bed, you can tell me how things went tomorrow"

"What I need my darling is a very stiff drink to help kill the pain before you operate on me."

Spinning around from the sideboard an empty tumbler in one hand and a bottle of scotch in the other she asks in apprehension, "What operation?"

Standing up I fling off my bowler, take off my jacket, undo my belt, push off my braces and turning around drop my trousers and drawers.

Betty is incredulous, "What on earth's happened to your bum, Detective Inspector? It's all red and spotty."

Pulling up my bottoms I turn to face her, "It's a long story. I fell off a horse and landed on a bramble."

"Well I never knew you could ride?"

"I can't. That's why I fell off."

"Why didn't you get yourself attended to at the station?"

"What and have some man poking around my backside while sticking his nose too close to my personals? No thank you, Betty. The only person I want to poke around my personal parts is you."

"But I'm not qualified," implores she.

"Do you need to be, just to pull a few thorns out?"

"Yes. Especially when they look as angry as yours do."

I am getting tired and a touch touchy. "Will you operate or not!"

"If you insist!"

"I do."

"Very well then, be it on your own head!"

"Good. Where do you want me?"

"Drink this," demands she handing me the tumbler full to the brim with scotch.

Downing it in one long swallow causes me to shiver right through my senses before I quickly feel very wobbly indeed. Betty refills my glass, and then surprise, surprise, she pours herself one.

"To a successful operation," smiles she, her eyes I suddenly realise are glazed. Horrified I realise there is another bottle of sherry laid down on the floor halfway under the sofa and this one is empty.

"Are you pissed?" slurs I.

"No, of course not. You just think I am, because you are."

Call me paranoid but I am certain she is pissed. However, I am desperate enough to ignore her inebriated state to have the thorns removed. "Where do you want me?"

"Minus your bottom half I want you on the kitchen table." She hiccups twice and either she is standing still while I am wobbling, or vice versa, or we are both standing still, or both wobbling.

Handing Betty my glass I kick off my shoes, drop my bottoms, fall back onto the sofa and pull them right off.

Betty hands me back my glass. "Hand me your revolver, Detective Inspector," demands she.

"Whatever for?" asks I in suspicion.

"If I can't operate successfully, I may have to put you out of your misery."

"You can go get …"

"No, I can't," scowls she swaying markedly. "Put it this way, Detective Inspector, If you were a surgeon would you operate on someone who may shoot you at any time should you make a mistake?"

"I don't suppose I would," admits I, while thinking that it really would have been safer to have had the Police Surgeon extract the thorns.

"That's that settled then," she grins all oddly. "Sit down and relax while I prepare the operating theatre. If anyone knocks on the door do not open it."

"Why not?"

"Because you are nude below the waist."

"What if it's your mother?"

"Then you had better hope she doesn't notice."

Ten minutes later I am laying on my front with only a thin sheet between my private bits and the kitchen table. Betty has bathed my cheeks with iodine and laid out her instruments of torture: one pair of tweezers with very sharp points; one pair with blunt points; one fine needle; and one long thick one in case she has to dig deep.

"White. I mean, right," slurs she with all the sternness of a hospital matron. "Grit your thief… teeth, I am about to extract the first thorn."

I grit my teeth fully aware that I am soberer now than I have ever been before.

"Have you gritted your teeth, Detective Inspector?"

Trying to stare up at her I give her the admonishing eye, "I had until you forced me to reply that yes, I had gritted my teeth."

"Well they're not gritted now because you are talking."

"What else could I have done?"

"In future, should I ask a question, just nod or hold up your hand."

"What if I wish to answer no?"

"Don't, comp… comp… makes things difficult, Detective Inspector. Would you like a chunk of wood or a bone to bite on?"

"No thank you I'm not that hungry. Just get on with it and cut out the chattering."

Betty pulls out the first one which has me wincing and tightening up my buttocks.

She puts her scotch scented breath to my nose, "How did that feel, Detective Inspector?"

I nod and hold up a hand.

"Good," laughs she. "Here we go for number two. It appears to be deeply embedded. You shouldn't have sat down so much it has exasperated the problem."

I yell at her under my breath, 'Well I couldn't stand up all bloody day, now could I?'

"I'll have to go in with the fat needle first," says she sounding suitably pleased. "Brace yourself."

There is pain and there is pain but I swear having a long fat needle jabbed right into you buttocks by a drunk, scores very high on the torture league.

At last it is over, by which time I am so stressed and exhausted the only place for me is my bed, sleep and freedom from nightmares of monstrous goblins stabbing at my buttocks with giant spikes.

As the first rays of sunlight filter through the curtains I am aware that the skin on my buttocks feels as if it's on fire. Other than that I am feeling rested but very hungry. I can hear Betty clattering about downstairs but can't smell any bacon being fried. A few minutes later she brings in tea and biscuits, sets them down on the bedside cabinet on her side and asks, as she gets back into bed, "How do you feel, Detective Inspector?"

"Marvellous," grates I. "Even better once I've had a good breakfast."

"Would you care for a starter?"

"I may have to pass on that for now," grins I.

"So, tell me all, Detective Inspector."

And I do, leaving nothing out I relate all that happened the day before. Betty's fury towards whoever was behind the murder of Patrick O'Connor is so vehement I have no doubt that if she could get her hands on whoever was responsible she would strangle them with her apron cord.

Once tea and biscuits are over Betty gets dressed and goes down to cook me a hearty breakfast while I get ready. Taking a look in the mirror reveals several patches of dressings over my buttocks, peeling one back exposes a slightly scabby looking spot that isn't anywhere near as inflamed as I thought it might be. I am on the mend.

By eight o'clock I step into Clump's office to find him sound asleep with his shoeless smelly feet up on the desk. There is an empty bottle of scotch on the desk with several cigar butts dumped into it. The place reeks of stale tobacco, alcohol and unwashed bodies. Clump half opens bloodshot eyes, absently brushes off a dead bluebottle from his beard and lets out a long yawn.

"Ah, Inspector," sighs he swinging his legs down and sitting up. "Be a gent and get someone to bring me a pot of coffee."

"You didn't go home last night then, sir?"

"Too busy. How's the backside?"

"On the mend, sir. I'll see about the coffee.

"Do I need this?" says Clump ten minutes later as grimacing he sips at his second mug of coffee.

"You did ask for it sir."

"Didn't I just. I have a tongue that tastes like a camel's armpit, Inspector. I am in dire need of a good soak in a tub followed by a hearty breakfast. While I do all that take yourself down to the morgue, Dr Shelley wishes to speak to you."

"He's in early."

"To his credit he was in with the dawn chorus. Anyway, get down there he has an exciting idea that he wishes to put to you for your perusal. He wouldn't tell me so I suspect it concerns stupid fingerprints and will be an utter waste of time."

I find the good Doctor sitting on one of the mortuary slabs enjoying a cup of tea. The place is spotless with no bodies out or gory bits lying about. We exchange the usual greetings and small talk before he pitches me with his 'idea'. In my eyes it is pure genius and I instantly agree to it. All we need is for Head to join us so that we can formulate a plan of action and then get to it.

Shortly after seeing Dr Shelley I am back in Clump's office to find Head has arrived and is talking to Clump.

"Take a seat, Inspector," says Clump. "I forestalled getting myself presentable in order to hear what Sergeant Head has to say," he waves an 'over to you' hand towards Head.

"How are you, Sergeant?" asks I noting that he does in fact appear to be fine.

"Fine, sir. In fact, I feel like I've just come out of hibernation."

"Just like a little dormouse," smiles Clump. "Get on with it, Sergeant."

"Right. Well I arrived at Waunepcy's place yesterday morning at nine. Waunepcy was pricing up items on his counter and as usual didn't look pleased to see me. I told him I was after answers and he had better start opening his mouth or he'd get my size elevens inserted up his rear end. Anyway, whilst I was grilling him I heard a noise coming from upstairs and demanded to know who was up there. It was Sadie Calver who, according to Waunepcy, doesn't go off to work until around lunchtime which set the brain box into gear. I went upstairs to question her before I carried on questioning Waunepcy."

"I'll bet she was surprised out of her drawers when you walked in," grins Clump.

"She was indeed, sir as she was sat on the potty with her nightie up around her knees."

"Lovely," laughs Clump.

"Anyway, I looked away while she finished peeing while moaning that I could have knocked first."

"You should have at least knocked," says I.

"The door was open…"

"Get on with it," grates Clump.

"Right, sir. Sadie pushed the potty under the bed, sat down on the bed and began to nervously wring her hands. Pulling over a chair I asked her what time she started work. She said about twelve. I asked did she always start at that time? She said yes. I asked her how often she stayed overnight at the pub and she replied never. I then asked her what she was doing there so early in the morning on the day Bert Dunn was done in and she replied she wasn't there."

"Meaning she had lied about being in bed with Sparks and Jenny, just as we suspected," puts in I. "She has blown Sparks' alibi out the window."

"Exactly. She started to cry and while shaking with fear she began to relate how she had been forced to lie by Sparks. Just then Waunepcy came creaking up the stairs carrying a tray with a bottle of brandy and two glasses on it. He said he knew Sadie would be in need of a fortifier and of course he knew I wouldn't refuse a tot or two. He poured me a glass and handed it to me and did the same for Sadie and then he went back downstairs. Sadie said cheers and we drank. Suddenly the room starting spinning around and I felt really odd. The next thing I knew I woke up in my own bed."

"Excellent work, Sergeant," beams Clump pushing back his chair and standing up. "The Inspector can fill you in on where we are at, while I go and get cleaned up and filled up."

It takes me two hours to bring Head up to date with everything that has happened since we were last together. The robbery and murders at the Soanes' household both intrigue and horrify him in equal measures. We end our session when Dr Shelley steps into my office to announce that he is ready. Head and I don our hats and jackets, holster our revolvers and the three of us set off in a hackney for the Neck Breakers Arms.

"Do you have everything you need, Doctor?" asks I.

He taps his brown leather bag perched on his lap, "Everything is in here," he grins.

"Excellent. Shall we go through it all again or are you both happy you know what to do."

They nod in unison.

"Then let us pray for the success of our mission."

The doors and windows to the Neck Breakers are open to allow air to filter in and create a draught. It is unusually hot for the time of the year, much more midsummer than midspring. Stepping into the bar we find it is quiet; just a pair of old men picking their noses and sipping tankards of cider in one corner and three off duty aged prostitutes conversing over gins while scratching at their crabs. Jacob Sparks is leaning over his bar looking suitably bored. His eyes light up on seeing the three of us come in and he straightens himself up while a condescending smirk plays on his lips. We go up to the bar.

"Good afternoon, gentlemen," smiles Sparks. "Twice in one week? You just can't keep away, can you?"

"It's the quality of your ale, landlord," smiles I. "Plus we need to ask you a few more questions."

He glares into my eyes trying to intimidate me before fixing them on Shelley. "You don't look much like a copper."

"That is because I am a doctor."

"Do you also wish to question me?"

Shelley shakes his head, "No indeed not, sir. All I wish for is a nice cool pint of best bitter. I shall go and sit by a window. Perhaps Sergeant Head, you might bring my drink over to me?"

"As you wish, Doctor," smiles Head as Shelley walks away.

"One pint of best bitter coming up," says Sparks as he reaches for a pint glass.

"Make that three please, landlord," says I.

"Three pints it is," smiles he, but his eyes do not smile.

The man is suspicious of us and obviously his brain is ticking over wondering what we are about. Head and I casually watch as the beer is pumped into the glasses while taking note of exactly where the landlord's left hand wrapped itself around each glass. Head picks up one of the glasses and carries it over to Shelley while I pay the bill.

"So, what do you want to know, Inspector?"

"Sadie Calver has disappeared. Do you have any idea where she might be?"

He shrugs, "None at all. What makes you think she's disappeared?"

"I don't think. I know. Any idea why she has disappeared?"

"None at all. She didn't turn up yesterday but was fine the day before and didn't appear to have any troubles about anything. My staff can always come to me if they have a problem, and as you know, Sadie and I are on particularly good terms. If something was bothering her she would have confided in me."

"So, she didn't turn up for work today either?"

"Obviously not or she'd be here, wouldn't she?"

"No need for sarcasm," grates I, meeting the landlord's eyes with rigid scrutiny.

"I apologise. Now, is that it, Inspector?"

"No, sir. Bray Waunepcy, Sadie's landlord has also gone missing."

"Perhaps they've eloped together."

"Perhaps. How well do you know Waunepcy?"

"I don't. I know of him. Well, who doesn't this side of the Thames?"

"So, you have no idea where he or Sadie may have got to?"

He shakes his head impatiently. "Didn't I just say as much?"

"You did indeed."

"Anything else?"

"Sally Dunn. Have you any idea where she is? Has she contacted you in any way?"

"It's a no to both questions," snaps he. "I take it this is about the murder of Sally's useless old man but what the hell you think it has got to do with me I have no idea. She may have slept with me and worked for me and Bert came in here fairly often but that is a far as my relationship with the pair of them went."

Head comes back to the bar, takes our pints and heads back to where Shelley is sitting.

"I take it you have read all about the murder at Billy Star's circus?"

"Indeed, I have. A dreadful act of unrivalled brutality, Inspector. If you want my opinion, I'd say whoever was behind it is so dangerous you and your Sergeant had best tread very cautiously during your investigations. Not just for your sakes but for your families also."

"Thank you for the advice, landlord," says I as a shiver runs up my spine. "You are aware that Billy Dunn, Sally's brother was almost certainly the intended victim and not Patrick O'Connor?"

"It didn't mention it in the papers," replies he casually. "If you want my opinion, Inspector I'd say whoever was behind the explosion intended to kill off all seven of the dwarfs not just one of them. I mean it's simple logic, the killer couldn't cherry pick his victim, going about it the way he did, so he decided that success would be more likely if he set out to kill the lot."

"My thoughts exactly," smiles I wanly. "Well, thank you for your time, landlord. If you hear anything please let me know."

"I'll keep my ears and eyes open, Inspector. But like I say, do be careful?"

I throw him a weak smile before joining Head and Shelley. Glancing behind me I spy the landlord going over to talk to the prostitutes, one of which promptly gets up and walks out.

"Any luck, Doctor?" whispers I leaning towards Shelley.

"I have an excellent print of the man's left thumb which I have no doubt will match the one Parker took."

"Absolutely wonderful," grins Head. "Did you notice, sir that Sparks had a nasty scratch in the palm of his right hand. A recent one at that."

"It is all coming together, Sergeant. All we need is for Clump to sanction a raid on this place and who knows we may find a pair of Sparks' boots whose soles match Parker's plaster casts."

"We may, indeed," smiles Shelley. "And if we are even luckier we may find a pair of tweed trousers with a tear in them somewhere around the seat."

Taking a long drink of my beer I ponder over how I am going to tell Head that Sparks has more or less just threatened not only us but our ladies also. Telling him right now might see him go for Sparks, thus ruining any chances of us remaining on the case. Having said that it would at least ensure Sparks would then subsequently leave us be. The man is seriously demented and without a shred of remorse for what he has done. This is a man who would kill his own mother if she put too much sugar in his tea. To my horror five noisy dockers suddenly come into the bar, pausing they glare over at us. No doubt Sparks sent the prostitute to summon them. "Drink up gentlemen it is time we left," orders I.

Heading back in a hackney I spy Andy walking along with another urchin. Having not seen him since the carnage at the circus I am relieved to see that he is alright. Shouting out to the driver to pull over I jump out to talk to him. "Andy, how are you?"

"Good boss. 'Ow are you?"

"Good. Have you found out anything yet?"

He shakes his head, "Sorry boss no one's 'eard nuffin'"

"Have you heard of a character known as 'Sticks'?"

"Yeah, I 'ave. Right greasy turd. Petty thief an' con man. Thinks 'es the bee's knockers."

"Knees."

"Knees. Knockers, what's the difference?"

"Probably none at your age. Do you know where this 'Sticks' lives?"

"No. But I can find out easy enough I reckon."

"When you do, come and tell me immediately no matter what the time of day or night."

He nods his compliance and fishing out a half crown I hand it to him.

"Cor, lovely. Thanks boss."

The other urchin jumps forwards, "'Ere mister, I could do wiv bein' ya snout. I'm good at snoutin', ain't I Andy?"

"Nick's good at snoutin' boss."

"Sorry lads I'm up to capacity with snouts."

"But I needs the dosh now, me ol' woman's up the puddin'," pleads Nick.

I am aghast, "How old are you, six?"

"Nah, I'm twelve I am, I think. Just a bit small for me age."

I hardly dare ask, "And how old is your 'misses'?"

He shrugs, "I dunno, 'bout thirty I think."

"Thirty! She's easily old enough to be your mother. She could go to prison for doing it with someone as young as you."

"Cor, really? That ain't fair she was only doin' what I asked 'er ta do."

"Whatever," sighs I. "Look son if I need any new snouts I'll keep you in mind. Now listen in. We are also looking for a Sadie Calver. A Bray Waunepcy and a Billy Dunn…"

"The short bloke from the circus?"

"Yes, one of the seven dwarfs. All of these missing persons will be in tonight's evening press. Sally and Billy Dunn's images will come from photographs. Bray Waunepcy's also, but from prison mug shots. Sticks' and Sadie Calver's will be from an artist's impression. Once the masses see the reward on offer for information we are going to be flooded with possible sightings…"

"'Ow much reward?" cuts in Andy.

"Five pounds."

"Five fuckin' pounds!" gasps Nick wide-eyed. "Cor if I 'ad five pounds I'd buy me ol' woman a bed ta 'ave the baby in."

"Doesn't she have a bed?"

"Nah, we don't 'ave no bed but we got a few sacks ta kip down on. They're alright but they make ya bum itch too much. Cor, yeah, a real bed would be like 'eaven I reckon."

His eyes go all dreamy and, call me a big softy, but I just can't help myself. Fishing out a ten shilling note I hand it to Andy. "Take this in lieu of the reward I hope you and Nick will be receiving between you. Buy him and his 'misses' a bed and a few things for the approaching baby."

Andy gazes up at me with eyes that say it all and I have to swallow a big lump of emotional pie as Nick starts to cry. At this point I need to get away fast before I really lose the plot and ask Nick if his 'misses' would like to move in with me and Betty until she has had the baby. On top of that I know I cannot keep chucking money around like confetti unless I can find a way to swell my own coffers. An idea springs to mind. "Andy, does your mate still have a key to the outside cellar door of the Neck Breakers Arms?"

He gives me a questioning look, "He does."

"Good. Get him to get a copy cut. They'll be a shilling in it for his troubles."

"'E won't like it if ya goin' in ta steal booze he intends ta steal."

"Vouch for me Andy, I won't be treading on his toes, trust me."

"I trust ya boss," smiles he.

"Good. Now piss off the pair of you before I arrest you for emotionally blackmailing a police officer."

Back at the Yard we hurry to Shelley's office where to our joy he matches Sparks' thumbprint from the glass to the one from the cannon.

"We have the bastard," growls Head.

"But we will still require more if we are to nail him," says I. "We must get Clump to agree to a raid on The Neck Breakers. And we desperately need to find our missing persons, and see if Mick has turned up anything."

We head to Clump's office where we find him, for once, chatting amiably to Mick.

"Good news men. O'Reilly, tell them what you have found out."

Shelley takes the only other seat leaving me and Head to stand.

"After visiting several companies, I eventually went to a Morton and Sons, licenced to sell explosives, so I did. Recently they had sold four small bottles of nitro to a legitimate demolition firm called Bombs and Roses. I went ta see the boss, a Mr Rose, who told me, after a few smacks, that he'd been blackmailed into securing the nitro for a Mr Smith? He described Smith as a big muscular bald-headed man with a lot of tattoos on his arms."

"Sparks?"

"To be sure. Now here's the rub, I reckon Sparks used two maybe three bottles of nitro at most ta blow the cannon."

"Meaning he still has at least one more bottle," puts in Clump.

"Exactly," says Mick. "That means our man is still one dangerous bastard."

"What did Sparks have on this Mr Rose?" asks Head.

"Nothin'. He just threatened to kill Rose's wife and kids if he didn't get what he wanted. He also said he'd come back if Rose opened his mouth to anyone, hence the reason I had to slap the man about a little. Anyway, I told him to take himself an' his family away for a while until this is all over."

"You have done well, O'Reilly," says Clump.

"Does this mean you're warming to me Irish charm at last?"

"No. How did you three get on with your bloody fingerprints?" frowns Clump to Shelley.

Shelley tells him about our match and our desire to organise a raid on The Neck Breakers. I go on to confirm just how dangerous Sparks is by relating how the maniac dared to threaten me, Head and our families. Clump listens in silence. You can see the fury in his eyes as he takes his time digesting all he's heard. At last he says, "The thumbprint will be inadmissible in court; therefore, I won't be able to get a search warrant on that alone." Mick attempts to butt in only to be prevented by Clump raising a 'wait a minute' hand.

"Mick has done well but the way he went about it wouldn't go down well in court. In fact, it's likely his findings will be quickly thrown out on the grounds of coercion. The other options are to raid the place and say to hell with procedures and suffer the consequences, or come up with something more solid to ensure a fully sanctioned raid. We need to find our missing persons, especially Sadie Calver, Sally and Billy Dunn, and get them talking. Meanwhile I suggest you all keep calm, keep digging for information and keep away from Sparks. Do not antagonise the man any further, you and your loved ones' safety is of the utmost priority. Trust me when I say, Sparks has friends in very high places and an awful number of nasty friends in very low places. To ensure there is no backlash from Sparks' cronies and cutthroats we must have the full weight of the law on our side. We will nail the bastard but for now we must be patient."

Of course, we all know he is right. Feeling deflated we leave Clump in peace and the four of us head off to the canteen for a bite to eat. Mick orders a double late breakfast while somehow charming the waitress into throwing in a huge steak usually reserved only for the higher ranks. Shelley settles for sausage and mash while Head and I opt for steak and kidney pies with mash and gravy. As we eat we go over everything we know between us while planning our next course of action. Mick comes up with a plan.

"All we have ta do is tell Shaun O'Connor that Sparks is his man and let him take over the investigation."

"Shaun won't investigate Sparks, he'll just kill him," says I.

"Exactly," grins Mick. "Job done."

"The trouble is Mick, it might not be Sparks laying on the mortuary slab but Shaun's entire family. How would you feel then?"

Chucking down his third cup of coffee in one go, Mick fixes me with a sombre look, "You're right, to be sure, Jerry me ol' darlin'. I'd feel real bad. But I'll tell ya this if it comes to it I'll kill that bastard meself, so I will."

"For now, I suggest we do as Clump has instructed us. We'll keep digging and keep away from Sparks and see what turns up once tonight's papers hit the streets."

Over the following five days, before it died down, half the police force in London was run ragged following up on possible leads and sightings of our missing persons, all to no avail. Head and I went through the Soanes case again along with several more unsolved burglaries committed around the same time, and achieved nothing. A return visit to Billy Star's circus, which is in the process of being taken over by Bassett's circus, revealed nothing new. Endless door to door enquiries around Cow Lane turned out to be a complete waste of time. By now Mick had been paid off, content to get back to his new lady but keen to rejoin us for the 'kill' should it ever materialise. Meanwhile the local plods who patrol around the docks area report back that The Neck Breakers Arms is carrying on in much the same fashion as always. Andy and Nick fail to unearth anything of worth and I am beginning to believe they are too terrified of Sparks to dig too deep. My plan of a clandestine raid on The Neck Breakers Arms to swell my coffers is shelved indefinitely as being far too dangerous. Despair seeps into my heart leaving me feeling as if my talents for catching criminals are seriously on the wane. But at least my buttocks have fully healed.

The breakthrough comes six days later when Andy and Nick turn up at my house, just as I am getting into bed, to announce they have found 'Sticks' and he is willing to meet me and may reveal where Sally and Billy Dunn are hiding out, providing the 'reward' is agreeable. 'Sticks' has requested I meet him the following evening at the Stuffed Monkey Inn over Brixton way. I hand Andy and Nick a half-crown each and tell them not to mention our meeting to anyone else. At last we might be getting somewhere.

The following morning me and Head head to the Yard and have a meeting with Clump to discuss the current turn of events.

"The Stuffed Monkey," frowns he. "I remember it well from years back when I was plodding the beat around that area. Got its name back in the seventies when the landlord got so drunk, so the story goes, he stuffed his pet monkey, and I don't mean by taxidermy stuffed. Before the stuffing the inn was known as the

Whistle and Flute. The area is away from the posher parts of Brixton and is as rough as guts and twice as nasty. A virtual maze of narrow alleyways, mostly three to six storey tenements and in places so damn dark even in the daytime you'd think it was night. Dark and so dangerous even the penny prostitutes go around in pairs while carrying weapons. You will need to take at least four armed uniform with you Inspector. This 'Sticks' character may well be genuine but I would not take that chance, you could be heading straight into a trap. Should you and the Sergeant get topped down there we may never find your remains…"

"Why not?" asks Head.

"Because you will be butchered, minced up and turned into dog food."

"The trouble is, sir," says I. "If we show up in force this 'Sticks' character is likely to be scared off. Plus, an armed uniform presence may just antagonise the locals enough to start a riot."

Clump raises his hand. "Alright. You can take O'Reilly with you. Just make sure you keep him reined in."

"Shall I put a bridle on him, sir?" asks Head.

Clump's eyes narrow, "Sometimes, Sergeant. Sometimes. Right you have several hours until you're to meet up with this 'Sticks' so get yourselves down to Tower Bridge right now while the tide's out. We had a report a couple of hours ago, while you were no doubt still snoring and farting in your beds, of a man jumping to his death into the mud below. I sent Detective Sergeant Brownly and Detective Constable Carter down there to investigate and they sent back word that they now believe it wasn't suicide but murder, with the victim being no other than Bray Waunepcy." He raises questioning eyebrows as do I and Head. "They also said the body will have to be retrieved from the mud within the next two hours before the incoming tide covers it."

"We best get going then," says I.

An hour later Head and I alight the cab at Tower Bridge and make our way down the stone steps to the foreshore where three plods and the two detectives are waiting. A small gang of mudlarks are sat back against the embankment idly watching, along with a mixed group of rag-bag adults. Thirty or more feet out I can clearly see a pair of feet attached to a pair of legs sticking up out of the mud from the knees up, the rest of the 'body' presumably being buried in the mud. The foreshore is solid for the first ten feet and we step up to the detectives to exchange pleasantries.

D. S. Brownly starts to fill me in on what he has found out thus far, "We have a witness who saw the victim thrown off the bridge around six o'clock this morning. The victim's name is Bray Waunepcy."

"How do you know the victim is Bray Waunepcy?"

"Our witness was crossing the bridge at the time and passed by the victim while recognising him as one Bray Waunepcy. He said he spoke to him but Waunepcy was miles away."

"If he was miles away how could he have been on the bridge at the same time?" asks Head.

"I don't understand the question?" muses Brownly.

"Sergeant Head is having a joke, Sergeant. Ignore him and please continue."

"Anyway, the witness kept walking but something made him look behind him where he saw a hansom carriage pull up beside Waunepcy. Two 'big men' jumped out, grabbed Waunepcy by the arms, lifted him up in the air and then hurled him screaming off the bridge. The witness then looked over the side to see the victim wildly flapping his arms in an attempt to fly. Course he didn't fly and hit the mud head first and went in up to his bum before sinking slowly to his knees, where thankfully he hasn't sunk any further since. Intent on finding a policeman to report what he had seen, the witness hurried on but as he neared the end of the bridge he heard the sound of horses' hooves coming closer and closer and realising the danger he was in, shinned up a girder hoping to escape but the hansom came to a stop, the men jumped out and began firing pistols at him."

"Not bullets then?" asks Head.

"Enough of the frivolities, Sergeant," remonstrates I. "Sergeant Brownly, please continue while ignoring my Sergeant."

"Right, sir. Anyway, the witness managed to evade being hit," he pauses to glare at Head, "by bullets or pistols, then the men jumped back into the hansom and fled."

"Can we speak to the witness?"

Brownly shakes his head, "After climbing down from the girder the witness bumped into a uniformed policeman at the end of the bridge. The witness told him in a trembling voice what he had seen, but before the officer could get the lad's details he ran off."

"Did he give descriptions of the two men?"

Brownly refers to his notebook and reads verbatim: "They was big bastards, one 'ad on a floppy felt 'at, the other a flat 'at. The floppy 'atted one 'ad 'is shirt sleeves rolled up, he 'ad a lot of tattoos. When he was throwin' ol' smelly off the bridge 'is 'at fell off an' he was bald." Closing his notebook, Brownly slips it into his jacket pocket. "That's it."

"Sounds like our main suspect, sir," comments Head.

"You know who the killer is?" asks Brownly.

"We have our suspicions but no iron proof as yet," says I. "Our suspect may have committed other murders, two of which go back several years."

"Interesting," muses Brownly. "Are we to hand this investigation over to you, sir?"

"Not fully. I'd appreciate your help, Sergeant. Question the mudlarks, see if they can put a name to the witness or can add anything to his account of events."

"Very good, sir."

"The floppy hat that fell off one of the killers, did you retrieve it?"

"I sent a pair of uniform up onto the bridge to look for, but to no avail."

"Um…" ums I. "Have you sent for forensics?"

"We have. They should be here shortly with duckboards so we can get safely out to the victim and pull him in."

"That being the case there is nothing we can do for now so let us question the mudlarks and the other bystanders."

"We spend several minutes questioning the mudlarks first, they were all out searching for 'treasures' left behind by the receding tide since first light and naturally had their heads down, but all of them heard the victim's ear-splitting scream and looked up to see Waunepcy fall and hit the mud with a loud plopping sound before he was swallowed up to leave only his legs sticking up. Not one would reveal the name of the witness or where he lives despite Head's threats of ringers around their lugs or my attempts to bribe them.

Forensics turn up with Blake the photographer and Dr Shelley. We exchange greetings before Blake sets himself up and starts taking photographs. The plods lay out the duckboards with the lightest of them ordered out to tie ropes around the victim's ankles so he might be dragged back over the boards. With a chorus of 'Pull me lucky lads' the victim is slowly but surely pulled from the mud and quickly reeled in on his back like a giant flounder. Covered in mud though he is, I confirm, the victim is indeed Bray Waunepcy. A couple of buckets of water are thrown over the body to wash away the worst of the foul smelling mud.

"At least he's free of fleas at last," grins Head.

Stepping forward a mudlark shouts out while pointing at the body's crotch area, "Look at that. 'Ees got a stiffy on an' it's movin'."

"Christ," gasps another. "Didn't know you could get a stiffy on after death. Perhaps he ain't dead yet!"

"He ain't dead! He ain't dead!" yells another so loudly it echoes half way across the Thames. "An' 'is thing's on the move!"

Horror etches their faces as they back away staring wide-eyed while pointing at the moving monster in Waunepcy's trousers.

"What the devil?" demands Shelley appearing as horrified as most everyone else appears to be.

"It's only a bleedin' eel," scoffs one of the plods, as at last the slimy creature's head pokes out of the bottom of Waunepcy's trousers before the rest of it slithers out and wiggles away over the mud towards the water.

"Thank Christ for that," sighs an old trollop who'd sidled up close to me. She fixes me with watery eyes. "Cor, I couldn't bear washing a dead man's body only ta see it get a stiffy on."

"I ain't never goin' ta eat jellied eels ever agin', says another old dear. "You don't know where they've been."

"Thank you, ladies for your pearls of wisdom," grates I. "Now bugger off back to the wall so we can get on." I wave my arms up in the air. "All of you get well back or clear off."

"Let us get to it," says Shelley bobbing down beside the body and opening his bag.

Leaving him to it I speak to Brownly, "Take as many men as you can muster, Sergeant. Have them question the street traders who would have been out when Waunepcy was making his way towards the bridge. See if any recall seeing him and from which direction he came. You may be able to retrace his footsteps and find out where he was staying. If by chance you do discover where he was staying, enter the place and search it. You may find one Sadie Calver hiding out there."

"Isn't she one of the missing persons we were instructed to look out for several days ago?"

"She is. If you find her escort her to the Yard and inform me immediately. Is that clear?"

"As glass, sir."

Leaving just one plod behind, Brownly gives the rest their orders and off they all go. There is nothing else for me and Head to do, so leaving forensics to it we head back to the Yard, calling in on the way at Mick's to request his help for later in the evening. He eagerly agrees to meet us at the Yard by eight o'clock.

"Another murder almost certainly committed by that bastard Sparks," grates Clump, when we finally report back to him in his office. "But still we do not have a single witness to take to trial or enough tangible evidence to arrest the suspect with. The man is walking on water, by God. Let us see if we can swing things more into our favour tonight. Meanwhile I suggest you send your partners away to a place of safety until this is all over."

"Already done, sir," says I. "They have both gone to stay with Betty's mother."

"Good. Well, gentlemen, we shall toast to your success tonight and then you can both bugger off for the rest of the day. Get some kip, you may well be up half the night."

The scotch and glasses come out, it is the good stuff and I'm thinking Clump has the same reservations about tonight's meeting with 'Sticks' as myself and Head. We could be heading into a trap and find ourselves in mortal danger.

After a couple of scotches each, Head and I head off to 'wardrobe' where we select suitable undercover attire for the night's venture.

On the way home, Head makes a surprise confession, "In case something goes horribly wrong tonight Gerald, I want you to know I am very sorry for how rude I was to you the other day."

"Apology accepted, Richard," smiles I.

We stop and face each other.

"But you don't know what I am about to apologise for."

"I can fathom a guess, Richard. Having reasoned you were in a troubled state of mind over something of obvious importance I racked my brains as to what it could be, and came up with the notion that you did not wish to upset me and subsequently acted in a rude defamatory way hoping for an argument to lessen the embarrassment to yourself. In short, I believe you have been struggling to inform me that Chloe is pregnant in case it upsets me and, particularly, Betty."

"Bloody hell, Gerald. So, you really do know everything about everything. How did you guess?"

"You have kept a tight rein on your spending of late and have often wandered off in your mind at times while not concentrating on the task in hand. All the actions of someone who is worried about their financial future. A child on the way means a wedding is also imminent. Correct?"

"Correct. That, along with the cost of baby things truly is very worrying. What savings we have won't stretch far and once Chloe gets too uncomfortable to continue her cleaning work we will quickly find ourselves financially buggered."

"Then we must do something about it, Richard. I too have found my finances somewhat stretched of late. We haven't picked up much in the way of 'rewards' lately and it's time we did. I have an idea but I have to put it to one side until we see how the band plays."

"Or even how the land lays."

"Exactly. One thing I must stress to you is do not worry about upsetting me or Betty about Chloe being pregnant. Betty will be thrilled for you both, trust me. And congratulations, Sergeant Head."

"Thank you, sir. Will you be my best man?"

"I would consider it an honour."

Walking on in silence we eventually reach my house where we shall wait until it is time to leave for the Stuffed Monkey.

Having been warm and sunny for several days by early evening thick rolling clouds cover the sky and the rising moon. The wind picks up and in the far distance you can just hear rumbles of thunder followed by cracking snaked lightning. All of which means that if it's coming our way, we are going to get very wet.

Mick turns up dead on eight o'clock wearing his steel enforced bowler and a long black raincoat that is bulging with God knows what beneath it. I just pray he hasn't got any dynamite with him. Head and I are sporting flat caps, long coats and workmen's boots. Beneath our coats we carry the usual array of weapons, but Head has left his sheaths behind as he no longer needs them now Chloe's pregnant.

I form a plan of sorts that is reliant on going to plan if it is to succeed. If things don't go to plan we shall have to think of a new plan really quickly or suffer the consequences. Mick thinks my plan sucks but he doesn't say what it sucks of or what the devil he is on about. He puts forwards his plan, which is the usual; brain everyone who gets in our way and kill everyone who looks even remotely threatening. Head admits to not having a plan except playing it by ear and running for it the second things look dodgy. We all agree that Head's plan is the best because it sounds less suicidal. With a half hour or so to go before we need to set off we decide to fortify ourselves by polishing off a bottle of brandy I'd been saving for a special occasion. The possibility of our imminent deaths is as good a special occasion as any.

Twenty minutes later Clump turns up in a paddy waggon with six armed uniformed officers and Superintendent Rant. We squash in the back and off we trot. We are to be dropped off at a local police station that's a quarter of a mile from the Stuffed Monkey Inn. Clump and the rest will remain at the station until ten-thirty where they will then make for the inn by which time it is hoped we would have met 'Sticks', taken the Dunns' under our armpits, and made it safely back to the inn ready to climb back on the waggon and head back to the Yard. Should we not be at the inn when Clump gets there, he will order his men into the slum area in search of us.

At nine-forty we are dropped off in a quiet little avenue and set off for the inn. The storm that threatened us earlier failed to come our way, the moon is out but is ringed by iridescent grey-green clouds which in turn are ringed by smoky-black clouds that appear to be going around in circles.

Head sees it as a bad omen, "Heaven is opening up ready to let us in," says he pessimistically. "We could be up there soon."

"We best say goodbye now then," grins Mick. "Cause sure as sure I'll not be heading upwards. I'd find it too bloody borin' anyway, what with all those harps, no boozers, no heads ta crack and no saucy women ta chase."

We walk on until the Stuffed Monkey comes into view beneath the wan light from a pair of gas lamps. As we cross a badly rutted road to the inn we start to appreciate the place is as rowdy as it sounded from across the street. There are several noisy villainous types outside drinking and smoking while mixing with some very rough looking prostitutes indeed. The language is beyond coarse while the physical interaction between one man and a woman, who's laid out on a rickety table with her skirts up above her knees and her legs wide open, verges on the absolute obscene, and is far too disgusting to relate to sensitive ears.

"Cor look at that, sir!" gasps Head. "That dirty bugger's got his head between her legs in full view of all and sundry. And she's groaning and wailing at the pleasure of it all."

"Some people have no shame, Sergeant, and I long for the day when such disgusting public displays of licentious behaviour will be frowned upon and the perpetrators will be so aggressively vilified by 'all and sundry' they will hang their heads in shame and subsequently join a religious order in an effort to atone for their sins, while taking vows of chastity and striving to rid the world of revolting male creatures who prey on vulnerable females forcing them to become nothing more than a toy for their perverted pleasures."

Mick is aghast, "Fucking hell, Jerry! That was one hell of a rendition, so it was. Can't ya not see the poor cow's givin' birth an' the only one sober enough ta 'elp her is me lad-o?"

I must admit I missed that bit. Moving on I notice the inn appears to be in a sorry state, at least on the outside. Timber framed, wattle and daub, most of the daub has long since fell off and lays where it fell years before. Several of the small windows in the walls are boarded up and what little paint still remains has peeled and faded to an unrecognisable colour. A group of thugs blocking the only entrance, part amiably as we approach, and I am beginning to realise that the locals couldn't care less who we are or why we are there.

Inside, the beamed ceiling is so low we have to duck to avoid brain damage. The place is packed with ne'er-do-wells, drinking, eating, gambling, shouting and swearing. The small bar is manned by a thick set, bushy-grey-bearded thug who gives us the evil eye as we approach. Beside him is a middle-aged very attractive dark-haired woman who's displaying half her voluptuous bosom which is barely held in decency by a strapless off the shoulder top that is perfectly see through. What amazes me is what on earth is holding her beauties up at her age, unless gravity itself has succumbed to her charms.

"By all that's bloody holy," gawps Mick. "Have you ever seen such a pair of beauties, Jerry me ol' darlin'? Cherries like cigar butts that I meself wouldn't mind drawing on if I weren't such a one-woman man."

"Let us remain focused," remonstrates I, trying not to stare at the barmaid's obvious pride and joys.

"Say what you will," says Head. "But nothing will keep a boozer freer from trouble than a beauty behind the bar. The trouble makers know if they start a ruckus the beauty buggers off and all they've got left to feast on is some ugly ol' git swinging a cudgel."

"You could be right, Sergeant, until that is, jealousy raises its ugly head. A barmaid has to be extremely good at hooking all of her customers into believing that she favours them above everyone else even if she can't abide any of them. Should she flirt with someone she fancies, while ignoring someone who is utterly transfixed by her charms then all hell can break loose."

"Good evening gentlemen," smiles the barmaid. "What would you like?"

We flick a glance at her big cherries, "Three pints of best bitter, luv," says I remembering to speak in local dialect.

"Three pints coming up," says she reaching for a glass while the barman gives us the evil eye before turning away to serve another customer. Mesmerised we watch the barmaid's assets swaying around as she pulls the pump and fills the glasses.

"'Aven't seen you fellas in here before," says she casually.

"Lady, if we'd have known you was pullin' pints in here, we'd have been in long ago," says Mick.

She throws back her head and laughs. She must have heard that one a hundred times before but obviously still relishes the compliment.

I pay the bill and ask, "Have you seen 'Sticks'?"

She appears mildly surprised by the question, "He's in the snug waiting for you. He said someone would come in looking for him, but you ain't one you're three."

"Is he alone?"

"Just him an' his mutt. I don't know you from Elsy, but whatever you're up to with him, take my advice, if it's to do with money he ain't to be trusted."

"Thank you for the warning," says I. Picking up our beers we head into the snug where we find it small, quiet and poorly lit with just a few chairs around a few square tables. There's a pair of old dears munching on bread and cheese and three nearly dead old men playing dominoes. Remembering Shaun's description, I see the man we are looking for is sat behind a table with his back against the wall, beside him sits a motley, scruffy black mutt busily scratching at its ears. We go over, grab a chair each and sit down opposite 'Sticks'. In a whisper I introduce us and then ask him what his real name is.

"Just call me 'Sticks'," says he, straightening up and meeting my steady gaze. "Thought you was comin' on ya own."

"You thought wrong. I am under the impression that you can lead us to Sally and Billy Dunn."

He takes a long drink of his beer before answering, "I can but I want the reward money up front. Three pounds, that's one for each of us."

"Us?"

"Yeah. It said in the rags they'd be a reward of one pound for information as to where each of the missin' persons are, an' I'm one of the missin' persons," says he, his eyes going all shifty. "I want the cash in advance or the deal's off".

"Fair enough," says I. Fishing out three pounds I hand them to him, he snatches the notes and shoves them in his waistcoat pocket.

"We best get goin' then," says he. Getting to his feet he is a good two inches taller than me. He leads the way outside and down the side of the inn, with the dog walking amiably by his side, before turning down a narrow passageway barely wide enough for two and quickens his pace.

"He's going to make a break for it," whispers Head.

I call out, "Stop a moment 'Sticks' I wish to talk to you."

Stopping he turns to face me, "What is it?"

Sticking my revolver under his nose I say, "You try and run and I'll shoot your legs away. Do you understand me?"

"I ain't got no thoughts of running. Trust me."

"Just slow the pace down a bit then."

With a shrug he turns and walks on. The passageway is dire, it stinks of damp, decay and animal faeces. What little light there is comes from a flickering gas lamp a good twenty yards ahead of us. A sudden crack of thunder makes us all jump, the lighting flash that follows briefly illuminates the passageway to expose eight-foot-high slimy green walls on both sides that are topped with broken glass.

"To be sure this is one spooky shit hole," hisses Mick stepping up alongside me. His sawn-off shot gun appears in his hand. "I got me a bad feeling about this, Jerry."

"As do I."

"And me," whispers Head who's bringing up the rear.

The walls come to an end and 'Sticks' turns left down an even narrower passageway where there is no light at all to help us see our way.

"Mind you don't trip in no holes," warns 'Sticks'.

It is difficult trying to define his outline as he blends into the darkness, while it is impossible to see the dog. If 'Sticks' runs for it now I'd probably lose sight of him before I can get a shot off. At last the passageway ends and we step out onto a road. Another flash of lighting exposes waste ground full of heaped up rubbish on one side, a sign that says 'unnamed' road and a row of unlit two-storey slum dwellings on the other side. In that moment I thought

I saw something, man size, skip across our path onto the waste ground.

"It's black as coal," hisses Head trying to push himself in between me and Mick.

"How much further, 'Sticks'?" calls out I.

"Just before the end of these 'ouses," calls back he.

The dog starts to growl and I can just make out he is directing his growling towards the waste ground.

"Sure, I am, the bastards settin' us up," hisses Mick. "There's someone out there."

"Well they won't start shooting at us as they'll be just as likely to shoot 'Sticks'. Keep your eyes peeled."

"I can't see bugger all anyway," grates Head.

The wind quite suddenly picks up, there comes a violent crack of thunder directly above our heads and then down it comes, blobs of rain as big as peas hammer onto us so loudly you can hear nothing else. We are drenched in seconds.

"In 'ere," yells 'Sticks'.

We find ourselves bundling into a narrow hallway that is lit by a single oil lamp on the wall. 'Sticks' slams the door shut and then bolts it leaving the dog outside. Bare rotting floor boards make crunching sounds as we follow 'Sticks' down the hall and into a tiny parlour that again is lit by a single oil lamp. The room boasts a tiny fireplace, mouldy distempered walls, a small table with two chairs and a tatty brown sofa. On that sofa sits a very surprised looking Sally Dunn beside her mouth-gaping brother Billy.

"You've stitched us up," cries Billy. "You rotten piece…"

"You have not been stitched up," snaps I taking off my bowler and shaking the rain from it. "If we can find you so can anyone and those anyones could be here right now slitting your throats instead of us not slitting your throats."

"I did it for ya own good," protests 'Sticks' holding out his hands. "You'll be safer with the coppers than hidin' out 'ere."

Sally gets to here feet, she is a very pretty little thing with soft eyes and tumbling golden locks. She looks so vulnerable and innocent my heart goes right out to her.

"Well ya could a fuckin' warned us you shit'ouse," snarls she. "Truth is ya could 'ave put us in even more danger by bringing this bunch a prat's down 'ere."

I decide that Sally may well appear angelic but beneath that outward appearance lies a common as muck mentality that is both nauseating and offensive to a gentleman such as I. "Madam, if you do not curb your foul tongue,

I shall shove my fist so far down your gob it'll come out of your bottom. Do I make myself clear?"

She immediately cracks up and starts to bawl, tears flood down her cheeks, she's shaking like a jelly on opium as a trickle of wee pools around her feet. The girl is terrified beyond belief and I realise that her disgusting language is born from that terror. Mick sorts it out by stepping forwards and giving her a slap instead of a cuddle. A slap from a normal person can hurt a bit, a slap from Mick is more akin to being hit with a brick and Sally is promptly knocked out cold.

"You hit my tart!" exclaims 'Sticks'.

"Sure, it was only a slap," pleads Mick.

"It was more than a slap," grates Head. "I'd say it was the equivalent to being kicked in the head by a demented bull."

"Now see you here me ol' darlin'," says Mick with deadly softness. "Ya can't go comparing me to no mad bull so you can't, unless you're willin' ta put ya money where ya fat mouth is."

Head's eyes glaze over. It isn't good and I realise as senior officer I need to retake control, calm everyone down and get us all back to the reality of the situation we are currently in. "Mr 'Sticks', do you have any whisky in this dump?"

Agog he stares at me, "No, but I've got some gin."

"That will suffice. Please fetch it along with six glasses. Have you any lemonade or similar to mix with it?"

He gives me a 'shouldn't you be in an asylum?' look "Got some ginger cordial."

"Marvellous," says I as he goes off. "Mick, get that bottle of scotch out and let's all have a few drinks."

"I was savin' that for later," moans he. "All for me little self."

"Greedy pig," grates Head.

"Sure, as a nun is not guaranteed ta be a virgin, you're not guaranteed to escape a good hidin', Sergeant Dick Head." warns Mick.

"Sure, as an Irish man is not guaranteed to be of any use in a brawl, you're not guaranteed to give me a good hiding, Mick the thick."

Well sometimes there is no other way to calm a potential violent situation than by being even more violent. I am not stupid enough to throw off my coat and roll up my sleeves as Mick and Head have, instead I take out my revolver and fire it into the ceiling, not once but twice for good effect. Head and Mick freeze on the spot. Billy cowers into the sofa while Sally doesn't do anything because she is still out cold.

"If you do not cease this stupidity I shall be forced to take drastic action," says I forcibly.

"What kind of drastic action?" demands Head.

"I will shoot you both in the legs."

"You just try it," warns Mick.

"Yeah," grates Head. "Try it and you are dead."

"You an' me should teach ol' Jerry pot a lesson," says Mick to Head.

"And a good one at that," spits Head.

Luckily, I am saved by Sally coming around, sitting up and groaning, "What happened?"

"You fell over an' bumped ya head," lies Mick.

"Sorry I was so rude to you. I'm just scared witless."

Billy goes over to her, helps her to her feet and over to the sofa. Everyone ignores the wee on the floor.

"Let's all have a drink," says I. "Where's that 'Sticks' got to?"

"You don't think he's made a run for it out the back?" says Head.

"He couldn't have," says Billy. "The only way out of this dump is via the front door or the windows. One down here and one upstairs."

"Sergeant, stay here and watch these two, Mick you come with me."

We are up the creaking stairs and into the front bedroom before you can blink. The room is lit by a single candle sat on a large packing case. 'Sticks' hasn't escaped through the window but is in fact lying prone on the floor with a bottle of gin in one hand and a bottle of ginger cordial in the other. There is a pool of blood on the bare boards.

Bobbing down I lift the tail of his frock coat.

"He's been shot in the arse, so he has," says Mick gazing down.

"He's been shot twice by the looks of it." Going over to the window I pull back the ragged curtains. It is still teeming down but the thunder and lightning have moved away. I fail to see anything clearly beyond a couple of feet but know someone is out there watching the house. But how the hell did they manage to shoot 'Sticks' if there's no bullet holes in the window pane? I meet Micks questioning eyes. "Someone or ones are out there waiting for us Mick and those someone or ones somehow managed to shoot poor old 'Sticks' in the bum without breaking the window."

Mick bobs down and sticks a finger into the floor boards, "I'm thinking Jerry me ol' mucker that you yourself shot the poor sod, these holes in the floor speak for themselves, so they do."

"How was I to know he was up here? I assumed he'd be in the kitchen…"

Suddenly Sally screams so loudly instant panic seizes me. We fly downstairs with weapons drawn. Perhaps I didn't shoot 'Sticks' and the real killer is actually in the house!

Billy has protective arms hugging Sally close to him while they both stare goggle-eyed up at the ceiling where blood has begun to drip through and plonk down onto the floor.

"What's going on, sir?" demands Head.

"Sorry everyone it appears that when I fired off a couple of shots into the ceiling the bullets went right through the boards and hit 'Sticks' in the bum."

"Is he dead?" gasps Billy.

"As a door knob," says Mick.

"Good," says Billy. "He deserved it for what he's done to my sister."

"What did he do?" asks I.

"Got her pregnant the rotten swine."

"But I loved him," weeps Sally. "What shall I do now?"

"Well he didn't love you, Sal' or he wouldn't have sold you out."

"Oh, it's all too much," wails she burying her head into Billy's chest.

"Never mind," says I soothingly. "Worse things happen in the Wild West. Sergeant nip upstairs and fetch the gin and ginger from 'Sticks' while I see if there's a bucket or something to catch the blood in. Going into what must be the tiniest kitchen ever built with its butler sink and nothing much else except for two buckets on the floor and a burning candle in a holder on the wall, I take a bucket into the parlour and set it down to catch the dripping blood. Head returns with the bottles and Mick takes out the bottle of scotch from inside his coat. It is time to try and relax until the rain eases. Taking off my coat and hat I hang them on a couple of nails in the front door alongside Head's and Mick's. Billy fetches whatever is available to drink out of; two chipped enamel mugs, one cracked wine glass and two wooden bowls.

"Gin and ginger or whisky and ginger?" asks I to Sally and Billy.

"Gin neat, please," sighs Sally.

"Scotch and ginger for me," says Billy.

"And me," says Head, as if we couldn't have guessed.

Mick does the honours and we settle down. Mick and I grab a chair while Head squashes up on the sofa beside Billy.

"Cheers," says I raising my wooden bowl. Cheers they chorus. "A toast to 'Sticks'. God rest his weary holes."

Several drinks later they all know I suspect the house is being watched and there might just be assassins out there waiting for us to leave. To ease the tension in the room I attempt casual conversation, "So, Sally, how far gone are you?"

"How should I bleedin' know?"

"Well you were there at the time, you must know?"

"Well I don't 'cause I don't know if it's his or that bastard Sparks."

"It weren't Sparks," says Billy with certainty.

"Well if it weren't him that messed about with me who was it?" demands she.

Confusion reigns. "Sally, can you tell us what happened between you and Sparks?"

She drops her gaze, "I could but I don't want to talk about in front of my brother."

"I must be honest here," says I. "If there are assassins out there waiting to get us, we may not all make it out of here alive. Chief Inspector Clump and his men will be looking for us by now, but in this weather in this rabbit warren he may not find us. That being the case I need to hear your and Billy's full confessions right now in front of everyone so that hopefully at least one of us will live to relate those confessions to the authorities, otherwise Sparks will escape justice, possibly for ever."

"Alright. Top up my glass first."

Mick tops up her glass.

"I cleaned for Sparks, cooked the meals and served them up when Sadie was off. I never did no servin' behind the bar 'cause I can't add up. Sparks was always nice to me an' never tried to get in me drawers. But he had a posh friend who used to come in a lot, ugly ol' git, all fat an' greasy with wandering 'ands. Anyway, Sparks kept tryin' to persuade me to be especially nice to the flatulent git but I kept refusin' saying I weren't that kind of girl. He got angry one day an' said it was important he keep this posh git happy an I'd best be nicer to him or I'd lose me job. I still refused, but one day Sparks asked me to join him in a drink to taste a new wine he was tryin'. Normally I don't drink durin' the day but I thought I'd best do what he wanted. So, I drunk a glass and the next thing I knew I woke up in his bed naked."

"The bastard," croaks Billy.

"Sure, the man's a monster," growls Mick.

"Please continue, Sally," says I.

She wipes a tear from her eye and takes a drink of her gin, "Cause I knew I'd been drugged an' then raped but there weren't nothin' I could do about it. But I could get revenge. I knew where Sparks kept the key to the safe in his bedroom so I got dressed and opened the safe. It was stuffed with notes wrapped in bank sleeves, jewellery in boxes and inside a velvet bag I found loads of little blue diamonds. I thought he won't miss a few, so I took five, put the bag back, locked the safe and put the key back. Then I went to the ol' man's 'cause I knew he was desperate for money as he'd got into debt with some real bad men. I gave him a diamond to get him interested and he agreed to rob Sparks' safe but knew he couldn't do it alone."

"So, he came to see me at the circus," puts in Billy. "But I wouldn't listen to his plan to rob Sparks. I lost my temper with him and he stormed off. I went around to his place of work to patch things up but all he was interested in was doin' over Sparks. I told him he was a fool to even think of crossing Sparks. Then I left thinking that was the end of it."

"Dad came to tell me he'd got a better idea," says Sally. "He told me that he knew Sparks had been in on the murders of two nobs some years back and he was goin' to blackmail Sparks over it."

"How did your father know Sparks was in on the murders?"

"I told him," sighs Billy. "After the robbery I was in a terrible state. I needed someone to talk to and as I was living with the ol' man at the time I told him in an attempt to unburden myself. I knew he'd keep quiet about it or I'd get done in by the gang for squealing."

"Dad went to see Sparks a couple of days later at the pub to blackmail him," cuts in Sally. "Sadie was there an' she overheard the conversation. Sparks just laughed at the ol' man and told him that there wasn't a shred of evidence linking him to any robbers, let alone murders anywhere, ever, and he could go to hell or he'd have him arrested for attempted blackmail. The ol' man was livid when he came to see me again and urged me to go see Billy and tell him what had happened to me so Billy would get angry and agree to help burgle the pub. But I couldn't say anything about the rape in front of 'Sticks' cause he'd have dumped me. I went to the ol' man's and told him I couldn't tell Billy what had happened to me. The ol' man went to see Billy at the circus and this time he came back with the biggest grin on his face and said, 'I got that bastard Sparks by the balls. Trust me daughter', he often called me daughter when he was in a good mood, 'He'll pay up, you mark my words'. He went back to the pub the next night but I don't know what happened between him an' Sparks. All I know is the next day he was dead."

"I know what happened," says Billy, guilt etched across his face. "The ol' man went for me the next time he came to see me at the circus. He said if I didn't help him rob the pub he'd tell the coppers I was in on the robbery at the Soanes' place. I told him it wouldn't work because I'd deny it and so would Sparks. He said what about the others in the gang? I told him the rest of the gang who were there at the time are all dead because you three," he points at me, Head and Mick, "blew them to smithereens some months back. Then the ol' man really went for it and tried to emotionally blackmail me, he said; 'How can you let that bastard go scot free knowing he'd not only raped that Soanes woman but had also raped your own sister?' I said he was wrong, there's no way Sparks would ever rape a woman. I wish I'd never have opened my mouth, if I'd have kept it shut none of this would have happened. See, I knew Sparks trusted me never to tell about what happened at the Soanes' and I proved it by going to prison and not saying anything. That's why they let me leave the gang and go into the circus. There's very few people who knows about Sparks' best kept secret, I'm one of them, so I know that if it got out he'd blame me and come for me." He takes hold of Sally's hand and squeezes it tightly. "It wasn't Sparks who raped you, Sally, though I've no doubt he set you up to be raped by one of his posh cronies. You see, the truth is; Sparks doesn't like the girls he likes the boys, but he's always been terrified of being found out. I made the mistake of blurting that fact out to the ol' man and I have no doubt he went to see Sparks to try a new line of blackmail that sealed his fate along with anyone else Sparks thought may now know his secret."

"You're saying that Bert Dunn, Patrick O'Connor and Bray Waunepcy's murders were down to the fact that Sparks was so obsessed about keeping his sexuality a secret he was, is, prepared to commit the vilest of crimes and kill anyone regardless." Billy nods. "That being so I have no doubt the man is out there now waiting to kill us all."

Head had been taking notes, pausing he asks, Sally, "Do you know where Sadie is?"

"No. Just after I gave Waunepcy a diamond to cover the rent I owed he went out and I knew he was going to see Sparks so I got me things together an' fled, stealing back me diamond as I went. I left a message in the room for Sadie to find saying come and see me. Sadie knew where I'd be because she'd been around here before. She turned up after you came to see her wanting me to know she was alright. She told me Waunepcy drugged you, Sergeant after overhearing her recant on giving Sparks an alibi for me Dad's murder. She was in dire danger and Waunepcy told her she'd best go with him to a secret place he'd got. He was sweet on Sadie an' didn't want her to get hurt. That's all I know."

I can see by the look on Head's face he believes that Sadie's body will turn up eventually. For myself I'm not so sure. Waunepcy was a slippery eel and no fool. He would have ensured his 'secret place' was exactly that. But how did Sparks and his accomplice know that Waunepcy would be on Tower Bridge at that particular time? Perhaps it was merely coincidence, either way it is very likely we shall never know.

Mick says softly, "The rain is easing off."

"Ah…" ahs I. "Let's you and I go upstairs and see if we can see anything."

We go upstairs, Mick blows out the candle and stepping over 'Sticks' goes to the window. After tripping over 'Sticks' I join him.

"Don't show ya face too close to the window," warns Mick. "If they're out there they might take a pot shot at ya."

"Movement, Mick. I saw something move over by that pile of rubbish on the right. Do you see it?"

"They're out there, Jerry me ol' darlin'. Three of them I reckon. But I can't make out anything more than just shadowy shapes. They could be anyone and nothing to do with Sparks."

"It's Sparks alright. 'Sticks' set us up for money. Money from Sparks, plus the reward money from the force. How do we play this?"

"Let's ask Dick."

"Good idea." Mick turns away for the stairs while I go through 'Sticks' pockets to retrieve my three pounds, on top of that I find a five-pound note as well, no doubt the blood money he'd received from Sparks. I decide it's a good job I accidently shot 'Sticks' dead because I saved him from being murdered, Sparks would never have let him walk away knowing what he knew. I go downstairs. The blood is still dripping down into the bucket. Sally and Billy still appear terrified and are as white as sheets. Head has dropped off and is happily snoring away.

"What next?" asks Billy.

"On reflection I think it best we stay here until daylight. Perhaps the Chief will have found us by then. Whatever, at least we will be able to see what's out there before we make a move. Failing that I need a pee. Where's your privy?"

"Across the road behind the rubbish," says Sally.

"What! Your privy is across the road behind the rubbish?"

"That's what I said."

"Why didn't you tell us this before."

"You never asked."

"And I take it, it is a communal privy between yourselves and the rest of the houses?"

"It is. Is that important?"

"Well now," says Mick. "I'd say we've been seeing shadows skipping around the place an' thinkin' they're the shadows of assassins when it's more likely, so it is, they're the shadows of people going for a crap, or whatever."

"Exactly," frowns I. Waking Head up I tell him we are leaving.

"Is that wise, sir," yawns he. "What if there are killers out there?"

"There won't be, trust me. However, let us err on the side of caution. Mick can you go get 'Sticks' down here we may need his help."

"How much help can a dead man give?" queries Head.

"You'll see. Let us get to it."

Mick goes upstairs to fetch 'Sticks'. A few seconds later there comes the thump, thump, thump sound of a body being thrown down the stairs. Mick then reappears dragging 'Sticks' in by his feet.

"Where do you want the bugger?" asks he as Sally passes out.

"By the front door please."

Mick drags 'Sticks' over to the front door, "What now?"

"We shall use him as a human shield. When I open the door you and the Sergeant will step out into the road while holding 'Sticks' up in front of you. If anyone should start shooting, hopefully 'Sparks' will take most of the bullets enabling you both to dart back inside unharmed. What do you think?"

"It stinks," grates Head. "Me and Mick could still get shot full of holes. Why don't I open the door while you and Mick go out?"

"I've a better idea, so I have," says Mick. "Why don't we get the little fella ta shove the body out. As he's so little there'll be less chance of him getting hit."

"He is under our protection, Mick. Therefore, we must do everything we can to protect him and his sister. Sergeant you can open the door and Mick and I will charge out with the body."

"What about them two?"

Billy has got Sally to her feet and is comforting her; their eyes are vacant and I realise they are in such shock they can't be relied upon to do anything correctly unless we guide them piecemeal. "Once we are outside and assured there are no assassins we shall bring them out and escort them away from the area. Is that clear?"

"As diarrhoea," groans Head.

"Good. Billy, you and Sally will remain inside until we say so while keeping away from the door and the window. Once we are assured it is safe we shall take you out. Is that all clear to you?"

"Yes. But what if you all get shot dead? What will happen to us?"

"You'll be fucked, so you will," says Mick.

"Right men, coats and hats on, check your weapons and we shall begin."

A sickly feeling wells up in my throat. If Sparks is out there, does he have the nitro glycerine on him? If he does, the second we open that door he'll throw it and we are all dead. Gazing around the room there is a trail of blood where Mick dragged the body, tipping over the bucket in the process to leave the place looking like an abattoir. Billy and Sally are now frozen in terror. But we have no option; if Sparks is out there he will not allow the current situation to carry on into the daylight and will blow us up anyway. It's now or never. "Billy, blow out the lamp and then get behind the sofa with Sally and lay right down."

He nods and does exactly what I told him.

"Ready, lads?"

"Ready," says Mick. "Been nice knowing you fellas." Smiling he bends down and slips his powerful arms under the body's armpits. Head pushes me away and moves to assist him in bringing 'Sticks' up onto his feet.

"Haul him back a bit," says I. "He is too close to the door."

They lift him back a foot, I wrap a sweating hand around the door knob while the other hand draws out my revolver. "Go!" I yank open the door, Mick and Head shove the body forwards and then hell itself opens fire on us, as Sally's scream pierces my eardrums. Falling back behind the wall as bullets fly straight through the open door, I see Head dive to the floor and roll away while Mick has flattened himself back against the wall, leaving barely inches of wall between him and the door frame. Dropping to the floor I kick the door shut, as bullets smack straight through the rotten wood. The window is smashed in by a flying brick, here it comes, the explosion that will end our lives. Mick opens the door a crack then one-handed, pokes out his sawn-off shotgun and fires off both barrels. There follows the boom from hell. The world lights up in a blinding flash. What glass is left in the window is shattered into thousands of splinters, while a blast of burning hot air floods in.

"Fuck me!" yells Mick. "I must have hit the nitro. The twats have been blown up by their own explosives."

Coughing and spluttering through the whirling dust and smoke I get to unsteady feet and venture towards the window where I cautiously take a peek outside. Across the road it is utter devastation. Most of the rubbish has disappeared or is spinning around in a cloud of black smoke and burning bits that light up the road and inside the parlour. There is not a sign of a living thing, including rats. But at least the rain has stopped.

"How is everyone?" asks I, realising my voice is shaking.

Billy's head pokes up cautiously from behind the sofa, half the ceiling has fallen down around him and he is covered in dirty white dust. But at least he is alright. Sally peeps up over the sofa and is also safe, if covered in dust. Groaning, Head struggles to his feet while holding both hands around his left thigh, saying, "I think I've been hit,"

Mick ventures outside and calls back, "It's safe ta come out. Sure as sure, there ain't a bloody thing left alive."

Head falls back on one of the chairs and I go over to him. He has been shot across the thigh, cutting a groove three inches long and about a quarter of an inch deep that is bleeding quite profusely. "Billy, do you have a first aid box in the house?" calls I.

"What's that?"

"Never mind," grates I. Taking off my coat, jacket and shirt I am about to rip the shirt straight up the back as Mick comes back in and gently pushes me away.

"Mick O'Reilly is always prepared," says he. Bobbing down he produces a pair of scissors from inside his coat and proceeds to cut out enough material from Head's trouser leg to expose the wound then hands me the scissors to hold. The whisky bottle appears and what's left is poured over Head's wound causing him to screw up his face with the pain, but he doesn't cry out and merely sucks in dusty air. Mick produces a bandage and wraps it tightly around the wound, snatches back the scissors and cuts a good foot down the centre of the bandage. He slips the scissors back inside his coat and then ties the bandage off. Standing up he steps back a pace to survey his work. "You'll live," grins he.

Wincing, Head gets shakily to his feet, "Thanks, Mick. Sorry I called you thick, you're anything but."

Mick slaps him on the shoulder and then taking off his bowler he shows me the indent in the metal where a bullet had hit, "It made my head feel like it was inside a church bell when it hit," grins he.

"I'll bet," grins I, putting on my shirt, jacket, coat and hat. "Let's go outside, it is nauseating in here."

'Sticks's' body, we find on turning it over on its back, is peppered with bullet holes. He had set us up and payed the price for it twice, but at least he saved Mick and Head from certain death. Crossing over to the waste ground we are amazed to see that the privy is near intact, although the door has been blown off and lays burning on the ground bright enough to light up the area. How many 'assassins' where killed is anyone's guess, there are bits and pieces of body parts all over the place and it will no doubt take forensics days to work out who's who and what piece belongs to whom. By now other residents have ventured outside but are careful to keep right back. Several windows have been shattered along the road and there are lots of little fires burning as far away as thirty or more feet.

"What now, Jerry?" asks Mick.

"I will just take a quick look around and then we'll head away from here and back to the Yard."

Searching over the debris reveals nothing of worth until I come upon the charred end of a length of cord. Following the cord for over ten feet takes me around the side of a high wall where bobbing down I can just make out a few rather large footprints. Someone was hidden behind this wall and that someone had hold of that cord. And what was on the other end of that cord? Of course, one or two bottles of nitro glycerine. Who was holding that cord? No other than Jacob Sparks I reason. The clever, devious bastard set up his own cutthroats and blew them to hell before making a break for it. Why? Simple. The net was closing in on him, he has faked his own death and by now will be where? Heading off to the ports intent on taking a steamer to France, perhaps? I go back to the group who stand patiently waiting.

"Sergeant, do you feel fit enough to escort Billy and Sally back to the Yard on your own once we get back to the Stuffed Monkey?"

"Yes, sir," says he, waving an improvised walking stick in my face. "So long as they don't run for it I'll be fine."

"Good." I address the Dunns. "Hold out your arms." They do so and I clap a handcuff on Billy's left hand with the other on Sally's right hand. "If you try and run my Sergeant will shoot you in the leg, Billy."

"Why me and not Sally?"

"Because she's a female and you, like it or not, are still implicated in a serious robbery and will have to stand trial for it."

He gazes forlornly up at me, "Will I go to prison?"

"We'll see. Sergeant, once at the inn, Mick and I will make for the Neck Breakers Arms."

"It'll be closed, sir, it's gone midnight."

"We are not going on the booze, Sergeant. If you bump into Clump tell him we have gone there to make certain that Sparks was killed here this day. If we find no evidence that he has fled, for example, his safe hasn't been emptied and his clothes are still in the wardrobe we can assume he is in bits around here. Otherwise he is alive and out there somewhere still taking the piss out of us."

Leaving 'Sticks' laying around we head off beneath a near full moon that has appeared from nowhere as if to assist us on our way. 'Sticks' dog leads the way.

Despite the time, the Stuffed Monkey is still open. Here the dog leaves us and hurries off inside. The woman who was giving birth earlier sits outside breast feeding her new baby, which appears healthy and happy. "God bless the little mite," says I. Shoving a sixpence in the woman's hand I ask her if a waggon load of policemen came by earlier. She thanks me for the money and then says, "They came and asked around which way you had gone, but no one knew so they went off that way," she points.

Completely in the wrong direction, sighs I to myself.

You can get a cab anywhere and at any time of day or night in London. Luckily there are two waiting for fares. After helping Head and the Dunns up on one, me and Mick take the other. "To the Neck Breakers Arms," orders I to the driver. As we trot along I ponder on what has happened to Clump? Perhaps they got lost or continued going off in the wrong direction? Whatever, all will be revealed eventually.

The Neck Breakers Arms is in total darkness except for a single lamp burning in a bedroom window. I pay the driver thus far and tell him to wait. We climb down from the cab and I lead the way around to the back of the inn. Taking out the key Andy got for me I unlock the cellar door and quietly lift it open.

"Sure, you're one sneaky bugger, Jerry," whispers Mick. "Where'd ya get the key?"

"Never you mind." Down the ladder I go. Mick closes the door behind him and we meet at the bottom of the steps. It is as dark as pitch until Mick lights a match. We cross over to the steps that lead up to the bar hatch and up we go. Cautiously I push the hatch open enough to peep out into the area behind the bar before opening it fully, while ensuring it doesn't slam onto the floor. Once up on our feet behind the bar Mick blows out the match, the light through the half-drawn curtains is adequate to see fairly well. He whispers, "Shall we take a tot ta give us courage? Sure, me tongue's as dry as a nun's nipple."

Taking a bottle of brandy from the bar I take a long swig and pass it to Mick. He swallows half the bottle before handing it back. I take a long swig and hand it back, whereupon he downs the rest before gently setting it down on the bar.

"I'm ready," whispers he.

Silently as we can, we make our way upstairs. Half way up we pause and listen.

I stick my mouth to Mick's ear, "Someone's moving about up there."

He nods, "A woman."

"How the heck do you know it's a woman?"

"Because I do."

We creep on ever upwards until we come to the landing where we pause again. We can hear a female voice humming a tune. Having been here before I reason it is coming from Sparks' bedroom. Drawing my revolver, I stride quickly to that bedroom and walk straight in to find Jenny stark naked while laid out on Sparks' bed reading a book.

"Good evening," says I.

Jenny jumps out of her skin slaps the book down to cover her secret place, lays a hand across her breasts and sits up. Surprisingly she quickly recovers her composure and says, "You could have knocked."

"Where's Sparks?"

"Gone."

"Where to?"

"He wouldn't say."

"How long ago did he leave?"

She shrugs, "Not long, an hour back, maybe."

"Just after he came in then?"

"Yes. He sent everyone out, closed the bar and handed me the keys. He said he was going off for a short break and I could run the place how I liked until his return."

"You know he has no intentions of returning?"

"Of course, I do. Who cares, by the time the brewery realises an unmarried woman is running the place I'd have made enough money to buy myself a little sweet shop."

"Why a sweet shop?" asks Mick stepping further into the room and gazing around.

"Because I love sweets."

"We shall look around," says I. "Meanwhile perhaps you could put something on while trying to think where Sparks may have gone. The station? The docks? Did he take a cab?"

"Like I said, I have no idea where he's gone but he did take a cab that headed towards the docks, but that don't mean a thing." Putting aside her book she swings off the bed as brazen as you want, goes over to the door and takes a very flimsy dressing gown from a hook and slips it over her nakedness, but she doesn't do up the cord and seems to be quite enjoying flaunting herself. It is clear by the lust in Mick's eyes that the only thing he wishes to search at the moment is Jenny. I have to admit that my turning away while Jenny crossed the room was more from my own arousal than any notion of being a gentleman. Then it comes to me.

"Madam!" snaps I, facing her square on while trying not to look below her chin. "I believe you are playing games with us in order to detain us long enough for your boss to get away. If you don't tell us what we want to know immediately we shall have to force it from you."

Pushing her gown away she shoves her hands on her hips and gives them a defiant wiggle, "When was the last time you saw a body as gorgeous as mine?" pouts she.

"Every night," smirks I, knowing I am winning the arousal battle as sadly it's shrinking back to normal.

Swinging around to face Mick she pouts even more, "And you?"

"Every night in my dreams, me darlin," says he pushing back the flaps on his coat.

"What the fuck is that?" demands Jenny stabbing out a finger.

"It's a stick of dynamite powerful enough ta blow this pub ta smithereens. Now, me darlin' as gorgeous as you are, you ain't as important to us at this moment as catching up with that murdering bloody bastard you call a boss. Now if ya don't sing loud and clear right now I'll blow this place up. After that is, I've thrown you out naked into the street. What's it to be, goodbye to ya sweet shop or hello sweeties?"

She wraps her gown tightly around her, the colour has drained from her face as she hurriedly muddles over her choices, "All right, he emptied the safe, threw a few things in a bag and left barely half an hour ago and headed for the docks. I know he's planning on going to live in the South of France so I assume he'll be catching the Sea Voyager as he knows the captain. It's due to leave before dawn breaks once fully loaded.

"Thank you, Jenny," says I.

"You're welcome," sneers she before turning to Mick. "Come and see me when you get back handsome, but don't bring your mate with you."

"Sure, I'll be up for that," grins Mick.

"I thought you was in love and had stopped chasing other woman?" grates I, as we head for the cab.

"I am in love and will always be in love with every beautiful woman I clap me eyes on."

We climb into the cab and head off for the docks. The sky has cleared of cloud, the moon is bright and the only sounds are the grinding wheels from the cab and the clip-clopping of the horse's hooves. The cab driver turns the horse onto the quay and heads towards the main loading area. Apart from a pair of patrolling plods going the opposite way there doesn't appear to be another soul around. A hundred yards further on I tell the driver to let us out. Paying him off with extra to forget he ever saw us, I send him on his way. The Sea Voyager is moored fifty or so yards further along. We walk towards it.

"What's ya plan, Jerry?"

"To capture or kill Sparks by whatever means."

"Does that mean I can be as dirty as I want?"

"It does, but don't you dare use that dynamite, Mick. The last thing we need is another massacre with bits of bodies strewn all over the place, especially if they are French bodies. Clump will have my head for it and yours too I shouldn't wonder."

"Don't worry ya little head me ol' darlin', my arse has got more chance of explodin' than that stick of dynamite. It's a dud, so it is."

Thank God for that, thinks I. The Sea Voyager comes fully into view, it is squashed between two other vessels, a full mast sailing ship fore-end and a Thames Barge at the stern. The gangplank is out and light fans out from the entrance where I spy a sailor smoking a pipe. We step up to the gangplank.

"Permission to come aboard?" calls out I in English because I can't remember the French.

"Oui," he nods.

We walk up the plank where I recall having met this particular sailor the last time I was here.

"Parlez-vous le capitaine," says I.

He grins broadly and points his pipe down the gangway. Remembering the way, I head into the ship with Mick close on my heels. Sparks could be anywhere on the ship, asleep in a cabin, talking with the captain or he could even jump out in front of us. Jenny may have fed us a lie and he might not even be on the ship. Who knows? But we shall soon be finding out. At the captain's cabin door, I take out my revolver, knock twice and press myself back against the bulkhead. To my surprise the door is quickly opened and the captain sticks his head out, glances up and down the gangway and then beckons us in. Quietly closing the door, he locks it. "You are the last man I expected to see at this time of night, Inspector," hisses he. "Who is this with you?"

"An associate of mine, Mr Michael O'Reilly."

"He looks more like an assassin than an associate to me. So, are you here to arrest Sparks or have you just popped in for another round of drunkenness?"

"We have come for Sparks."

He nods, "Of course you have. He is up on deck enjoying the air and I would prefer you to arrest him there and not inside the ship. Why? Simple, if you start firing bullets they will ricochet off the iron bulkheads and could hit one of my men, plus it easy to swab blood off the deck. We set sail in an hour, so my men are up and having onions and goats' cheese with bread before they stoke the boilers right up to build up enough steam in readiness to cast off. Be careful Inspector, Sparks is a very dangerous man."

"No one knows that better than me, Captain. Is he armed?"

"He is always armed. He has a pistol in the carpetbag he has with him."

"Does he have his own cabin?"

He shakes his head, "This is not a cruise ship, Inspector. If he wants to lay down he will have to take a bunk up with the others."

"From what we know of him," says Mick, "he'd like nothin' better than a bunk up with your sailors."

"I do not follow you Monsieur O'Reilly?"

"No matter," says I. "Which way to the deck?"

Opening the door, he peeps out, glances both ways and then ushering us out points up the gangway towards the bows. "Go to the end and up the steps, you will find him there. If he resists arrest will you kill him?"

"We will."

"Good. Then I too will be free from his evil."

The distance from the captain's cabin to the iron stairway that leads up to the deck seems like miles when in fact it is merely yards, such is the way fear can muddle reality. Sparks has got so far into my psyche; my legs are leaden while my heart pounds in my chest.

"You're not going ta chicken out on me?" whispers Mick, fixing me with accusing eyes. "Cause judging by the smell that just sneaked from ya arse I'd say you're on the point of fillin' ya pants."

I take a deep breath. The hand holding my revolver is trembling and I fear death is imminent, at the same time I am desperately trying to keep my cheeks squeezed together.

"I'll be alright, Mick. Just a bit nervous that's all."

Climbing the steps, we find the door to the deck is wide open. Mick takes a peek before pushing me back out of sight, "He's sat out on a lounger with a big smoking cigar in one hand and a balloon glass of spirit in the other. Sure, he's in the land of nod with his back to us. There's a large carpetbag by his side. Go on and take a peek."

I do so. Sparks has indeed got his back to us. He has on a floppy hat; the collar of his dark coat is turned right up and he appears to be staring out over the water. If it is him? It could be anyone sat back on that lounger and the second we show ourselves Sparks could spring out from where he's hiding and shoot us to pieces. But we are here now, and I will not allow my fear to turn me into a coward and run for it. Besides I could do with a nice fat reward from whatever treasures are in that carpet bag. Swallowing hard I step stealthily out onto the deck with Mick alongside me. Mick's shotgun appears and holding it at waist height he marches forwards as if he were a soldier on a battlefield walking straight for the enemy, he reaches the figure on the lounger a good three steps in front of me and sticks the end of his barrels in the back of the figure's neck.

"The end of your barrels, are cold," says Sparks stiffening up. "Do you mind removing them?"

"Not in the least," says Mick, and retracts them an inch.

Taking a long draw on his cigar, Sparks turns his head to the side and blows smoke towards me, "Well, well. Detective Inspector Gerald Potter no less. I must admit I did not even comprehend the thought of your catching up with me before the ship sailed. I commend you. Now clear off and leave me in peace off before I lose my temper."

"We are going nowhere without you, Sparks. Now, you can make this easy or hard, which is to be?"

"Let's make it easy. How much do you want to go away?"

"How much are you offering?" asks I.

"Pass me my bag and let's begin bartering."

"I don't think so. Put down your glass, stand up and put your hands behind your back."

Swallowing his drink in one go he sets the glass down, swings his legs off the lounger, stands up and faces me. "There is no point in you arresting me, Inspector, you know how it will end. Arrest me, charge me and throw me in a cell. I go to trial where the evidence you present will be crushed by the best legal defence anyone could possibly have and it won't cost me a penny. Of course, I will be exonerated and will be on my way to France, albeit a few weeks later than planned, all because of what I know about who I know. And you, and fellow me lad here, will be made to look worse than stupid. You may even find yourself demoted back to the beat. If you're lucky."

"You wouldn't be fleeing the country if you were cocksure you'd get away with all you have done," sneers I, taking a step back from him as he has ever so slightly edged his way closer to me. "No, this time, Jacob Sparks, you realised you'd gone too far. The murder of Patrick O'Connor particularly sealed your fate. The public are up in arms about it and demanding results. It would be a very foolish person who tries to use his clout to get you off this one. You are done for Sparks, you have nothing left to bargain with and will be swinging from a rope before the end of the month."

He draws hard on his cigar before tossing it away and blowing smoke into my eyes, "I have a lot left to bargain with, Potter. Do you think you can cross me and get away scot-free? Even if I am sentenced to death, I will ensure that you and your pretty little wife, what's her name, Betty? will receive a one-off visit from a few of my less savoury acquaintances before I swing. I ask again, how much for you and your Irish idiot to go away and report to all and sundry that you are certain I perished in that unnamed road along with my men?"

"Mick, pass me that carpet bag and lower your weapon."

"Now you are beginning to see sense," sneers Sparks.

Mick's eyes are brimming with fury as he grabs the bag and thrusts it at me. He would have much preferred I gave him the nod to kill Sparks.

Taking a few steps even further back from Sparks I shoulder my revolver and bobbing down I open the bag. Extracting Sparks' weapon, I place it behind my back into my belt. Apart from a single change of clothes the bag is stuffed with bank notes, jewellery in fancy boxes and of course the bag of little blue diamonds. I stand up again. "Before we negotiate, I would like to ask you a few questions merely for my own satisfaction, if you don't mind?"

"Ask away, Inspector."

"You drugged Sally Dunn so that one of your flatulent customers could do what they wanted with her. I want the name of that person."

"No chance."

"Do you have any guilt for using that poor girl in such a vile way?"

"None at all. What else do you wish to know?"

"How did you know that Bray Waunepcy would be walking across Tower Bridge at that time of day?"

"I didn't. All I knew was that having double-crossed me the decrepit little fleabag was hiding out somewhere around that area. It was pure chance that we ran into him."

"Why kill him?"

"He wouldn't tell me why Sadie Calver didn't turn up for work or where she was. In fact, he told me to; 'Go shove a cucumber up ya hole.' No one talks to Jacob Johnathan Aldridge Sparks like that, especially as cucumbers are out of season. So, we threw the piece of shit off the bridge."

"And Sadie, did you find out where she was hiding?"

"Yes, but unfortunately not before the police did."

"She was going to retract the alibi you forced her to give you and no doubt would have given evidence against you."

"That was what I eventually reasoned myself, when an hour or so after throwing the fleabag of the bridge we spied Sadie being put into the back of a police waggon just off Bermondsey Street. Too many uniformed police for us to get to her."

"Obviously you intended to kill everyone down that road, including 'Sticks' and your men. How did you get 'Sticks' on side?"

"He came to me, he wanted out when he realised the danger he was in by harbouring Sally. I paid him to help set you all up. The intention was that my men would kill you all and then I would pull a cord that would set off the nitro glycerine, thus getting rid of everyone else who might later testify that I didn't die with them."

"Brilliant," smiles I. "Do you have any regrets about any of this?"

He smiles ruefully, "It's a shame the wrong dwarf got killed but how was I to know Billy would be substituted because he had a gammy knee?"

"You weren't. What if you had killed all the dwarfs?"

He shrugs, "It didn't matter. Who cares about dwarfs, they are nothing but freaks of nature."

"They're blessed, so they are," snarls Mick raising his shotgun. "And worth a million scum like you."

With his eyes glazing over Sparks takes a step towards us and for the first time I see the true evil in his eyes. The man is without fear or remorse and is a psychopath of the highest order.

"Take one more step," warns Mick. "An' this idiot Irishman shall blow your…"

"No," hisses I. "You fire that shotgun Mick and it will make one hell of a mess." Taking out Sparks' revolver from the back of my trousers I cock it and aim it straight at his black heart.

"You wouldn't dare," sneers he.

But I do dare and shoot him. The look of disbelief in his eyes as his hands slap automatically to his chest is a joy to behold. The punch he receives from the bullet would have dropped a normal man, especially at such close range, but although it rocks him he remains standing. Time has run out for him and he knows it. Slumping to his knees he holds out a bloodied hand, his eyes plead for mercy; 'Finish it'. Only I can't finish it. I want to watch him die. A deathly quiet moment passes before he slumps forward onto the deck. I hurl the revolver over the side.

Mick's questioning gaze meets my eyes, "It's over so it is."

"For some it will never be over," says I, thinking of the O'Connors and the Dunns.

Dawn is breaking as Mick and I head back on foot to the Neck Breakers. My official report will state that Sparks perished by his own hands down unnamed road. To ensure my report is believed I have no option other than to return Sparks' money and jewels to his safe, minus of course 'expenses'. The captain readily agreed to incinerate Sparks' body in the ship's furnace, for a large fee of course, until he was nothing more than ash. Mick, Head and myself will receive one-hundred pounds each. I will need to pay Jenny off and of course compensation to the O'Connors.

There will be an inquiry over Sparks' criminal activities and his death. Hopefully Billy Dunn will never be tried and Sally, along with whatever diamonds she has left, will be allowed to walk away to pick up the threads of her life. As for the O'Connors, well they are only just beginning their life sentences.